WARNING FROM WITHIN

Waiting for her coffee to brew, Deidi smoked a cigarette and picked out the clothes she would wear that day, a gray pin-striped suit she always wore with a frilly red blouse. But when she reached for the blouse, her hand shrank away from it as if it had tried to bite her. The red material had brought back the bloody vision, and this time she had seen the old man's eyes, how they'd been filled with intense pain and horror. And something else. Confusion.

Deidi stepped back from the closet and took a deep drag of her cigarette, shuddering as her mind gave birth to an ugly idea. The woman who'd killed Larry Patton had killed again, last night. But Deidi couldn't understand why she should know this. She wasn't psychic and never had been. Yet she'd known that Larry Patton's body was nude, and that inner voice had whispered soon, very soon. . . .

DON'T MISS THESE OTHER
MASTERPIECES OF HORROR BY
D. A. FOWLER,
AVAILABLE FROM POCKET BOOKS!

WHAT'S WRONG WITH VALERIE?

"Unforgettable! One of the best horror debuts I've come across in a long time!"
—Douglas Clegg, author of *Neverland*

"Bizarrely original, darkly humorous, and downright spooky! Fowler expertly creates a genuinely nightmarish atmosphere and leavens it with a weird, dry wit."
—R. Patrick Gates, author of *Grimm Memorials*

"A grabber! I read it in two hungry gulps. Here is a unique blend of graphic horror, limber psychological twists, and mystery: is this dame nuts or is she living in a haunted house—and adapting rather nicely?"
—Sean Costello, author of *Captain Quad*

"A nightmarish rollercoaster ride into hell. A unique blend of madness, terror, and humor."
—Patrick Whalen, author of *Death Walker*

"Darkly delightful. **A giddy rollercoaster ride through the mind of a madwoman, full of horrors and pitch-black humor. Great cringing fun!**"
—Chris Curry, author of *Winter Scream*

WHAT'S WRONG WITH TAMARA?

"*What's Wrong with Tamara?* is bone-chilling, suspenseful. . . ."
—Matthew J. Costello, author of *Darkborn*

"This is the art of superior characterization and good storytelling, combined with horror, suspense, and dark humor."
—Ron Dee, author of *Dusk*

THE DEVIL'S END

"A wicked, wicked delight!"
—Douglas Clegg, author of *Neverland*

THE BOOK OF THE DAMNED

"A brilliant dark read, and a provocative blend of V. C. Andrews and Freddie Krueger."
—Patrick Whalen, author of *Death Walker*

"Imaginative terror . . . tantalizing."
—Andrew Niederman, author of *The Devil's Advocate*

"D. A. Fowler's a darkly funny twisted sister with balls. She's a comer. Fowler's got the goods!"
—Rex Miller, author of *Chaingang*

"Blood-curdling terror . . . The characters flew from the pages and urged me to join them on this dark and suspenseful journey."
—Ron Dee, author of *Dusk*

Books by D. A. Fowler

The Book of the Damned
The Devil's End
Flesh and Blood
What's Wrong with Tamara?
What's Wrong with Valerie?

Published by POCKET BOOKS

Most Pocket Books are available at special quantity discounts for bulk purchases for sales promotions, premiums or fund raising. Special books or book excerpts can also be created to fit specific needs.

For details write the office of the Vice President of Special Markets, Pocket Books, 1230 Avenue of the Americas, New York, New York 10020.

FLESH AND BLOOD

D.A. FOWLER

POCKET BOOKS
New York   London   Toronto   Sydney   Tokyo   Singapore

The sale of this book without its cover is unauthorized. If you purchased this book without a cover, you should be aware that it was reported to the publisher as "unsold and destroyed." Neither the author nor the publisher has received payment for the sale of this "stripped book."

This book is a work of fiction. Names, characters, places and incidents are either products of the author's imagination or are used fictitiously. Any resemblance to actual events or locales or persons, living or dead, is entirely coincidental.

An *Original* Publication of POCKET BOOKS

POCKET BOOKS, a division of Simon & Schuster Inc.
1230 Avenue of the Americas, New York, NY 10020

Copyright © 1993 by Debra Fowler

All rights reserved, including the right to reproduce this book or portions thereof in any form whatsoever. For information address Pocket Books, 1230 Avenue of the Americas, New York, NY 10020

ISBN: 0-671-76045-9

First Pocket Books printing December 1993

10 9 8 7 6 5 4 3 2 1

POCKET and colophon are registered trademarks of Simon & Schuster Inc.

Cover art by Vince Natale

Printed in the U.S.A.

FLESH AND BLOOD

1

She was sitting alone at a corner table in a small, dim nightclub, smoking a cigarette with a half-finished drink in front of her. She didn't remember how she got there, or what she was doing with a cigarette between her fingers—she'd quit smoking three years ago. She'd quit going to nightclubs three kids ago, and she'd never been much of a drinker—alcohol only put her to sleep.

She didn't know what time it was—the watch she usually wore was missing from her left wrist—but she had the impression that it was very late, well past midnight. There were just a few other people in the club: the male bartender, who was either deep in thought or sleeping in an upright position with his eyes open; a cocktail waitress with bleached blond hair, who was busy cleaning abandoned tables; and two men in business suits, one at a table across the room, squinting over a newspaper, the other sitting at the bar, nursing his drink, from time to time glancing in her direction. He looked to be in his mid-forties, not handsome but not ugly, either; he had an accountant's face, a forgettable face, dark receding hair, wire-rimmed glasses. She knew he was working up the nerve to come over to her table and introduce himself.

Although that was exactly what she wanted, she didn't offer him an encouraging smile. She wasn't that good an actress. It was all she could do to hide the hate.

Finally Mr. Accountant Face picked up his glass and slid off his perch. An uncertain smile appeared on his thin lips as he approached her. She held his gaze steadily, boldly, not blinking even once.

"Are you waiting for someone?" he asked in a coarse tenor voice.

She almost said *Yes, I've been waiting for you, whoever you are,* but all that came out was "No."

"Mind if I join you? I'm Larry. Larry Patton."

She briefly shook the damp hand he proffered, but didn't give her name in return. She didn't dare, in case something should go wrong. "No, I don't mind."

His smile became less uncertain as he pulled out a chair for himself and sat down facing her, ice cubes tinkling against his glass. "And you are?"

"Very horny," she said, deadpan.

Mr. Accountant Face surely hadn't heard her correctly. His smile faltered, his cheeks flushed slightly, and the ice cubes in his glass clinked because the hand holding it began to shake. "P-Pardon?"

She found his display of discombobulation amusing. As if having sex with her had been the furthest thing from his mind. But she had no trouble believing this was the easiest pickup of his meaningless, monotonous life. His own wife probably wasn't even this willing, and the band on his left ring finger testified that he was married. Which was no surprise.

"You heard me," she answered in a sultry voice, then drew deeply on her cigarette. Exhaling, she stared hard at him through the spiraling smoke. "Well?"

Larry Patton lifted his glass to his lips and sucked down the remaining amber fluid. "I think I need another drink," he said. "How about you?"

"Long Island tea." She took another drag on the cigarette and watched through narrowed eyes as he got

FLESH AND BLOOD

up and made his way back to the bar. Absently her other hand moved to her lap, feeling the smooth leather of her purse. Inside, her fingers rambled over an assortment of shapes and textures until they located the wooden handle of a steak knife and then carefully worked their way up to the cool serrated blade.

As she touched it, a secretive smile emerged on her face.

2

Just when Deidi Marshall thought it was safe to go out for lunch, a carnivorous shark named Tom Fitzgerald glided hungrily through the conditioned air toward her cubicle. Only he wasn't actually gliding; in fact, he was probably causing plaster to fall on the offices below. Tom wasn't just fat—he was obese. He was also editor-in-chief of the *Danville Chronicle,* and he had an insatiable appetite for news as well as anything unable to crawl off a plate.

"Deidi, there's a hot one going at the Sea Breeze Motel on Camden Avenue." Hardly giving her enough time to respond, he clapped his fat hands. "Come on, get a move on! I'm talking about a front page headliner!"

Deidi's eyebrows rose. "Okay, okay, don't doodie in your didies, I'm going. But I doubt if there's enough time to get it into this afternoon's edition, if that's what you're hoping for." She didn't ask for further details. She already knew that the only thing Tom got this excited about was murder, which was probably all the information he had: someone was dead, and the circumstances looked suspicious. The details were hers to discover.

"Hope I don't faint from starvation on my way

FLESH AND BLOOD

down there," she tossed blithely over her shoulder as she headed for the door. There were three other staff writers at the *Chronicle,* all of whom were out to lunch. Their computer monitors were blank, keyboards silent. Even the teletype machine was silent for once.

"Should I get out my violin?" Tom retorted, not the least bit sympathetic. This from a man who would let his own mother drown if the slightest craving for a Hostess cupcake surfaced the same moment she went under. Deidi pursed her full red lips in disgust, barely resisting the temptation to slam the office door with its frosted-glass window marked NEWSROOM behind her.

As usual, the house was a mess. There were toys scattered all over the place among dirty socks and tattered canvas shoes. There was dust on all the secondhand furniture, dirty dishes piled in the sink and on the table, greasy skillets with charred residuals on the stove, and pots ringed with mysterious crusts. The mistress of this filthy manor, Camisa Collins, was in the master bedroom with the door shut, lying in bed with a suspense novel. She had no idea what her three young children were up to, nor did she much care. She'd fed the brats their lunches, now she deserved a little time to herself.

In spite of her interest in the paperback she was reading, her thoughts kept wandering to the dream she'd had the night before. It wasn't usual for her to remember her dreams at all, and this one had been particularly vivid.

After Mr. Accountant Face had returned to the table with their drinks, she'd sent him back to the bar for an extra slice of lemon. As soon as his back was turned, she slipped a large tablet into his glass. It dissolved quickly, and although she didn't know what it was, she knew what it would do. Unaware of the extra ingredient, he drank his bourbon on the rocks and talked while she pretended to listen, watching for the first sign of drowsiness. As it turned out, he wasn't an accountant, but a software salesman, and according to him, so far this month had really been the pits. When the drug began to affect him, evidenced by a bleary gaze, she suggested that they dispense with the bullshit and go to his room.

Camisa was still amazed at the details of the dream. How the Long Island tea had tasted, the feel of taking the cigarette smoke into her lungs, the smell of the salesman's cologne mixed with stale sweat. Suddenly there was a loud commotion on the other side of the thin wall, followed by Michael's distinctive, piercing wail. Michael was three and a half and a perpetual crybaby. Camisa's oldest, Aaron, was five, and she was convinced he had somehow wormed himself into her womb from Hell. (And to think there had almost been two of him, but his twin didn't make it—thank God for small favors.) Felicia, who should have been named Disaster, was only thirteen months old and into anything her grubby little hands could reach. She'd unrolled miles of toilet paper, poured several bottles of shampoo and conditioner out on the bathroom carpet, sprinkled the whole house with baby powder, and fingerpainted on the walls with her shit. It gave Camisa a headache to think of all the other things she'd done.

Michael was now calling for her between screams. Scowling, Camisa dog-eared the page she was on, slapped the book down on the rumpled bedspread and got up to see what the hell was going on in the next room.

The moment they entered the motel room, he grabbed her and began pawing her, even though he was obviously having trouble standing. His breath stank and his kisses came with slobber. She could almost hear the thoughts that had to be running through his murky head: Gotta hurry before I pass out ... last drink was really potent ... whaddya know, finally got lucky this month, too bad I'm not getting paid . . . is she expecting me to pay her?

Aaron was trying to stuff Michael into the toy chest. All Camisa could see of her three-year-old was his red, squalling face; Aaron was pushing the chest's lid down over his younger brother's neck. Felicia was gnawing contentedly on Aaron's G.I. Joe, even though a noxious smell in the room indicated she was sitting in a dirty diaper. Camisa was tempted to take all three of them into the bathroom and drown them like unwanted kittens. Stepping into the room, she wished for the millionth time that she'd had a tubal ligation done as soon as her periods started.

"Aaron! Just what the hell do you think you're doing?"

His face a mask of guilty surprise, Aaron spun around, then immediately jumped back from the chest as if she could be fooled into thinking the scene she'd walked in on had been an optical illusion. He landed right on top of Felicia, and now Camisa had two kids screaming their heads off.

Might as well make it unanimous, she thought, and she reached for Aaron.

Patton never made it to the bed. He collapsed on the floor with his slacks pulled down around his knees. She slid his wallet out of his left hip pocket and sat on the edge of the bed to open it. He didn't have much cash, only about fifty dollars. Robbery wasn't her motive, but she stuffed the bills inside her purse anyway. There were several photos sealed in plastic—pictures of his family, no doubt—and she studied them coldly. The woman she assumed was his wife, posed with him and two teenage girls, was a sow with frizzy red hair and a nose job. One of the teenage girls looked just like her, except that her frizzy hair was blond. The other girl resembled Larry, and for that she was undoubtedly profoundly grateful, considering the course nature could have taken—but she still would have been much better off as a boy.

She tossed the wallet down on the nightstand and took the steak knife out of her purse.

"Mommy, don't! Don't, Mommy, no!"

Aaron struggled to get away from her but had no chance of succeeding. When his mother was mad she was also very strong. Camisa had dragged him out to the garage, which was a sweltering oven in the mid-August heat, and now she was preparing to force him into the large dog carrier. The collie it had been purchased for had died mysteriously the summer before.

"Shut up, Aaron. You knew you were being mean to Michael, now you're going to get punished for it. The madder you make me, the longer you're going to have to stay in there. It's already going to be an hour. You want to make it two hours? Three?"

The small boy shook his head vigorously, a tear sliding down his cheek. "But it's hot out here."

"Yes it is," Camisa agreed. "It's hot in Hell, too, a lot hotter than this garage even, and if you go there when you die because of being bad, you can't ever get out again. How would you like that, Aaron? You want to go to Hell and live with the Devil forever?"

The light green eyes that so often sparkled with malice now reflected only fear. How innocent and vulnerable he could look when the tables were turned on him, Camisa thought. But she didn't allow herself to be taken in by it. He wouldn't truly be sorry until he'd spent some time in that cage, in this heat.

How many times had she stabbed him? Forty, fifty? She'd stopped counting after ten . . .

"We counted fifty-nine stab wounds," homicide detective Judson Hendricks related to Deidi Marshall. They were standing on the balcony outside Room 216 of the Sea Breeze Motel along with a camera crew from the local television station. Uniformed officers were posted by the stairwells on either side of them.

FLESH AND BLOOD

"Looks like she used a small knife, with a blade about five inches long."

Deidi's dark coffee-bean eyes drifted for a moment as she thought of her next question. "What's the suspect's description?"

Hendricks began to recite what the club's night bartender had told him. He hadn't yet talked to the cocktail waitress who'd worked last night; by day she was a student working on her Bachelor of Arts degree in drama. "The motel employee who saw Larry Patton leave the bar late last night with a woman has described her as being about twenty-five years of age with dark shoulder-length brown hair and brown eyes, around five feet, six inches tall, one hundred and twenty pounds, no distinguishing marks or scars, but at the time she was wearing bright red lipstick. She had on a pink-and-gray jogging outfit and one of those purses that are worn like a belt, also gray. White running shoes."

Deidi smiled wryly. "Except for the outfit, you just described what I look like. I just turned twenty-seven."

A light wind whirled around them, ruffling Deidi's dark brown shoulder-length hair, carrying with it the smell of the sea. The white beaches of Danville were only a quarter mile away.

"I guess I did," Hendricks said, also smiling. "So where were you last night around two A.M.?" His mouth was smiling, but his voice was not. His voice was level and coldly professional.

Deidi's smile quickly wilted. "Are you serious? You really want an answer to that question?"

"Would you rather have a lawyer present?" he asked amiably.

The journalist stared at him open-mouthed, aware of a flush creeping its way up her cheeks. The sonofabitch really was serious, and that damned news camera was right up in her face.

At that moment, two burly men toting a stretcher began backing out onto the balcony, and she and the camera crew had to move away from Hendricks to give them room. On the stretcher was a black body bag which gave no hint of the horror within, but an idea suddenly struck Deidi and she vocalized it before thinking.

"He was nude?"

Hendricks looked at her, his expression suddenly grim. "How did you know that? I didn't tell you he was nude."

Deidi's mind raced for an explanation. She couldn't have known, but somehow she'd figured it out.

"The stab wounds," she said. "You told me you counted fifty-nine stab wounds. How could you have done that if he'd had his clothes on? I wouldn't think you'd take them off here."

There was still some activity going on in the room. One man was dusting for fingerprints, another was going through the contents of Larry Patton's suitcase, another was on the phone ordering a large pepperoni and mushroom pizza.

Her explanation seemed plausible enough, although Deidi wasn't sure if it was the right one. Some of the hardness melted from the detective's gaze. Some, but not all. He was still waiting for his other question to be answered. "You're right about that. Okay, I'll buy it. You made a logical deduction and came up with the right answer. Color me impressed."

"I was in bed asleep by eleven last night," Deidi said stiffly, "and I'm sorry, but the only one who can corroborate that is my Doberman pinscher, Hughman. I happen to live alone. Now if you don't mind, I'd like to get finished here so I can grab some lunch on my way back to the *Chronicle.*" She turned her attention to her notebook. "Do you have any ideas on the motive for this killing?"

Hendricks sighed and looked out over the courtyard below, in the midst of which glimmered an inviting pear-shaped pool. It was presently empty of swimmers. "I'm still working on that. Could've been robbery, but she didn't take his watch or ring. And if it was just a robbery, there would've been no need for the fifty-nine stab wounds. Most of those went into a corpse. So maybe it was a crime of passion, but it was the bartender's impression that Patton had met the woman for the first time last night."

Another salty breeze swept through Deidi's hair, and a dark voice whispered in the back of her mind. *She killed him simply because he was a man, and for some reason she hates all men, but not only men. She is completely ruled by hatred, loving nothing other than herself and the insidious deeds that give her pleasure. Look in any mirror and you will see her.*

"Do you think she'll do it again?" Deidi's voice was trembling. Where the hell were such insane, crazy thoughts coming from? It was as if a demon or some evil spirit had whispered to her, sowing seeds of madness with malicious fantasy. Fuck it. She just wouldn't listen.

Of course she will do it again. You know she will. And soon, very soon.

"Serial killers are usually men, but I wouldn't rule out the possibility."

Deidi put her notebook away with unsteady hands, suddenly anxious to get away from this place, away from Judson Hendricks's penetrating gaze. Away from the dark voice that whispered things she didn't want to hear.

"Thank you for your cooperation. I'll be in touch for further developments." She turned and walked away, heels clicking on the cement floor of the balcony, feeling both the TV camera lens and the detective's eyes following her, burning into her with suspicion. She had a childish urge to raise an extended middle finger over her shoulder but couldn't quite get up the nerve. After all, she was a professional and a lady. And Hendricks was only doing his job. If he had a sister who fit the suspect's description, he would question her, too.

The uniformed cop standing at the northeast stairwell smiled at her as she passed. Deidi smiled back, but behind the smile she was gritting her teeth. She was guilty of nothing other than oversleeping now and then, and sometimes being a slob at home (and so what, most of the time Hughman was the only one around to notice, and he never complained). Maybe she smoked a little too much and didn't go to church like she should, but no one was perfect, so there was absolutely no reason for her to suddenly feel like a dirty criminal. What Hendricks was thinking shouldn't affect her, even if she was somehow picking up on negative vibes he was throwing in her direction. She tried to shake the feeling off, but it persisted the rest of the afternoon.

Camisa was in the kitchen feeding Felicia and watching the five o'clock news on the small black-and-white TV sitting on the counter. Aaron was still out in the garage locked inside the dog carrier. On and off since a quarter of one, when she'd put him in there, he'd cried and screamed to be let out, which had invariably started Camisa giggling like a deranged hyena. He'd been quiet for a while now, over an hour, and she was thinking that after Felicia was fed, he could come back into the house. Michael was in the living room with his coloring book and crayons, deep in concentration, his tongue sticking out the side of his mouth as he gave Snow White a purple face. Camisa's husband Harlan was a truck driver only home on the weekends, so there was no worry about him coming through the door any moment and hollering for the kids to come give Daddy a big hug. She didn't think Harlan would agree with Aaron's punishment, even if Aaron could have broken Michael's neck.

Camisa was spooning pureed apricots into Felicia's

eager mouth when a story came on the news that snatched her full attention. Half the spoonful dribbled down Felicia's chin.

"A murder late last night in Danville," said the local anchorman, Bob Duran, a young Clint Eastwood with curly brown hair and deep-set green eyes. "Police sources say that sometime between two and five A.M., a man staying at the Sea Breeze Motel was brutally stabbed to death. He's been identified as Larry Wayne Patton, forty-three, of Nashville, Tennessee. Mr. Patton was a software salesman doing business in the area."

The screen was suddenly filled with a white stucco wall that bore a colorful sign, shaped like an ocean wave: Sea Breeze Motel, parenthesized by palm trees. A slender blond-headed woman stood in front of it holding a microphone. The wind was blowing her hair.

"According to the club's bartender, Patton left the bar just after two A.M. with a dark-haired woman approximately twenty-five years of age . . ."

Camisa almost knocked the highchair over in her haste to get up and turn off the set. Her heart was pounding, eyes bulging from their sockets. "Shit!"

"Sheee," Felicia gurgled happily, patting the metal tray with her gooey hands.

Camisa began frantically pacing the dirty kitchen floor, the man's name resounding in her ears. *Larry Patton*. The dream. Larry Patton, software salesman. Dark-haired woman approximately twenty-five years old. No dream. Real! She'd actually left the house last night after she'd gone to bed. And she'd killed a man, a man named Larry Patton who had a pig-faced wife with frizzy red hair.

Shit *supreme*.

"What the hell am I going to do?" she asked the floor, her voice becoming hysterical, hands clutching at her dark greasy hair. Dark hair. She pulled two limp sections in front of her face and had a sudden inspiration: bleach. But what about the other evidence? What had she done with that jogging outfit, the gray purse, the money she'd taken out of Larry Patton's wallet? (And where had she gotten the outfit and purse to begin with?) Maybe she had a whole other life she knew nothing about.

And the knife.

She turned and dashed to the drawer where she kept the silverware and jerked it open. While she was taking a frantic inventory of the steak knives, Aaron began yelling again from the garage. Camisa ignored him; this was by far the number-one priority at the moment. Felicia knocked the jar of apricots onto the floor. Camisa ignored that, too.

Then the telephone rang.

Camisa jumped and spun around, staring at the white instrument with total dread, fearing it was the police. But given a few moments to think, she decided it wouldn't be them. They would come to her house with a warrant for her arrest, or at least show up in person to ask some questions first.

Still, her hand was trembling when she picked up the receiver on the fourth ring. "Hello?"

"Camisa." It was her mother, and her voice sounded strange: flat, subdued. Maybe the police had been to her house asking questions.

"Mother? Is something wrong?" Camisa held her breath, eyes closed, and behind the lids watched a vision of herself hurriedly packing a suitcase. She could leave the kids with Mrs. Ryder next door, for "half an hour," she'd say, just while she ran to the store for a few things, and then she'd simply disappear, perhaps into her mysterious other life.

"It's your father, Camisa. He's . . . he's had a rather severe heart attack. I'm at the hospital now, the intensive care unit. You'd better come."

Camisa felt relief wash through her. Then guilt for feeling relieved. But the guilt didn't cling for long. She and her father had never gotten along very well anyway. "All right, I'll get there as soon as I can, but you know how it is with these kids." Any time she said the word "kids," it came out sounding like a profanity.

Her mother issued a long sigh. "I guess I'd better let you go, then. Anyway, I've still got to call Sabrina."

At the mention of her younger sister's name, Camisa felt a tightening in her chest. Camisa was night and Sabrina was day. Camisa gets married right out of high school to Mr. Nowhere Man and starts popping out babies to carry on the Nowhere name and tradition; Sabrina goes to college and earns an M.A. in business administration, and at the age of twenty-two has a top management position in *the* largest corporation in Danville. Camisa's hair is almost black. Sabrina's is golden blond. Camisa reads suspense thrillers and Sabrina reads romances.

The romance books Camisa could do without, but given the opportunity, she'd trade places with her sister in every other respect without blinking an eye. She'd never wanted this dreary housewife's existence, and was still trying to figure out how she'd allowed herself to be sucked into it.

Her mother had already hung up. Camisa replaced the receiver in its hook and looked disdainfully at the apricot mess spread out on the floor. Felicia had grabbed the spoon upside down and was waving it around in jerky, spasmodic movements that almost promised an injury to one of her eyes. In the garage, Aaron's hoarse screams and pleas had mellowed into sobs. Michael came into the kitchen with his completed artwork: Snow Purple and the Seven Martians.

"That looks like shit, Michael, now go find your shoes. We've got to go to the hospital, your granddaddy is about ready to kick the bucket."

3

Deidi Marshall lived in what had once been a large beautiful house by the sea, now divided up into four apartments and pretty much gone to seed. Nothing was done about the salt corrosion or the algae on the outer, light pink stucco walls, the weeds in the courtyard, or the sagging shutters.

Deidi and Hughman lived on the lower level, in the section that had formerly served as a recreation room, with a small kitchen, wet bar, and bathroom. Two walls had been added to make a private bedroom, leaving on one side a spacious living area with a fireplace and sliding patio door through which she came and went, on the other side a smaller dining area. The floor was parquet, and when Deidi had first moved in, she'd spent half a day getting off the old wax and polishing it anew. It had looked really good for a few months. After four years it didn't look so hot anymore, and although Deidi had promised countless times that one of these weekends she was going to make it pretty and shiny again, the job remained undone.

She was in her small kitchen fixing a crab salad for supper, thinking about the police composite she'd obtained from Judson Hendricks late that afternoon.

FLESH AND BLOOD

It would be printed with tomorrow's story about the murder, along with a photograph of Larry Patton. Just as she'd feared, the composite had resembled her, but not so much that anyone who knew her would take one look at it and say, "My God, that's Deidi Marshall!" And not so much that Judson Hendricks wanted to detain her for further questioning, although he had given her a few strange sidelong glances.

Floorboards groaned over the sparsely furnished living area, victims of Flora Bushbaum's heavy tread. Lying stretched out beside the patio door, Hughman looked up momentarily, then returned his muzzle to his paws with a grunt. Deidi also looked at the ceiling and wondered how long it would be before a section of it caved in under Flora's massive body. The woman had to weigh at least four hundred pounds, and whenever she went down to the beach for some sun, Deidi couldn't help but think of a beached whale, and was mildly surprised that someone didn't come along and start shooting harpoons at her. Deidi had pictured doing it herself. How could people like Flora and Tom let it get that bad? Didn't they ever look in a mirror? Did they think everyone wore size twenty clothes?

Flora's patio door slid open; she was coming down. Deidi could hear her thunderous footfalls on the redwood stairs. She tried to turn her attention back to the salad she was making, but instead she heard a voice.

A strange woman's voice yelling at her. "What is wrong with you?" And Deidi looked down to see what was in her lap, only she couldn't see it because it was too terrible to remember, but she did see something, a man's face covered with bleeding gashes, mouth open and tongue split. Larry's face, Larry Patton's dead face.

Deidi jumped. Someone was pounding against the glass of her patio door. Hughman had sprung to his feet and was growling softly at the closed drape.

"Take it easy, boy," she said as she maneuvered

around the counter to see who it was, and she silently gave the same advice to herself. She was shaking badly, feeling a dire need for a cigarette even though she'd just put one out a minute ago. She wished her next appointment with Dr. Jordan, her psychologist, was tomorrow instead of next week.

Pulling the drape aside, she saw that her visitor was Flora, or as Deidi sometimes called her, Baby Shamu. She was holding an envelope in the fat white sausages she called fingers. Deidi assumed it was a piece of her mail that the carrier had misplaced in Flora's box, which was typical. She wondered why Flora didn't just slip it into the correct mailbox. But she knew. Any excuse Flora could come up with to be neighborly would be used to full advantage. She was a recent widow (she had probably rolled over on her husband in bed) and by her own admission was very lonely. Deidi had suggested that she could make lots of friends at Weight Watchers meetings or an aerobics class, but Flora apparently had an invisible force field that kept such words from reaching her ears.

Deidi had calmed down somewhat by the time she opened the sliding door, but Hughman was still on guard, his black lips pulled back from his teeth, a low growl rumbling deep in his throat. Deidi ignored it; she knew the dog wouldn't attack unless she gave the command: *Hugh, cut 'em up!*

Flora, her face a pocked, cheesy moon, beamed Deidi a smile, which she grudgingly returned. "Postman give you some of my mail again, Flora?"

Nodding, Flora handed the envelope over. "Letter from Fort Lauderdale, looks like. Nice handwriting, so I don't suppose it's from a young man. I used to be a schoolteacher you know, and I'll swear I never gave a boy anything higher than a C in penmanship."

"Well, thank you, anyway, I was just—"

"Saw you yesterday evening around eight o'clock down on Market Street, and I waved, but I guess you didn't see me." Market Street, near the bus depot, was a curved avenue of open shops, most of the items for sale handcrafted or secondhand. Deidi hadn't been anywhere near it in almost six months.

"I stayed at home last night and watched television," she said patiently, in spite of the fact that she was anxious to close the door and get back to her supper. "It must have been someone who looked like me, but it definitely wasn't me."

Confusion bloomed on Flora's full-moon face. "But I could've sworn . . . she looked just like you, the spitting image, and I wasn't that far away, but the street was crowded and I lost sight of her after I waved. Could've been your sister, maybe?"

Deidi sighed, feeling her patience slipping away like sand through her fingers. "As I've told you before, I'm an only child. And at the moment I'm a very hungry only child. I was just fixing my dinner when you came."

Suddenly Flora looked extremely apologetic. "Oh, I'm sorry. I won't keep you any longer, then. I just wanted to bring you your mail." Flora had short gray hair that looked pin-curled; she patted it absently with one of her meaty hands and looked off toward the sea for a few moments in which her pale blue eyes misted over with memory. "I think I'll take me a walk," she said, and giving Deidi a brief parting smile, headed toward the beach, her huge lumpy buttocks jiggling obscenely inside the tight pair of yellow stretch pants she wore. *Thar she blows!* Deidi thought. Unaware of the grimace that had crept over her face, she pulled her patio door shut and locked it.

Hughman finally stopped growling and looked up at her expectantly, licking his chops. It was time for him to eat, too. But Deidi wanted to open and read her letter first. It was from one of her college roommates, Suzanne Weiss, perhaps the closest friend she'd ever had. Tearing across the top of the envelope with a fingernail, Deidi plopped down on her couch, not bothering to move aside the articles of clothing scattered over the cushions with Hughman's rawhide bone, an unfinished novel, and the section of yesterday's newspaper containing the crossword puzzle. Before diving into the letter, she reached for her lighter and pack of Virginia Slims on the cluttered coffee table, lit one and inhaled deeply. Hughman came around and lay his head across her knees, his brown eyes staring at her soulfully.

What is WRONG with you?

Deidi took another long drag on the cigarette and noticed that her hand was shaking again. What *was* wrong with her? So far Dr. Jordan hadn't been able to tell her. But she knew there was something, something very ugly buried down deep that wanted to surface. For years she'd been fighting to keep it from doing that, and had done so successfully, but for some reason she was starting to grow weak, or that ugly something was starting to get stronger.

She wondered if the dark voice she'd heard today at the Sea Breeze Motel was part of it, and if it had caused her to see that terrible vision of Larry Patton's ravaged face. She hadn't gone to the police morgue and looked at his body, but she had a dreadful feeling that if she should ask, Judson Hendricks would tell her that Larry Patton's tongue had been sliced open. But of course she wouldn't ask; how could she explain knowing something like that?

What is WRONG with you?

There was pressure now on both her temples as she tried concentrating on the letter from Suzanne. She and Kurt had split up. Her idea. Now he was bugging the hell out of her. Wouldn't leave her alone. Made a big ugly scene where she worked. Had to call the police three times now. She wanted to come down and stay for a week, if it wouldn't be too much trouble. Maybe Kurt would get his shit together if she wasn't around.

Deidi took another drag on her cigarette and tapped

the ashes in an overflowing ashtray. The pressure at her temples was getting worse, and now she had the disturbing sensation of being closely watched. She looked down at her lap and Hughman's eyes rolled up to meet hers. Covering them *(Peek-a-boo! What's WRONG with you?)* with her hand, she waited to see if that made any difference, but obviously it was not Hughman's gaze that was bothering her.

She looked toward the partially open drape to see if Flora had returned, or if Judson Hendricks had decided to drop by and pay her a not-so-friendly visit. But there was no one standing behind the glass.

Deidi tossed the letter on the coffee table and went back to the kitchen area behind the orange Formica counter to first open a can of Alpo, then to finish getting her own supper prepared. To drown out her own thoughts as well as any unwelcome voices that might decide to speak, she turned the radio on and tuned it to a rock station. It would be the last thing she remembered doing before waking up the next morning.

As she stared up at the bedroom ceiling, her mind danced with visions of herself on a bus, plane, train, cruise ship. There was no wedding band on her finger, no kids clinging to her clothes, no potbellied slob attached to a chain around her ankle. She savored the fantasy of freedom until a soft whimpering from the boys' bedroom rudely popped her rosy balloon.

What a drag that hospital scene had been. Felicia was cranky because of a new tooth she was cutting, Michael was unusually hyper in the strange surroundings, and then Aaron had acted like he was the one dying.

"What's the matter with Aaron, Camisa? He doesn't seem well at all. Looks like he can barely stand, and why is he so sweaty?" Fetched by a nurse, her mother had come out of the ICU room to the waiting area, and this had been her greeting. The old lady didn't look so well herself, complexion pasty, hair a mess, dark circles under her eyes.

Camisa had warned Aaron not to say anything about the dog carrier or the garage. He didn't open his mouth, but he didn't have to, as much as he was saying with body language.

"He's fine, I think he just spent a little too much time in the sun today," she answered sharply, glaring at Aaron and struggling to keep the wiggling, whining baby in her arms from doing a backflip onto the floor. "So how's Father? Still with us, I presume?"

"He's stablized, but he's in a coma. Go on back; I'll look after the children," her mother said, reaching for Felicia. "It's the fourth room on the left. Sabrina's in there with him now."

Camisa opened a heavy beige metal door and entered another carpeted corridor. Up ahead to her right, nurses flitted around their station like honeybees on a hive. Camisa counted the open doorways on her left and stopped inside the fourth. The room was rather small; the adjustable bed on which her father lay between railings was taking up most of the space. Along the right wall was a bank of machines. One of them was breathing for him through a plastic tube secured to his mouth with tape. His chest rose and fell in an unnatural, almost jerky way. A heart monitor at the far end had a green screen with a line through its center, and every second or two it made a peak and a blip. Forrest Murray: takes a licking and keeps on ticking.

Sabrina sensed her presence and turned around, still holding their father's limp left hand. Her lips curved slightly in a sad smile. "He's going to be okay. I just feel a real peace from God."

What you feel, my dear sister, Camisa thought, is the peace of knowing your savings account's about to get a little fatter. Maybe a lot fatter. Hard to say what the old man was worth since he never discussed

FLESH AND BLOOD

financial matters, even with his wife. A pretty nurse came in and wrote something on a chart hanging beside the heart monitor, then took a penlight and one at a time lifted the pads over Forrest Murray's eyes and shined the light into them.

"Are his pupils responding yet?" Sabrina asked in a small voice.

The nurse shook her head and walked out.

"If his pupils aren't responding to light, that usually means brain damage or brain death," Camisa said matter-of-factly. "I read that in a book once. *Murders of the Full Moon*, I think it was."

Sabrina looked at her as if she'd just spat on a statue of the Virgin. "You don't even care, do you? It doesn't matter to you one way or the other if Daddy lives or dies."

"Watch it," Camisa said. "If he isn't brain dead, he can hear everything we say."

Then she could hear Felicia squalling in the waiting area, and her mother's flustered voice telling Michael to leave something alone. "Kids," she said with disgust. "You were smart not to have any, Sabrina, and if you ever have any second thoughts, come over and babysit mine for a few hours. You'll be cured for at least a year." She left with Sabrina's eyes burning into her like hot coals, and as she passed the nurse's station, one of them glanced up at her and did a quick double-take.

The murder at the Sea Breeze Motel, Camisa thought with a sudden pang of paranoia. The description of her on the news. Maybe they'd even shown a composite drawing based on the memories of the bartender and cocktail waitress after she'd turned off her set. Hanging her head so that her hair would at least partially cover her face, she hurried down the corridor to the metal door.

Michael was running in circles around the middle island of cushioned chairs, giggling and squealing and repeating the new word he'd learned today, *shit*, short chubby legs flying, with Grandma a pace behind in hot pursuit, her expression grim as she hissed at him to sit down and behave himself. Felicia was getting quite a ride on Grandma's hip, and obviously didn't like it one bit. Her face was red and puckering for the next scream. Aaron was laying on the floor like a rag doll.

Camisa became aware that she was clenching her teeth and her fists, and rage was boiling up inside her like a volcano. How she managed to restrain herself from killing her three children on the way home would forever remain a mystery, especially considering the little scene she'd had with her mother before leaving the hospital. It had nearly pushed her over the edge, standing there listening to galling accusations about being a bad mother and an uncaring daughter.

She remembered giving all three of them a tablespoonful of Harlan's Jim Beam and putting them to bed, and even though it was early yet, she went to bed as well. But before she climbed under the covers with her new suspense novel, she pulled out a strand of hair and secured one end with spit to the bedroom door, the other to the doorjamb. Then she took an old pair of panty hose from her lingerie drawer and tied her left ankle to a post on the footboard. She thought she'd perhaps read through two chapters, then the next thing she knew, she was dressed in jeans and a sweater and walking along Palm Grove, the strap of a black canvas purse slung over her right shoulder.

It was still light out, but the sun was going down. She guessed it was about eight o'clock, maybe a little later. Looking to her left, she saw that she was coming up on Gravitz & Sons Mortuary. It was a low, stern gray building with black trim, set in the midst of several towering palm trees. Beneath a wide carport on the left was parked a white hearse and white limousine.

She didn't think she had intended to go inside the funeral home, but her feet, with minds of their own,

FLESH AND BLOOD

turned up the front walk and carried her to the double black doors. The one on the right was unlocked.

Inside, her tennis shoes sunk into plush maroon carpeting. The air smelled faintly of roses, and soft music was playing, piped in from a mysterious source. It was a blending of mournful, subdued organ notes, the kind of music you'd only expect to hear at a funeral or in a place like this. To her left were the ornate doors of a chapel, and one of them was propped open by a slender podium that supported an open book. A guest register, she thought. So everyone can see how much the deceased was really loved. Or not loved. Either way, the world still turned.

A tall, slender man with aristocratic features suddenly materialized at her side. "Are you here to see Mrs. Wilheim or Mr. Giles?" His dark eyes flicked over her attire in obvious disapproval.

"Mr. Giles," she said, and with a curt nod he turned to lead her down a corridor on the right, past a lacquered black door that said OFFICE.

There were three state rooms along this corridor, and Mr. Giles was in the middle one. She entered the small room with its soft, strategic lighting, and the tall snob left her alone with the corpse, which was laid in a bluish-gray metal casket with dark blue handles and inner lining. Both ends of the casket were flanked with large flower arrangements.

Mr. Giles looked about sixty or so, bald on top, black hair generously peppered with gray on the sides. On closer inspection he looked like something made of wax, which never had been alive. She hadn't known him, but she was glad he was dead anyway.

"You fucker," she hissed in his pale, waxy face. And then a smile crept to her lips, the child of a deliciously wicked idea. After a surreptitious glance over her shoulder to make sure she wasn't being observed, she reached into the canvas purse and fished around until she located a hard, slender tube. She brought it out and removed the top, turning the base until the tip of the red lipstick protruded half an inch above the casing. Clamping one hand over her mouth to suppress a rising fountain of giggles, she began applying the lipstick to Mr. Gile's sealed, lifeless lips.

Next she took an eyebrow pencil and drew a large pair of eyes on his closed lids—after discovering they'd been sealed shut with some kind of glue, maybe Elmer's—every few seconds tossing a furtive glance toward the doorway, unable to keep the giggles down.

She supposed she could get into a lot of trouble for doing this, but she didn't care and she couldn't stop herself anyway. Maybe this time it really was just a dream, a very bizarre dream.

Mr. Giles was quite a sight with wide-open cartoon eyes and ruby lips; if any family members saw him like this, they'd shit a truckload of bricks. But she still wasn't satisfied. Scrounging around in the purse, she came up with a thin crumpled box containing a few Luden's cherry cough drops to cram up his nostrils. Seeing them in place spawned a fresh burst of fiendish tittering; she clamped both hands over her mouth, watery eyes darting over her shoulder to check the doorway again.

The tall man was standing there with his hands clasped behind his back, staring at her with a very solemn expression. He couldn't see Mr. Giles's face; she was blocking his view. But he obviously suspected that something was amiss.

She quickly turned her giggles into tortured sobs, relying on the tears standing in her eyes to authenticate the facetious sounds of woe. "He was such a good man, it just isn't fair!" she wailed, turning back to the corpse. When she chanced another peek at the doorway a few seconds later, the tall man was gone. A slight smile appeared on her lips, and her pretentious sobs ebbed into quiet malevolent laughter. Returning her attention to Mr. Giles, she decided what the crowning touch should be, the final insult to this glorified slab of meat. She arranged (with some difficulty) for one of his cold, stiff hands to shoot the bird, and when she was finished working the rigid joints, an unexpected chill seeped into her along with a terrible notion: what if he wasn't as dead as he should be, what if he was aware of what she had done, incensed, and his hands suddenly started to move on their own, what if—

His eyes slowly began to open in spite of the glue, and his red lips began to twitch and separate, releasing a putrid stench. His waxy head shifted slightly on the satin pillow, nostrils flaring around the cherry cough drops as his voice bellowed at her from a bottomless pit: *"What is wrong with you?"*

She stared down at him wide-eyed, her body trembling. Of course, he hadn't really moved; her imagination had just played a dirty trick on her. She spat in his face and left the mortuary, the snobbish undertaker nowhere in sight.

Later, sitting on a deserted pier, she was swinging her legs over the foamy green water. The only light was given by the moon, shining full and bright over the expanse of calm sea, swatches of diaphanous clouds drifting across it from time to time. The only sounds were the metallic clangings and wooden creakings of the boats moored in their stalls, the occasional cry of a night bird, and the water lapping gently against the docks. The breezes coming off the Atlantic were very cool, and whenever they blew, she shivered inside her bulky sweater. She was smoking a cigarette and wondering if the old man who lived in the trashy fishing boat was asleep yet; there was still a dim light burning inside the cabin, but she'd seen no movement for a while now. He'd been out on the deck earlier when she was taking a walk along the pier, and had issued a wolf whistle in her direction. Bad mistake.

She had somehow stepped back into her other life, her secret life, the one in which she was truly free of the stifling tethers of motherhood and marriage. In this life she did terrible things, things over which she had no control, but she didn't feel bad about doing them. Quite the opposite.

Another cool, salty breeze ruffled through her hair. Looking to her right, she saw that the light was still on in the fishing boat's cabin, but she rose to her feet, tossed the remainder of the cigarette into the water and began walking up the dark pier; she was tired of waiting, and surely the old man was asleep by now. The wooden slats creaked softly beneath her footsteps and the canvas purse rubbed against her thigh, making a swishing sound. Other than that, she could only hear the sound of her own breathing, all other night sounds blocked out. A gray ghost ship drifted across the moon full sail, temporarily deepening the shadows surrounding her. She felt her pulse quicken with excitement as she reached into the purse for the serrated steak knife. An inner voice suggested too late that she should have carved something into Mr. Giles's forehead, like "Death Sucks" or "I'm in Hell." Maybe next time, at a different mortuary.

Before stepping over the railing of the decrepit boat, she held her breath and listened for any sound coming from within the cabin. All she heard was the vessel's groans as the waves gently rocked it, the rhythmic bumping of its starboard side against a wall of tires. But after several more moments of intense listening, her ears picked up something else, the faint but unmistakable sound of snoring.

Very quietly, very carefully, she climbed onto the deck. The moon gave enough illumination so that she could move around without bumping into anything, but she couldn't define the odd shapes scattered around her. The cabin roof was low, and up close the whole thing looked like it had been slapped together with tin and a prayer. She moved up to the leaning doorway over which a heavy black tarp had been hung, and paused, the knife gripped tightly in her left hand. The old fisherman snorted loudly, startling her,

FLESH AND BLOOD

but then he went back to his regular snoring and she felt her tightened muscles relax somewhat. After taking a few deep breaths to calm herself further, she pulled the tarp aside and stepped silently into the cabin.

The light she'd seen from the pier was coming from an old oil lantern. It was hanging over a makeshift wooden table that looked like it could be toppled with a gust of wind, but it was apparently strong enough to support the weight of an almost empty whiskey bottle, a glass, and an ashtray overflowing with brownish hand-rolled butts. The cabin was crowded with all kinds of junk, probably everything the man owned, and it reeked with a collection of unsavory smells: sweat, fish, urine, spoiled food, stale tobacco, and a few others that defied definition. She grimaced in disgust.

The old man's bed was directly across from the table. It was a mattress settled into a box framework almost as high as the table, with flaking, ill-hung cabinet doors below it, which were kept closed with a frayed piece of rope, indicating that it doubled as a storage compartment.

The old man was lying on the bed in a filthy pair of boxer shorts, partially covered by a sheet that probably hadn't seen a washing machine in twenty years. He was lying on his back, hoary head sunk into an uncovered feather pillow, mouth hanging open, eyelids twitching with dreams. She wondered what a useless old goat like him would be dreaming about. Being the captain of a glorious ship? Getting marooned on an island full of brown-skinned women who'd never learned the meaning of shame? Having his smelly old cock sucked by a beautiful mermaid?

She carefully set the purse down on the built-in bench next to the table and crept to the edge of the bed with the knife, suppressing the urge to gag from the man's sweat-fishy odor. He must have sensed her presence then, on a subconscious level, for he spoke in a whiskey-roughened voice, though his eyes remained closed.

"Good catch today, eh, Cyrus? Damn lucky the net didn't break."

She decided to play with him. Even if he awakened, he didn't stand a chance against her youthful strength, determination, and the sharp blade of the knife in her hand. Not this drunken, worn-out old coot.

"Catch yourself a mermaid today, old man?"

He snorted again, one hand reaching up to scratch at his scraggly gray and white beard. Probably has fleas, she thought, fervently hoping none of them jumped on her. The other hand scratched absently at his crotch, tugged at the stained sheet until his chest was covered, and then he was still except for the snoring.

She leaned over him, knife hand twitching. "Old man," she whispered, sickened by the heavy wax buildup in his left ear, "tell me about the mermaid you caught in your net today. What did she do for you?"

"Pirate ship dead ahead, Cyrus!" a loud voice squawked, and she nearly jumped out of her skin. Her head whipped around to the corner from which it had come, and there in the shadows, half hidden by a coat tree heavy with garments, was a large bird cage, and within it a green parrot paced in slow motion back and forth along a perch, its head cocked in her direction.

"Pirate ship dead ahead, Cyrus!" the bird repeated loudly.

"Ah, shaddup," the old man grumbled, reaching down again to scratch his crotch. His eyes fluttered open, closing quickly to shut out the offensive light of the lantern, but reopening in a squint a moment later to get another look at the unfamiliar shape he thought he'd seen standing next to his bed.

He'd thought correctly; there was something there. A woman, her features cast in shadow because her

FLESH AND BLOOD

back was to the light. Rufus Bagget felt his old ticker lurch into overdrive. "Sara? Is that you?" Sara was his daughter, whom he hadn't seen in over fifteen years. It was damned unlikely for her to suddenly show up on his boat like this, but who else could it be? Anna from the tavern? No, Anna would have no reason. She flirted with him, but she flirted with all her male customers and none of it meant anything, it was just good for business. And it certainly wouldn't be any of the dancers. They all went for the virile young sailors, if not for each other.

"Sara, is that you?" the parrot mimicked from its corner.

"Yes, it's Sara," she said, fingers tightening around the steak knife's handle. "So how's it going, old man? Seen any mermaids lately?"

Rufus's head was spinning and he couldn't make it stop. There was a fire down somewhere in his guts, and his tongue felt like it was covered with fungus. Maybe it was. He hardly knew up from down, and at the moment probably couldn't recite his social security number if his life depended on it, but he knew the woman standing before him wasn't really his Sara. He hadn't heard Sara's voice in fifteen years, but he remembered it as being very soft and feminine, almost melodic. Whoever this was, claiming to be her, had a fairly low voice for a woman, coarse and menacing, although he supposed some men would consider it sexy.

"You're not Sara," he said, swallowing something acrid and slimy that had crawled up his throat.

"Hell of a storm brewin' up, Cyrus!" the parrot squawked.

She glanced toward the cage, where the parrot was doing lazy calisthenics on his perch. "Smart bird you've got there. He's right, you know. There is a hell of a storm brewing. In fact, it's already here, old man, in full fury. In me." And quick as a lightning flash, she slashed at him with the knife and cut a deep, wide gash across his throat. Blood instantly began to flow from the wound, coursing like crimson rivers down the sides of his neck to the bare feather pillow beneath his head. His bloodshot eyes bugged out in horror although his brain had yet to fully realize what had just occurred. Automatically his hands flew to his neck, and there his trembling, tobacco-stained fingers slid over the warm wetness being pumped from his carotid artery. At the same time, he became aware of a sweet coppery taste in his mouth, but it quickly became rancid and he rolled over to the edge of the bed to spit it out on the cabin floor. When he did, she stabbed him savagely in the back, the blade sinking in at least three inches. Rufus screamed, and with the scream a large blood clot flew out of his mouth, landing on the woman's right tennis shoe.

She pulled the knife blade out, having to wiggle it a bit, and watched a second as the new fountain erupted. Then she plunged the knife again, this time in the back of his neck, and the blade went all the way through, the tip sticking into the wooden bed frame. He was impaled like a bug specimen.

"Pirate ship dead ahead, Cyrus!" the parrot said in its queer voice over the old man's gargling screams. The old man was attempting to grab the knife's handle, but she kept slapping his bloody hand away, amazed that he still had any strength left. Didn't the old fart know when to give it up and die? But she was in for an even bigger surprise: the next thing she knew, he was getting up on his hands and knees, and with what had to be nothing but sheer willpower, pulled the blade's tip from the wood by yanking his neck upward. She was so surprised by this—surprised and frightened—that she stumbled backward, bumping into the table and knocking over the whiskey bottle. It rolled off the table and fell to the floor with a loud clunk, its remaining contents spilling from the uncapped lip.

Humped over his knees on the bed, whose sheets

FLESH AND BLOOD

were almost totally bloodsoaked, the old man worked to remove the knife from his neck, all the while coughing and spitting up phlegmy blood clots the size of dried prunes, a wild, desperate look in his eyes. As he tugged at the knife's handle, grimacing in agony, he turned those eyes on her, taking in the features he could now see, asking her silently how she could have done such a thing to him. He didn't know her; never saw her before in his life. Did she think he had some treasure secretly stashed in this floating rat's nest? If so, she was going to be greatly disappointed.

He could feel unconsciousness gnawing at him. He'd lost a great deal of blood, and he knew he was dying, but wished he could know why. She'd missed his windpipe, but he still couldn't speak, couldn't ask what he'd done to deserve such a brutal, painful death.

The knife wouldn't come out. Hurt too much. He held a hand caked with sticky, dark red blood out toward her, and initiated an effort to climb out of the bed. Her eyes widened, her mouth opening in a gasp. Then she ducked, picked up the fallen whiskey bottle by the neck and swung the base at him like she was Babe Ruth going for a home run. The bottle cracked against the side of his head, knocking him back against the wall of the cabin with an explosion of stars, and when their lights faded away, there was nothing for Rufus Bagget but the darkness of night.

She stood staring down at him, waiting for him to move again. There was quite a crater in his skull where she'd bashed him with the liquor bottle, and blood seeped from a wide gash in its center as the surrounding area rapidly turned purple. "You dead, old man?" she asked the still, bloody form, not wishing to get any closer to find out for sure.

One of his legs twitched. Muscle spasm? She brought the whiskey bottle up, cradling it, prepared to use it again if necessary.

The parrot rattled the bars of its cage with its beak

and made a series of nonsensical sounds and whistles. She thought about killing it, too, but decided it would be more trouble than it was worth, and she might get bitten. What she really wanted to do was stab the old man a few dozen more times, like she'd done with Larry Patton. The storm within her was not yet quieted. Holding the whiskey bottle firmly, she cautiously approached the edge of the bed.

"Can you hear me, old man?"

"Can you hear me, old man?" the parrot echoed.

She glowered toward the cage. "Shut up, you stupid bird."

"Shut up, you stupid bird."

She scowled and poked at one of the old man's legs with the bottle. After a few seconds she heard a low groan followed by a raspy, bubbling intake of breath.

"Fuck this, I'm getting out of here," she muttered, turning to throw the bottle at the parrot's cage before leaving. Her aim was true; the heavy glass smacked straight into it, resulting in a frantic flurry of wings that sent feathers and other debris sailing into the air, the bird screeching and squawking in rage.

4

Deidi Marshall awoke the next morning feeling like she'd just put her head down on the pillow. And besides feeling unrested, she felt surrounded by the dark, clinging aura of a nightmare, although she couldn't remember having any dreams.

Hughman was nuzzling her with his wet nose. *Let me out to pee, and I mean right now, or I'll do it on the wheel of your exercise bike.* "All right, boy, hold on, I'm getting up," she said groggily, but first she treated herself to a leisurely stretch that included a groaning yawn. She tried to remember what time she'd gone to bed last night and realized that she couldn't even remember doing it, which bothered her. Bothered her a lot. Her mind continued to paw through the cobwebs for that memory—which had to be in there somewhere—while she put on her robe and led Hughman to the sliding glass door.

While he was doing his business on his favorite palm tree, she stood in the open doorway taking deep breaths of the cool morning air, still trying to chronicle her activities of the night before, when a terrible vision flashed before her eyes. It was gone almost as soon as it appeared, but the picture had registered. An old bearded man covered with blood, kneeling on a bed with bloody sheets, reaching out to her. And she wasn't sure, but she thought she saw something sticking out of his neck.

"God," she said aloud, shaking her head. She didn't know where that had come from, just that she didn't want to see it again. Hughman trotted back inside, looking proud of himself with his black stub of a tail wagging. Deidi closed the glass door and trudged into the kitchen area to put her Mr. Coffee to work. Maybe with a little caffeine in her system she'd be able to think.

Waiting for her coffee to brew, she smoked a cigarette and picked out the clothes she would wear that day, a gray pinstriped suit that she always wore with a frilly red blouse. But when she reached for the hanger on which the blouse was hung, her hand shrank away from it as if it had tried to bite her. The red material had brought back the bloody vision, and this time she had seen the old man's eyes, how they'd been filled with intense pain and horror. And something else. Confusion.

Deidi stepped back from the closet and took a deep drag of her cigarette, shuddering involuntarily as her mind gave birth to an ugly idea. The woman who'd killed Larry Patton had killed again, last night. But Deidi couldn't understand why she should know this. She wasn't psychic and never had been. Yet she'd known that Larry Patton's body was nude, and that inner voice had whispered soon, very soon . . .

"I think I may be cracking up for sure, Dr. Jordan," she said to the light pink blouse she picked out instead. Hughman, who was lying across the foot of her bed snoozing, raised his head, pointed ears turned in her direction. *Talking to yourself again, you silly human? Maybe you should get checked for distemper.*

"I don't believe so, Deidi," she answered herself, mimicking Dr. Jordan's deep voice with its slight Southern accent. "You're just getting a little paranoid, due to the conflict between your id and superego, or in

Jung's terms, your shadow and your persona. When we've found out what all's lurking in that vast subconscious terrain of yours and analyzed it in the cold light of the present, you'll be just fine. All it takes is a little understanding. It's like looking into the closet and finding that what you thought was a hairy monster with big sharp teeth is in reality your winter coat."

Deidi took one last drag on her cigarette, crushed it out and replied in her own voice on the way to the bathroom to shower, "You don't know what a relief that is to hear, Doctor, especially since I can't remember one fucking thing I did after I fixed my dinner last night."

Hughman settled his head back down on his paws and whined softly.

Before heading for the *Danville Chronicle*'s large green-brick complex on the corner of Florida and Third Avenue, Deidi was required every morning to first swing by the police station and get the info for the daily police blotter. The female officer who usually supplied this information was a dead ringer for Sandy Dennis, although Deidi was fairly certain both of Carla Wilson's eyes were real.

As usual, Carla was sitting behind her dark particleboard desk, its imitation wood grain surface all but hidden under various piles of paper. This morning she was busy keying traffic tickets into the computer system, the machine barely keeping up with her speedy fingers.

Deidi cleared her throat to get Carla's attention. "Anything exciting happen yesterday? I mean, besides the murder?"

Carla went on with her work as if she hadn't heard, but Deidi knew that she had. Nor was Carla being rude; it was just impossible for her to stop in the middle of something. Deidi wondered what Dr. Jordan would think about that. A few seconds later Carla finished filling in the blank spaces on the glowing green monitor, slapped the ticket facedown on the correct stack, and turned to greet Deidi with her bright Sandy Dennis smile.

"Good morning to you, too."

Deidi feigned a scowl. "Screw the amenities, pig. Just give me the information and I'll be on my way."

Carla's eyes narrowed, the bright Sandy Dennis smile replaced by a sinister grin. "I think I'll lock you up right now for impersonating a human being. And I'll bet you didn't feed your parking meter. So, I'd say you're in some real trouble, lady. Care to ask me a little nicer?"

Deidi looked suddenly contrite, and clasped her hands together as if in prayer. "Oh, please, please don't put me in jail," she responded in a little-girl voice. "I'm sorry, Miss Piggy. I'll be nice. Can I please take a look at your log?"

Carla chuckled as she rolled her swivel chair toward the counter Deidi was leaning on to get the dispatcher's logbook, which was kept on a shelf behind it. The sheets were turned in individually at the end of each shift.

Deidi heard a man's soft, throaty laughter suddenly join Carla's, and whipped her head around to see Judson Hendricks standing at the head of a brown-carpeted corridor that Carla once told her led to the detective division's offices: Robbery, Vice, Homicide, Narcotics, and Fraud. Deidi had never seen him at the station before, but then, the detectives usually didn't show up until eight at the earliest, and she was always gone by a quarter of.

She felt her cheeks begin to flame; apparently he'd heard what she'd said to Carla in that little-girl voice. It was a game she and Carla often played, and no offense was ever meant or taken. And until this morning, it had been a very private game.

"If I were you, Carla, I'd go ahead and lock her up," he said with a glib smile, sauntering into the large central office with his hands in his pockets. He had a slight, lean build that didn't quite fill his beige leisure suit, and a face that had yet to show any permanent emotional scars from his profession. He looked more like an artist or musician, especially with his wheat-colored hair worn on the long and shaggy side, but his intensely inquisitive eyes definitely belonged to a detective.

"I would, but I'm really behind on the traffic tickets," Carla said, hoisting the logbook up on the counter. "I'd have to fill out all that paperwork, and then she'd just turn around and post bail. Maybe you can just take her down the hall and wash her mouth out with soap for me."

Deidi looked warily at the detective. "I think that would go under the heading of cruel and unusual punishment, not to mention a violation of my right to a fair trial."

Hendricks shook his head and tsk-tsked. "Sorry, Carla; she seems to know the law. We don't want the ACLU coming down on us."

"I know, take her to lunch at Julio's Burrito Barn." Carla grinned, a devious matchmaking gleam in her baby blues. "That'll teach her a lesson, one she won't soon forget, and what could a Civil Liberties attorney say about that?"

"Plenty, if he's ever eaten there," Deidi muttered, remembering her assignment to investigate the rumors that Julio's burritos were being made with dog meat. They weren't, but one would never know from the taste.

She could feel heat blossoming in her cheeks again. *Fuck you very much, Miss Cupid Piggy,* and quickly veered the conversation away from the prospect of Hendricks taking her out to lunch. "So how's the investigation on the Patton murder going? Any leads yet?"

A sudden weariness settled over the detective's

features. Frowning, he pulled his right hand from its pocket and rubbed his temples as if she'd given him an instant headache. "Nothing solid. We lifted several good prints in the motel room, but most of them belonged to Patton and the maid. The few that didn't weren't on file. I spent last night tracking down the people Patton had contacted that day, but none of them could give me any information about the brunette he was seen with at the club. Got a few calls on the composite, but the women those led to all had solid alibis."

"Did you know about the complaint filed by Gravitz and Sons Mortuary last night?" Carla asked him, her usual cheerfulness subdued by the grim subject, like the sun hiding behind a dark cloud. An oppressive pall was hanging over all three of them now, in steep contrast to the jocular atmosphere of a few moments ago. Hendricks's expression indicated that he did not know about the complaint, and Carla stood to open the thick logbook.

Reading from one of the entries on the last page, printed on light green computer paper in dot matrix, she continued in a serious tone: "The call came in at eight thirty-two, made by Arthur Gravitz, one of the owners. About half an hour earlier, he'd let a woman in to view the body of Edward Giles." She paused, turning to sift through some papers on her desk. Finding what she wanted a few seconds later, she removed it from the pile and brought it over to the counter. "Officer Greg Crouch was dispatched to take the report, and this is what he wrote: 'Body's left hand arranged in obscene gesture. False eyes drawn on eyelids with brown pencil. Red candy inserted into nostrils. Red lipstick on lips. Description of suspect: Early to mid-twenties, average height, dark brown shoulder-length hair and brown eyes, wearing jeans, bulky gray sweater, and white running shoes, carrying a black purse.'" Her eyes left the page and rose to meet the detective's attentive gaze. "Well, what do you think?"

He snorted. "I think she must have one hell of a grudge against the guy, or else she's a total nut case."

Deidi's mind formed a picture of what Carla had just described, and for some unfathomable reason it struck her as being hysterically funny and she had to make a concerted effort to keep from giggling. "Except for the clothes, that was the description of the woman seen leaving the Sea Breeze club with Larry Patton," she said, a forced look of seriousness on her face. She was certain that the similarity had not escaped Hendricks, as he feigned; neither had the fact that, except for the clothes, she also fit the description. But so did dozens, maybe even hundreds of other women in this city. Still, she could almost hear Hendricks thinking at her, *So where were you last night between eight and eight-thirty p.m.?* "I think I'll get my hair cut and bleached platinum-blond today," she added with a sour smile, letting him know that his train of thought could be seen coming down the tracks and she was ready to meet it head-on. Briefly returning his piercing stare, she got out her notebook and pen. "What time did you say that was, Carla?"

Carla turned the report around so Deidi could read the information for herself. While she was jotting it down, Hendricks leaned against the counter and rubbed his chin thoughtfully. "I don't know, could be the same woman, I suppose, but I don't think it's likely. There's certainly no similarity in the crimes. I guess it wouldn't hurt to swing by the mortuary and show Mr. Arthur Gravitz a copy of our composite, though. So anyway, Debbie—no, it's Deidi, right? What time should I pick you up for lunch?"

Deidi was so startled by the question, she almost dropped her pen. Her mouth fell open slightly and she felt suddenly weak in the knees. Was this a continuation of their previous game, or was he for real? And if he was asking on the level, why? Was he attracted to her or was he thinking of it as a chance to investigate her without her knowing it?

"Sorry, but I'd rather eat a live iguana than one of Julio's burritos."

He and Carla both laughed, then Carla went back to her desk, sat down in her swivel chair and resumed entering traffic tickets into the computer system as if her life depended on getting it done before eight o'clock. Deidi wasn't fooled. Maybe Carla did need to get on with her work, but she'd clearly taken a conscious step out of nature's way. Deidi's brain instantly went to work on coming up with a solid excuse as to why she couldn't have lunch with Judson Hendricks until the year 2000.

"Same here," he said, still chuckling, although his eyes retained the look of a predator. "But I don't care much for live iguana, either. How about the Cyprus Gourmet? You like seafood?"

"Breaks me out in hives," Deidi lied, then added apologetically, "Thanks for the invite, but it's really impossible for me to make a lunch date; my schedule's just too erratic." She went back to her note taking with a vengeance, hoping like hell he wouldn't counter her refusal with an offer to take her out to dinner.

He didn't. He shrugged the whole thing off as though he hadn't cared one way or another, then excused himself and returned to his office down the corridor. As soon as he was gone, Carla looked over her shoulder at Deidi with a reproving frown.

"He is single, you know. Divorced with custody of his two kids, but nobody's perfect."

"Beware the ulterior motive," Deidi muttered under her breath.

"What?"

"Never mind. Better get back to your stack of tickets before they start mating and reproducing themselves."

* * *

FLESH AND BLOOD

The constant ringing of the telephone finally coaxed Camisa out of her dream. In it she had been leaning over a porcelain sink trying to get the old man's blood off her right tennis shoe, but the more she scrubbed, the bigger and darker the stain became, until finally fresh blood was flowing from it as if from a gaping wound.

Her eyes opened and she became aware that she was covered with cold sweat. Besides the telephone, she could now hear Felicia crying from the nursery, and the Looney Tunes cartoon jingle blaring from the living room.

Nyah, what's up, Doc? I taught I taw a tewwible twime. I did, I did!

Camisa bolted upright and looked toward the foot of the bed, where she'd tethered her left ankle to the footboard. One end of the panty hose was still attached to the post on the footboard, but the rest of it was dangling on the floor.

You waskelly wabbit.

"Fuck," Camisa breathed, staring at her freed ankle in horror. She couldn't remember taking it off. Maybe one of the boys had come in and done it? Or she might have had to get up and go to the bathroom last night, and was still half asleep, barely conscious of what she was doing. Or she'd assumed her other identity and freed herself so she could go out and kill the old man in the fishing boat. And that wasn't all. Just then she remembered what she'd done before going to the pier. In that mortuary. To that dead body.

You're dethpicable.

The phone stopped ringing, but Felicia's wails grew louder. The sound pierced Camisa's brain like a laser. She pushed herself out of bed and stomped over to her bedroom door, which was slightly ajar, and she distinctly remembered shutting it before going to bed. She was wearing the same cotton nightgown she'd gone to sleep in, but she didn't suppose that meant anything. As soon as she got Felicia shut up, she'd throw on her robe and go out to check the mileage on her old Chrysler.

The nursery reeked of shit, and she clenched her teeth together so tightly it was a wonder they weren't ground to powder. Moving toward the crib with a murderous look on her face, Camisa violently shook the collapsible side onto which Felicia was clinging and screamed *"Shut up, you little shit!"* in the baby's face, which only made her cry louder.

Camisa flung her down on the crib's mattress and roughly yanked the cohesive tabs apart with Felicia kicking and screaming, small arms flailing, her face and neck flushed a deep red. Camisa bent down, grabbed a pacifier that had fallen to the floor and jammed it into Felicia's open mouth, but her lips wouldn't close around it. The frightened baby continued to scream, and Camisa was fast reaching the end of her rope.

"Take it, damn you!"

Felicia turned her head to escape the rubber object being forced into her mouth, which was the proverbial last straw. Camisa threw it at her, then slapped her hard across the face, shocking her into a brief silence that was followed by cries of such high pitch and intensity that Camisa thought her eardrums would shatter. In her mind's eye she saw herself jerk her baby daughter up and hurl her to the floor as many times as it took to make her be still. And she might have actually done it, but something strange happened just then, something that shoved Felicia and her intolerable crying completely out of Camisa's mind.

She had a vision of herself at a very young age, no older than two or three, being tossed playfully into the air by a man she assumed was her father. She was squealing and giggling with delight as he tossed her up again and again, catching her firmly with his big strong hands.

Then the phone started to ring again, and the vision with all its pleasant nuances dissolved, the sound of

Felicia's wailing returning louder than ever, but Camisa was no longer bothered by it. Looking down, she saw the angry handprint on her daughter's cheek and felt a sudden pang of guilt.

"Aaron, answer the goddamn phone!" she bellowed over her shoulder, then leaned over and gently caressed the ugly mark she'd made on Felicia's rose-petal skin. "Hush now, Mama's going to change your diaper," she cooed, "then we'll go to the kitchen and have some breakfast. Mama's sweet angel hungry for her breakfast?" Then she went about changing the dirty diaper with the usual scowl on her face. Felicia continued to cry, but not as loudly. The phone was still ringing, and Camisa wondered why the hell Aaron wasn't answering it like she told him to. Damn kid wasn't worth a plugged nickel.

"Aaron! Get the phone *right now!*"

Her thoughts returned to the vision, or memory or whatever that had been, and she vaguely recalled the man's face, which had been rather fat, now that she thought about it. Fat and greasy-looking. So the man couldn't have been her father, who'd always been "skinny as a broom" according to her mother. Must have been an uncle or some other relative who'd died or gone away for good when she was still very young. Or maybe her imagination had just thrown that up at her to stop her from seriously injuring or even killing Felicia.

By the time the diapering job was finished, Camisa's anger had been rekindled by the fact that Aaron had blatantly ignored her demand to answer the phone. After twenty-something rings, it had finally stopped ringing on its own. She carried Felicia, who had finally allowed herself to be plugged by the pacifier, into the living room, where Camisa's narrowed eyes found only Michael sitting cross-legged on the dilapidated couch, watching cartoons with a forefinger buried halfway up his nose.

"Michael, stop that," Camisa barked at him, frowning in disgust. He looked up at her like he didn't know what in the world she was talking about, he was just sitting there watching cartoons. He was trying his hardest to be a Good Boy, because he didn't want to be put out in the garage like Aaron had.

"Get your finger out of your nose!" Camisa bellowed when he didn't react, which made Felicia start crying again; the pacifier fell out of her open mouth and landed on the floor between Camisa's feet. She angrily kicked it away, still glaring at Michael, who hadn't until that moment even been aware of his present booger expedition. He quickly pulled his finger out, and finding nothing on it, clasped his hands together in his lap and offered her a tentative smile.

"The next time I catch you picking your nose, I'm going to cut that nasty finger off," Camisa threatened, and Michael's tentative smile quickly vanished, replaced by an expression of cold fear. Most little boys his age would instinctively know that their mothers were kidding when they said something like that. Michael did not. In fact he was pretty sure she wasn't. "Where the hell is Aaron?" Camisa continued in the same surly tone of voice, jostling Felicia on her hip to quiet her. It wasn't working.

"Aaron's still in bed," Michael answered solemnly, the same finger that had been rooting in his nostril going subconsciously to his mouth.

Giving him the same scathing look that a pious nun would give to a flasher, Camisa put the baby down on the floor and jammed the pacifier into her mouth. Just then Sylvester the cat got completely flattened by an elephant's foot on the color television screen. There was no blood, of course, and no death either; four legs suddenly appeared beneath the smashed cat and carried it comically out of sight. Sometimes, like right now, Camisa wished the same thing would happen to her three kids, only for real.

As Michael had said, Aaron was still in bed. He was lying very still on the double bed he shared with his

FLESH AND BLOOD

younger brother, eyes closed, limbs splayed out and uncovered, his skin a clammy, pasty gray. Studying him from the doorway, Camisa was reminded of the way E.T. looked when he was found on the riverbed by Elliot's big brother. Her heart fluttered uneasily. Aaron didn't look well at all. Maybe she shouldn't have left him out in the garage for so long, hot as it had been yesterday. The outside temperature reached 103, so it might have been as high as 110 inside the garage. She'd literally baked him.

"Aaron?" She called his name softly as she entered the room, a coldness seeping into her bones. He didn't answer, nor did he move a muscle. Surely he wasn't dead. Aaron couldn't be dead, because if he was, she was in a hell of a lot of trouble. But then, that business with Larry Patton was hardly an insignificant worry.

Moving close to the bed, she could see that Aaron was breathing. Very shallowly, but breathing nonetheless; he was still alive. She poked him on the shoulder. "Aaron, wake up. It's time to get up and eat breakfast."

He stirred slightly and moaned, but didn't open his eyes. Camisa poked him again, a little rougher. "I said wake up, Aaron. If you're pulling this just to make me feel sorry for you, it's not going to work."

His eyelids parted slightly, and so did his lips. His lips looked dry and scabrous, like in the movies when someone's been stranded out in the desert. All day in that hot garage with no water. He'd become badly dehydrated, and Camisa knew that could be serious. It could be fatal. Checking his pulse, she found it to be much faster than normal. She had to get some liquids down him, and if she had to attach the garden hose to his mouth to do it, she would.

"Aaron Joseph, you get out of this bed right . . ."

The telephone shrilled.

". . . now," Camisa finished weakly. She leaned over and shook him, patted his face, then shook him again. All he did was moan. "Christ," she muttered, wondering as she left the room to answer the phone what would happen if she took him to the hospital.

In the kitchen she jerked up the receiver and spoke into it brusquely. Taking Aaron to the hospital was out, she'd just decided. Too many questions would be asked. Someone was bound to get suspicious.

"Hello?"

"Camisa, I've been trying to call you for twenty minutes, letting the phone ring off the wall. Why didn't you answer it?" It was Sabrina's voice, and Camisa knew she had to be calling about the old man. She never called just to be sociable. Her voice was accusatory, as if there was a law about people answering their phones before a certain number of rings.

"Become a mother of three children, then see if you still need to ask me that question," Camisa responded sourly. "Anyway, I've answered it now, so what's all the panic about? No, don't tell me, let me guess—Dad's gone off to that big board meeting in the sky, right?"

"You are such a bitch! I hope Daddy didn't leave you anything, which by the way is the reason I'm calling. The reading of his will is this morning at ten o'clock, Wendell Swihart's office in the Tower Plaza office building on First and Everglade. And don't be late."

There was a loud click, followed by the dial tone. Camisa hung up, disappointed that she hadn't gotten the chance to needle Sabrina about the peace she'd felt last night, her heavenly assurance that their father would be all right. But she already knew what Sabrina would have said. It was God's will that he "go home," and the peace had been given to her for strength. If a huge meteor from outer space entered earth's atmosphere and creamed the whole state of Florida, Sabrina would put that on God's tab, too. Except she'd have "gone home" with everyone else.

Camisa stared fretfully at the clock on the oven. It was almost two hours until her presence was required

FLESH AND BLOOD

at the Tower Plaza, which was plenty of time to get herself, Michael, and Felicia ready, but there was no way Aaron was going to be fit for an outing by then. She supposed she would have to leave him here by himself, and tell anyone who might ask that he was being watched by a neighbor. Considering the way he usually behaved, that was entirely feasible.

As she filled a glass with tap water to force down Aaron's throat, she wondered how much money the old man had bequeathed her, having completely forgotten, at least for the time being, about the old man in the fishing boat and whether or not she had actually killed him.

5

The sky was a cloudless, azure canopy over the La Croix harbor, with at least a dozen white sea gulls circling lazily overhead, crying to each other in a language only they knew. Zeke Sawyer shuffled along the weather-beaten docks, paying attention only to his feet. They were inside a pair of brown penny loafers that looked ready to fall apart any moment. He wore no socks, and the bottoms of his ragged navy-blue slacks barely covered his ankles. Over his scrawny chest, which was brown and leathery like the rest of his skin, he wore a stained muscle T-shirt, and his balding head was covered by a frayed straw hat. In his right hand he carried a small duffel bag containing a fifth of cheap whiskey, a full package of Lucky Strikes, a transistor radio, and some food he'd scavenged from the Dumpster behind Dunn's Cafeteria, which he'd wrapped in an old newspaper.

He was oblivious to the activity around him, fishermen preparing their vessels for another long day of back-breaking toil under a blazing sun. Zeke was too busy thinking of how he was going to break his news to Rufus, his friend and companion of almost twenty years. Zeke's oldest son had invited him to come live

FLESH AND BLOOD

with him and his family; they'd just bought a new house with a small but very nice guest house in back. It was an offer Zeke couldn't refuse. He was tired of living in his crummy roach-infested room at the boardinghouse, having to steal his cigarettes and scrounge his meals from garbage cans whenever the sea decided to be stingy, and that turned out to be fairly often. Surely Rufus would understand, and it wasn't as if he would be entirely alone. He would still have Cyrus.

Looking ahead, he could see that Rufus wasn't out on the boat's rear deck, as he usually was by this time, chugging a cup of coffee that looked like crude oil (and could probably bring the dead back to life) while he checked the nets for damage. Zeke didn't think that much of it. Several times in the past few months Rufus had overslept due to a severe hangover. Apparently he'd hit the bottle a little too hard again last night.

Climbing over the railing, the boat rocking slightly under his weight, Zeke called out to his friend. "Rufus! Come on, get your sorry ass out of bed! The whole harbor is loaded with giant lobsters!"

His only answer was the cry of the sea gulls, and Zeke shook his head, setting his duffel bag down carefully on the deck floor. Old Rufus must have drunk himself clean into another world, he thought as he pulled aside the canvas drape and stepped inside the dim, malodorous cabin. He had to wait a few moments for his eyes to adjust from the brightness outside, and when they did, and saw what was on the floor between the table and bed, Zeke Sawyer felt his blood turn to ice water.

Rufus lay faceup, his wide-open eyes fixed on the cabin's tin ceiling, his mouth frozen open in a grimace of agony. There was a deep, ugly gash in his forehead. Dried blood was smeared over most of his near-naked body, and the bed looked like a pig had been slaughtered on it. The bloody fingers of the old fisherman's right hand were curled around the wooden handle of a knife, its five-inch blade a dull brown that lay guiltily across his bloated stomach.

"Catch yourself a mermaid today, old man?" Cyrus squawked from his cage. Zeke jumped as if he'd been goosed. He'd been so shocked by the sight before him that he'd completely forgotten the bird even existed.

Stupid as it would be to do so, Zeke had an impulse to ask the parrot what had happened, but he couldn't find his vocal chords. The dank coppery smell of the blood rose above all the other odors in the cabin and made Zeke's stomach do a slow, queasy rollover. "Jesus Almighty," was all he managed to say in a whisper, still not quite able to believe that his eyes were telling him the truth.

"You're not Sara," Cyrus piped up, doing a slow sidestep on his perch. After taking a few languid bows, he said it again. "You're not Sara."

Zeke's horrified eyes darted from the bloody remains of his dead friend to the bird's cage, and his mind pulled out of shock far enough to think about what he had just heard. *You're not Sara.* Sara was the name of Rufus's only daughter, though Zeke couldn't remember him mentioning her in many years.

Zeke looked back down at the body, specifically at the knife Rufus was holding in his dead hand. There was no way, no way in hell, that Rufus had done this to himself. Sometimes Rufus would say something like, "When I die, Zeke, you just dump me in the sea and feed me to the fishes, then I'll know I was good for something." But he never mentioned suicide, and even if Rufus had decided to kill himself, he couldn't or wouldn't have done himself in this way, Zeke thought. Someone else had done this to him. Rufus had been murdered. And Cyrus had witnessed the whole thing, and had heard Rufus say to whoever it was, "You're not Sara." So he hadn't been murdered by his daughter Sara, but very likely by a woman he might have originally mistaken for Sara. Zeke won-

FLESH AND BLOOD

dered what else the bird might have heard. Maybe enough to help the police catch the killer, if they could just get him to play back everything that had been recorded in his little pea brain last night.

The bird craned his neck. "Pirate ship dead ahead, Cyrus!"

"Who did this to Rufus?" Zeke asked him with a trembling voice, feeling a little foolish, but he was willing to try anything that might help bring Rufus's killer to justice.

"Shut up, you stupid bird."

Zeke had never heard Cyrus say that before. But it was hardly a clue. Getting anything useful out of the parrot could take all day or even longer, supposing there was any useful information to get. Zeke issued a long sigh, tears forming at the corners of his eyes. He couldn't stand this another minute. He had to get out of here, he had to find a phone and call the police. He had to get some whiskey down his gullet to dull his senses.

Stumbling from the cabin and the scene of violent death, he hoped Rufus would forgive him for not feeding his body to the fishes, as he'd been made to promise at least a dozen times. Damn the old coot's worthless drunken hide, he should know he would just make them sick.

Deidi was sitting at her desk going through the mass of information that had come in from UPI and AP wire services, judging which to toss and which to pass on to her lard-ass boss when he buzzed her extension and ordered her into his office pronto. Rolling her eyes to the acoustic ceiling, she took a drag of her cigarette, and left it burning in the ashtray while she went to see what he wanted.

"There's been another homicide," he said when she appeared, his voice carrying the same enthusiasm he would evince had he just discovered that a huge UFO had landed on top of the building, and that it was made out of chocolate eclairs. "They're on their way to La Croix harbor," he went on, glancing at his scribblings on the legal pad before him. Behind him distorted voices spoke to each other in code on the police band radio. Naturally, Tom knew their language, and whenever he heard the words "signal fifteen," he had an instant orgasm. "Fishing boat on dock sixteen. A man named Zeke Sawyer called it in, said the victim had been brutally stabbed." Tom smiled. "He told the dispatcher he thought a woman did it."

Deidi felt the room tilt slightly, and for a second she thought she was going to faint. For the third time that morning an old man with a knife blade protruding from his throat reached out to her with his bloodied hands, and in that terrible moment she knew instinctively that he was the one who had been murdered in La Croix harbor. She had an impulse to run out of the newsroom, out of the building to the parking lot, jump in her car and burn rubber all the way to Dr. Jordan's office so he could tell her why the hell this was happening to her. She didn't like it one bit, especially since she still had no memory of last night. But even so, she was absolutely positive she couldn't have committed a murder. No.

"Well, thank you for sharing that with me, Tom. Can I get back to my desk now?"

He smirked. "Very funny, Deidi. You're on your way to La Croix harbor, and I want you to find out if this murder was done by the same woman who did in Larry Patton. If my gut feeling's right, we've got a hell of a sensational story going here. Maybe as big as the Gainesville slayings. Give the wire stuff to Linda."

Deidi gave him a mock salute with a halfhearted smile and slumped out of his office like an overburdened mule, although she was feeling slightly better due to Tom's gut feeling about the same woman being responsible for both crimes—with a gut like his, how could he go wrong?—which would mean that she was unquestionably in the clear; she'd had no memory lapse the night before last, when Larry Patton was killed. So she had nothing to worry about, except this sudden gift of ESP that she wished would go away. She didn't want to know anything through a mysterious sixth sense or voices in her head. She didn't want to see old men drenched in their own blood reaching out to her with haunting looks in their eyes, or to hear, as she had some five or six years ago, teenage boys with deep teeth marks on the heads of their penises screaming curses at her, which was the reason she'd started seeing Dr. Jordan in the first place. There had been other times, too, in her early teens and once when she was about ten, that terrible images had jumped at her from out of the blue, but they had never been connected to actual events, and within a week she'd forgotten all about them.

Linda Honeycut gave Deidi a dirty look when she piled the wire services printouts on her desk. Linda was working on an article for the Lifestyle section that was clearly requiring a great deal of concentration, but Deidi knew the dirty look wasn't because she'd interrupted Linda's train of thought. It was for killing any spare time she might have had later to secretly work on that Nobel Prize–winning book she was writing.

"Hey, what gives?" Linda asked hotly. She had a long horsey face that attained a sluttish kind of beauty with all the makeup it bore, but her frosted hair, teased outwardly like a rat's nest, drew the most attention.

"Tom told me to give you this stuff, so if you have any complaints, go to him," Deidi said, and added with an exaggerated frown, "He's sending me out to cover another damn murder. Lucky me." Deidi could see in Linda's eyes that she was eating her ambitious little heart out, which made her feel better. She turned and went back to her own cubicle, stuck her lit cigarette between her lips, grabbed her purse, notebook, and Nikon camera, and headed for the door.

Flies were swarming over the corpse when Judson Hendricks stepped through the canvas tarp into the boat's tin cabin. His nose immediately wrinkled in protest of the smell, a potpourri of blood, fish, urine, feces, and general filth.

Zeke Sawyer was right behind him; the coroner and crime lab investigator were still coming along the pier, lugging their heavy cases past a line of curious gawkers kept away from the scene by two uniformed officers.

"There's Cyrus," Zeke said, pointing to the cage suspended in the far right corner. Hendricks had asked him as they walked to the boat what made him think Rufus Bagget had been murdered by a woman, and Zeke told him. The detective had looked at him skeptically.

"Even if it could give a detailed deposition, I rather doubt that a bird's testimony would hold up in court," Hendricks said, and he could almost hear the D.A. laughing his ass off at him now. Returning his attention to the corpse, his eyes were drawn to the knife it was clutching in its right hand. A couple of flies had lighted on the blade and were feasting on its bloody surface, probably pooping maggot eggs while they were at it, he thought with disgust. Nasty creatures. "That knife look familiar to you?"

The fact that he'd never seen such a knife in Rufus's possession before had escaped Zeke until now. He shook his head. "No, Rufus ain't got but one knife, and it don't look anything like that."

"Hell of a storm brewin' up, Cyrus!" the parrot squawked at them.

Zeke shook his finger at the cage. "You tell him what you heard last night, Cyrus! Who did this to Rufus, huh? 'You're not Sara.' Remember that? And, 'Shut up, you stupid bird.' Now what else did you hear?"

FLESH AND BLOOD

"What else did you hear?" Cyrus mimicked, dipping his slick green head.

It was quite an effort for Hendricks to maintain a straight face, and he only managed to do so by putting a hand across his mouth as if he were in deep philosophical thought. He'd dealt with a lot of crazy shit in his eighteen years as a policeman, but trying to get information on a murder case from a fucking bird was just too much. When he was no longer in danger of cracking up, he asked Zeke Sawyer in a solemn tone, "Did Bagget have any money or valuables stashed away that someone would kill him to get? The place looks like it might have been ransacked."

Zeke stopped glaring at Cyrus and turned to face the detective, shaking his head. "No, Rufus hardly had a pot to piss in. Most valuable thing he owned was this here boat. And it always looked this way. Rufus wasn't much on housekeepin'."

The boat rocked slightly as county coroner Ed Cooke and crime lab specialist Lyle Walden climbed onto the rear deck with their equipment. There wasn't enough room in the cabin for all of them to move around, so Cooke and Walden, who had a five-dollar bet going on whether the stiff's eyes were open or closed, waited out on the deck for Hendricks to get finished.

"Rufus have any enemies you know of?" Hendricks asked.

Again Zeke shook his head. "Long as I knew him, ol' Rufus lived by the golden rule: don't step on anybody's toes, and they won't step on yours. Far as I know, I was his only real friend, but he didn't have no enemies. I gotta admit, though, I was gonna tell him today that I was leaving soon to go live with my son in Orlando. I was gonna go off and leave Rufus all alone, except for that damn Cyrus. So maybe I can't say that I was a real friend. I don't think Rufus woulda done that to me."

Looking down at the filthy wooden floor, Hendricks

saw the empty whiskey bottle in the corner under the parrot's cage. What appeared to be dried blood was smeared along one side of its base. His eyes trailed over to the bashed-in area of Rufus Bagget's forehead, which was presently serving as a picnic table for several flies. Removing a ballpoint pen from his shirt pocket, Hendricks crouched below the cage and inserted half the pen's length into the bottle's neck, then carefully picked it up.

"I'd be willing to bet this is what made that gash in his head. If we're lucky, maybe we can get a good print off of it." Hendricks watched the old man's face carefully for his reaction. At the moment, Sawyer was Hendricks's number-one suspect. Robbery had not been eliminated as a motive just because Sawyer had claimed that Rufus Bagget hardly had a pot to piss in. Just maybe he'd found out otherwise, and Bagget had refused to share. And this thing about him suddenly going off to live with his son in Orlando. He was going to tell his old pal Bagget about it today. What immaculate timing. And the bird thing. Had Sawyer killed Bagget and afterward trained the parrot to repeat misleading clues?

Sawyer nodded, looking at the bottle with obvious and justified disdain, but his expression showed no hint of apprehension or paranoia. And why should it bother him for his prints to be found on this bottle? He was Bagget's boozing bosom buddy. It crossed Hendricks's mind that they might even have been lovers. It was a sickening thought, but it wouldn't be the first time two old scuzzies had gone for each other.

"Can you hear me, old man?" Cyrus squawked quietly from the corner.

Both men looked toward the parrot's cage. Zeke's faded blue eyes widened with excitement. "That's a new one. Never heard him say that before, and I know he never heard it from me or Rufus. We never called each other old man. Old coot, maybe, old fart; I think

FLESH AND BLOOD

Rufus called me an old woman once, a long time ago. She must have said that to him last night, the woman he said wasn't Sara. The one who killed him."

Hendricks glanced at Sawyer with a look that said *yeah, right*. And then they both felt the boat rock and bump against the tires around the docking slip as someone got on or off the rear deck. A moment later Hendricks could hear a familiar female voice speaking with Ed Cooke and Lyle Walden, though he couldn't determine whose it was.

"You just keep right on talking, Cyrus," Zeke Sawyer told the bird in a pleading voice, encouraging it with a desperate come-on gesture. "Tell us what else you heard last night. You gotta help us. Rufus took better care of you than he did hisself, you damn bird, so now it's your turn to do something for him."

Hendricks was thinking he could use some fresh air, and he was also curious to see who was out on the rear deck talking to the coroner and his assistant. But before he could get Sawyer's attention away from the parrot, the tarp covering the cabin's entrance was pulled aside, letting in a wash of bright sunlight that momentarily blinded him.

Deidi Marshall took a timid step inside, letting the tarp close behind her. She was immediately overwhelmed by the cabin's foul stench, and it was all she could do to keep from making a hasty retreat. What made it worse was remembering what her friend Suzanne had told her when they were going to college —that whenever she smelled something, tiny particles of it were going up her nose. The temptation to pinch it closed was great, but she certainly didn't want any of those nasty particles on her tongue instead.

"Well, if it isn't Lois Lane. I should have guessed."

Deidi peered at the shadowy silhouettes before her, which gradually attained features as her eyes adjusted to the dimness. "Dick Tracy. What a surprise."

"There's a piece of rubber nailed on that wall there,

to your right, if you wanna tie back the tarp," Sawyer said, pointing. "Guess Mr. Tracy here could use a little more light."

Hendricks gave him a withering look. "My name is Hendricks."

Deidi was more than happy to get some fresh air into the place. She turned and gathered the tarp aside, tying it with the piece of rubber that looked like it had once been part of a boot. Under other circumstances, she might have laughed at what the old man had said. But in the presence of a murder victim's bloody remains, only the most depraved of minds could find anything funny, in her opinion.

As much as she didn't want to, she turned back around and took a few steps forward to look at the corpse in the cold light of day. At once she felt every inch of her skin crawl into gooseflesh. It was him. It was the same old man she'd seen this morning in her visions, or whatever those had been. And although his beard covered up most of his throat, she could see a stab wound caked with blood near the base and just to the right of his windpipe. Silently she screamed.

And Cyrus the parrot suddenly went wild in his cage, squawking loudly and frantically beating his wings against the bars, sending up dozens of feathers that floated on the air like confetti and made Judson Hendricks sneeze like a trumpet.

With Felicia riding on her left hip and Michael in tow, Camisa arrived at Wendell Swihart's law office in the Tower Plaza five minutes early, to discover that everyone else was already gathered and, when she walked crookedly into the plush room with its thick burgundy carpeting, everyone was glaring at her as if she were half an hour late. Only the silver-haired attorney offered her a smile, and it was completely devoid of warmth.

"Have a seat, Mrs. Collins," he said, gesturing to the only empty chair in the room, which happened to be the one nearest his massive oak desk. There were six others present: her mother, dressed traditionally in black; her sister, clutching a hanky, looking, as always, like a bitch; her father's two younger brothers, Anthony and Lance; his older sister, Marie; and last but not least, his faithful secretary, a war-horse named Francine Lowery, who looked like a man wearing makeup and a wig and who could probably hold her own with a rampaging gorilla.

Camisa sat down, transferring Felicia to her lap and making Michael sit on the floor at her feet. He sat very rigidly, with his lips sealed tight and his hands clasped over his crossed ankles, only daring to move his eyes around. He'd been warned in the elevator that the slightest misbehavior would result in a severe spanking that would turn his bottom black and blue.

Now that everyone who had been mentioned in the will was present, Wendell Swihart put on his bifocals and began reading, mumbling over the preliminary paragraphs, which began with the standard line, "Being of sound mind and body . . ."

Camisa was only half listening, another part of her brain fretting about Aaron. She hadn't been able to get very much water down him; most of it had run out of his mouth and soaked into his pillow. Compounding her worry was the fact that this was Friday and Harlan was expected home sometime this evening. He would insist that Aaron be taken to the hospital, and then she would have those damn know-it-all doctors to face, and their intimidating questions to answer. And if she lied, they would know it. But she couldn't tell them the truth. Either way, she was going to get reported to the welfare department or maybe even the police. Definitely to the police if he died. Aaron wouldn't die, though. She had to think positively.

". . . to my daughter Sabrina, the sum of ten thousand dollars," Swihart said, and he glanced up from the papers in Sabrina's direction, offering her a brief congratulatory smile. Sabrina covered her face with her hankie and let out a sob. Camisa rolled her eyes to the ceiling, scornful as ever of her sister's cheap theatrics.

Ten thousand dollars. Camisa straightened in her leather-upholstered chair, assuming that she would be mentioned next (although she should have been first; after all, she was born first), and that she would receive the same amount as Sabrina. Ten thousand dollars wasn't all that much, but it wasn't exactly pocket change, either. It might be enough for her to somehow buy her way out of the trouble she was in.

Felicia was wanting down, and was starting to make little grunting noises. Swihart ignored the disturbance and went on to read what Murray had left to his sister Marie, which was his coin collection, valued at sixty-five hundred dollars. Marie lowered her head, a grateful smile appearing on her colorless lips. A look of confusion came over Camisa's face. Had she missed something? Did she not hear when Swihart read the part about her inheritance? Felicia's little grunts had evolved into squealing whines, and she began flailing her arms and kicking, and in so doing, accidently bopped Camisa's nose hard enough to hurt. Camisa responded before thinking, and smacked the baby on one of her naked thighs. Everyone looked at her with either shock or disapproval, including Swihart, who had just started reading what his deceased client had left to his brother Anthony.

Felicia started to wail loudly, and Camisa felt like screaming herself. "Can you just skip to the part that concerns me," she said to the attorney between clenched teeth. "As you can see, I've got a slight problem here."

"Give Felicia to me," her mother said coldly, but Camisa refused to even look at her, being in no mood to see the condemnation that was sure to be written all over her face.

Wendell Swihart cleared his throat and returned his attention to the will. Adjusting his glasses, he began skimming down the page with a forefinger. Camisa could tell by the way his jaw muscles were working that Felicia's wailing was getting on his nerves even more than it was hers.

When he found the clause he was looking for, he cleared his throat again, then looked up at Camisa with an expression that indicated she wasn't going to like what he was about to say. Her mind raced ahead. What had the old man left her, his damn golf trophies? His membership to the country club where she and Harlan would stand out like a couple of hillbillies, supposing they could even afford to eat dinner there? Then her mind reeled back in time, remembering some ugly scenes between her and her father. She'd said some very nasty things to him in anger, but all teenagers did that to their parents, didn't they? And their parents didn't hold a grudge against them for the rest of their lives because of it. Did they?

I hate your guts. I wish you weren't my father.

He'd grounded her for a week because she'd come home two hours past her curfew and he hadn't known where she was.

"To Camisa Dawn I give the truth, which is also the fulfillment of her wish that I had not been her father. I was not her natural father. My wife and I adopted her at the age of four after attempting unsuccessfully for several years to have a child of our own. Then, as frequently happens after an adoption, my wife conceived Sabrina. I did my best to love both children equally, but—"

Camisa came out of her initial shock and exploded. *"What?* Is this some kind of joke?" She carelessly dropped Felicia into Michael's lap, which brought an immediate and tense silence to the room.

Swihart looked up from the paper and removed his glasses. "I'm afraid not, Mrs. Collins. It was Forrest Murray's will that you be told the truth about your heritage, that you were adopted and not of his own flesh and blood. Shall I continue?"

Now Camisa turned to face her mother—adoptive mother, surprise surprise—her dark eyes filled with hatred. "All my life you've been lying to me. You said all my baby pictures had been lost in a fire. And those cute little anecdotes you told me about when I was learning to walk—*lies*. You just made all that up, because you weren't around when I was learning to walk. No wonder you've always been partial to Sabrina. She's your very own *flesh and blood*." She said the last three words with venomous sarcasm, then added in the same spirit, "I'll bet that after you got pregnant with her, you wanted to take me back to the orphanage or wherever the hell I came from."

Elyse Murray did not look at all guilty, as Camisa thought she should. Instead she boldly met Camisa's glare with one of her own. "You made both of us want to do that a thousand times, Camisa. In spite of all the love and affection we gave you, you were a horrible child and you've grown up to be a horrible woman. I didn't know Forrest was going to do this, but I'm glad he did. It's exactly what you deserved."

Part of an old folk song floated through Camisa's head, *If I had a hammer*. If only she had an Uzi. She'd mow them all down in a relentless spray of bullets, every last one of them. Suddenly these people she'd known all her life were not only total strangers, they were her enemies and their eyes had turned into weapons. In those cold, dispassionate mirrors she had become an outcast, unwanted and abhorred.

With so much rage boiling inside her, it took a considerable amount of willpower for Camisa to paste on a smile, but she didn't want to suffer any more humiliation than she already had. Every fiber of her being urged her to scream profanities at her ex-mother, and/or to leap over to her chair and slap the living shit out of her, but that would only validate what her mother had said about her growing up to be a horrible adult.

So Camisa smiled and said, "Well, I think it was

FLESH AND BLOOD

rather tasteless of the old man to have the truth laid on me like this, and I think Ann Landers would agree, but you can't imagine how happy I am about the news. I feel like the ugly duckling felt when he discovered he was really a swan."

"Oh, God," Sabrina muttered contemptuously.

"Mrs. Collins?"

Still smiling, Camisa looked back at Wendell Swihart, assuming he was anxious to go on with the reading of the will. But he was looking under his desk wearing an irritable expression, and when she turned around, he said, "Your children, Mrs. Collins. Would you please do something with them?"

Felicia was playing with the tassels on his shoes, and Michael was making a game of pulling the man's socks up and down. Although normally Camisa would have wanted to knock their heads together, under the present circumstances she couldn't have cared less if they set him on fire. But Swihart didn't have all day, and with Aaron still in dire need of liquids, neither did she.

As soon as she got Michael and Felicia out from under the desk, Felicia started crying again, and Camisa could feel her self-control rapidly slipping away. "Just tell me one thing, Mr. Swihart, if you know it. The name of the agency or institution through which I was adopted."

Swihart did know, and as soon as he told her, Camisa politely thanked him and left, dragging Michael faster than his legs could keep up, and carrying Felicia under one arm like a football.

6

By the time Deidi got home at twenty after six that evening, she felt like she was on the verge of a nervous breakdown. The last thing she was in the mood for was company, but her friend Suzanne's cherry-red Z-28 was parked in the small gravel lot on the west side of the courtyard, and Suzanne was sitting on the hood looking mildly peeved. A large green suitcase stood next to the front wide-tread tire.

It had been months since Deidi had seen her, and the sight of Suzanne's pixie face should have been a welcome sight, a cause for celebration. But Deidi felt resentment for her friend's presence rise up within her like a black cloud. Some nerve Suzanne had, taking it for granted that she could come on down before receiving a response to her letter. Maybe the answer would have been no. Maybe she could have just met an irresistible hardbody and been in the middle of a euphoric sexfest to which three would have definitely *not* been company. Unlikely but possible.

Or, Deidi thought, she could have been in the middle of a major crisis that required peace and solitude. Which she very definitely was. But it looked like there would be no peace or solitude forthcoming for at least a few days. With an inward groan, Deidi

FLESH AND BLOOD

stepped out of her canary-yellow Corvette and tried her best to work up a smile. "Well, what a surprise. I thought you'd wait to hear from me before you came, but that's cool. Unless Kurt followed you down here. That I couldn't handle. At all."

Suzanne hopped off the hood of her car, her peeved expression replaced by one of utter disbelief and confusion. Her pale blond hair had been permed into a mop of curls since Deidi had last seen her, and her eyes had changed from blue to emerald-green. Colored contacts, Deidi guessed. At least once a year Suzanne did something radical to her appearance.

"A surprise?" Suzanne strode up to Deidi with a hand on her hip, her eyebrows knitted together. "Are you kidding me, or what? You called me last night and told me to come. You even said you'd leave me a key in the rubber plant's pot so I could get in if I got here before you. That was just last night, Deidi. Don't tell me you completely forgot. But I guess you did. The key isn't there."

Now it was Deidi's turn to look confused, but she couldn't bring herself to admit that she didn't know what the hell Suzanne was talking about. Since she had no memories of last night at all, she had to assume that Suzanne was telling the truth. Deidi didn't believe she'd just stood in the kitchen like a stone statue until she'd gone to bed. "I'm sorry, Suzanne. It's just that I've had a really rough day. I think the police suspect that I may have committed a murder."

Suzanne's eyes widened and her mouth dropped open slightly, her hand falling away from her hip to hang limply at her side. "My God, Deidi, why?"

Deidi sighed, staring for a moment toward the sea, watching the foamy waves breaking on the shore as if playing a lazy game of leapfrog. "I'll tell you about it inside, although I really don't even want to think about it. Anyway, I've got to let Hughman out to pee before his eyeballs start floating."

Fifteen minutes later, while Deidi was behind the

kitchen counter fixing them both Bloody Marys, she told Suzanne about what had happened on the fishing boat, the way Judson Hendricks had looked at her after the parrot had finally calmed down. It had obviously witnessed the murder, although Deidi seriously doubted it could have comprehended what was happening. At any rate, the detective and a friend of the deceased had gone into the cabin and the bird hadn't panicked, but the second she'd come within sight of the cage, the winged reptile had gone ape-shit. And when Hendricks was ready to leave the scene, he'd taken the bird with him, staring at her as if he thought she might try to come back and kill it.

Suzanne, stretched out on the couch in the living room, where she was being thoroughly sniffed over by Hughman, shook her head. "I can't believe he suspects you just because that bird freaked out. That's the stupidest thing I've ever heard."

"There's a little more to it," Deidi said, frowning as she squirted a little lime into each of their glasses. "A woman fitting my description is believed responsible for the murder the night before last of a traveling salesman named Larry Patton. This may be totally unrelated, but some woman who also looks like yours truly went into Gravitz and Sons Mortuary last night and desecrated one of the corpses. I fully expect any minute now to be escorted to the police station and put in a lineup. To tell you the truth, I hope I'm right. I'm starting to wonder about me, too." *Look in any mirror and you will see her see her see her . . .* She picked up the glasses and took them into the living area.

Suzanne sat up to make room for her on the couch, and let out a nervous little laugh. "Good grief, Deidi, you should know whether or not you committed a murder. It's not like being unable to remember if you'd taken your birth control pill or unplugged your curling iron."

Deidi took a big swallow of her Bloody Mary and

closed her eyes, wondering if she should tell Suzanne about the other things, the voice and the visions. She decided not to. Suzanne wouldn't have any answers or explanations for her; it would be pointless to bring them up. But Suzanne could help her to fill in last night's big blank. Maybe if they talked about their conversation last night, it would jog her memory.

"What time did I call you last night?" Deidi asked, hoping Suzanne would drop the previous subject. As long as she didn't remember what she'd done last night, anything was possible. Even murder, she supposed with an imperceptible shudder.

"About seven," Suzanne replied, licking her lips. Hughman was sniffing at her drink; she dipped a finger in it and held it up to him. He nosed it, sneezed, and then turned away, no longer interested in her or what she had to offer. He lumbered over to the hearth and lay down with a groan.

"Seven," Deidi repeated thoughtfully.

"You don't remember, do you?"

Deidi ignored the question. "How long did we talk?"

"Half an hour, I guess." The words came out slowly, and in a softer tone of voice. Suzanne was looking at her as if she were trying to obtain the information she wanted by telepathy. Deidi wouldn't have been surprised to learn that was precisely what her friend was doing. Trying to do, anyway. Suzanne was always into something weird. TM, primal screaming, channeling, spoon bending, tarot cards. This week telepathy, next week auras or reading people's stool samples. *Nice and firm, I see. Yes. You should go ahead and invest in that stock. Uh-oh, there's a lot of green in it, and look at the way it's pebbled. Better hold off on those wedding plans. Jesus, what a stink. Are you holding a grudge against somebody?*

Deidi's mind was still a blank, refusing to be jogged. But she was determined; if nothing else, she would have Dr. Jordan pull it out of her next Tuesday through hypnosis. He'd been wanting to try that on her for a long time anyway, but she'd never been comfortable with the idea. If that was what it was going to take, though, to fill in this maddening void, then hypnosis it would be. "So what all did we talk about? I was really zonked last night. Totally. But I guess you've already figured that out." Reaching for her pack of cigarettes on the coffee table, she noticed that her hand was shaking badly.

Suzanne gulped half her drink down and carefully sat the glass on the other end of the coffee table, turning back to Deidi with an expression of deep concern. "Hey, are you all right? I have the feeling you're holding something back from me. You know that's what always drove me crazy about you. You keep all your bad feelings locked up inside, and I promise you, that's just begging for cancer. But I guess you're begging for it anyway, with those cigarettes."

"Don't start lecturing me about smoking again," Deidi warned, drawing deeply on the cigarette she'd just lit. She exhaled the smoke with a rebellious look of satisfaction. "There might be a truck bumper out there with my name on it. One of these nights that two-legged whale who lives above me might crash through the ceiling and flatten me like a pancake. You never know. I say enjoy life to the fullest while you have it, and I happen to enjoy smoking. So now that we've gotten that out of the way, tell me what we talked about last night. I think it'll come back to me if you'll just give me some specifics."

Above them, a muffled plumbing sound indicated that Flora Bushbaum had just flushed her toilet. Across the room, Hughman's ear pricked up, twitching back and forth like a pair of radar scanners. Suzanne remained silent for several moments, staring sullenly at her unfinished drink. Deidi knew she'd hurt her friend's feelings, but didn't really care. The way she saw it, Suzanne had deserved a little verbal

FLESH AND BLOOD

slap. What she did with her own body and emotions was really none of Suzanne's business.

Finally Suzanne said, "We talked about me and Kurt for a while, and then you started talking about when you were a little girl. Something about a cat you had then, that it had gotten hit by a car."

Deidi looked at her strangely. She'd been about to take another hit off her Virginia Slim, but the filter paused at her parted lips, then drifted slowly away as Deidi placed the smoldering cigarette down in one of the ashtray grooves. "A cat? I never had a cat when I was growing up. Mother was extremely allergic to them."

"Well, you said you had a cat," Suzanne asserted, reaching for her drink. "In fact, I distinctly remember you calling it your kitty-cat, so I couldn't have misunderstood. Its name was . . . Mittens."

Hearing the name Mittens, Deidi felt like a blowfish had suddenly sprouted inside her brain. Her temples began throbbing, her heart pounding in erratic rhythm. From somewhere within the unfathomable blackness of her subconscious, a voice was pressing to be heard. Try as she might to close her mind's ears, its message came through, carried in on a wave of contempt.

What is WRONG with you?

"I think I need to lie down for a while," Deidi said, her face completely drained of color. "Just make yourself at home."

Suzanne watched her get up from the couch and nearly stumble out of the room as if she were about to throw up. A few seconds later the sound of retching could be heard from the hallway bathroom.

Michael and Felicia had been put to bed at five o'clock that evening with another dose of Jim Beam. Camisa was afraid Harlan would get suspicious if only Aaron were in bed so early; this way she could tell him the kids had all played so hard today they'd pooped themselves out. She didn't want to tell him that Aaron was sick, in case he'd want to go in and check on him. Aaron wasn't doing so well. When she'd gotten back from Swihart's office, she thought he was dead; it seemed to have taken her forever to find his pulse. She couldn't get any water down his throat at all. He was obviously in a coma.

Camisa marveled at how much shit could hit the fan at once. Here was Aaron, about to die on her; then this morning she finds out, at the age of twenty-seven, that she'd been fucking *adopted;* and splashed on the front page of the *Danville Chronicle* she sees the headline: MAN FOUND SLAIN ON BOAT. Beneath the caption was a picture of the docked boat, and Camisa had recognized it at once. She'd done it again. Actually murdered someone, a man she didn't even know. In cold blood. And that wasn't all. According to the police blotter, she'd really gone to that funeral home, too, and done those sick things to that corpse.

The notion of having a whole other identity still appealed to Camisa, but not if these criminal acts continued. Eventually she'd get caught and sent to prison, where she'd be raped with giant dildos every night, and God only knew what else those dirty lesbians would make her do. There had to be some way to unsplit her personality, to gain full control of her life again.

There also had to be a way to get Aaron out of that coma. Camisa had been looking at her watch every few minutes with dread, knowing Harlan was going to pull his detached rig up any minute. Suddenly she had an idea, and rushed out to the garage. On a shelf where Harlan kept a lot of his tools was an old radio that didn't work anymore, but Camisa didn't think its problem was not getting any electricity. Using a small pair of pliers with a cutting blade near the base, she clipped off the cord and scraped the rubber tubing away from the end of the wires. Pulling them apart,

FLESH AND BLOOD

she went back into the house and down the hallway to the boys' room.

Michael was lying on his stomach, clad only in his Mutant Ninja Turtles pajama bottoms, one arm dangling over the side of the bed. Next to him, Aaron lay faceup with the sheet drawn up to his neck, just as Camisa had left him. His mouth was hanging open, and there were large purple halfmoons under both eyes. Looking down on him, Camisa flashed on seeing him in a small casket, dressed in his Sunday suit with his hair neatly combed back, surrounded by white quilted satin. She quickly shook the image away and turned to plug the cord into the electric outlet, and was for a moment tempted to hold an exposed wire in each hand to see what a hundred and ten volts felt like, but she couldn't quite get up the nerve.

Hoping and praying that this would bring him out of his coma—she'd already tried shaking and slapping him—she pressed the wires against Aaron's temples to pass the current through his head.

His body stiffened, eyes popping halfway open with only the whites visible. A spreading stain on the sheet below his waist indicated that his bladder had released. Camisa frowned, unable to imagine how his body had even come up with that much fluid, as much as he'd sweated and vomited in the dog carrier. She would have bet a hundred dollars that he couldn't have filled a thimble.

Looking back at his face, she saw that bubbles were forming around his mouth. His back was arched and his eyes were open a little wider than they'd been a few seconds earlier, but they were still rolled back in his head. Deciding he'd had enough, maybe a little more than enough, Camisa terminated the shock treatment. Aaron's body immediately went limp.

Leaning over him, Camisa patted his cold cheek. All day his body temperature had seemed way below normal. "Aaron? Can you hear me now? Say something to me. Anything. Tell me to eat shit and die."

Several months ago, when she'd belted him for feeding Felicia earthworms, he'd told her exactly that, which had earned him several more licks. She would be ecstatic to hear him say those words to her now.

But he said nothing, and after concentrating on his small chest for several moments, it became clear that Aaron wasn't breathing. Her own heart palpitating with fear, Camisa put her ear to his chest and listened.

All she heard was the sound of Harlan's rig pulling up in front of the house.

7

"Pirate ship dead ahead, Cyrus!"

Jeremy and Lacey Hendricks both giggled. The talking bird their father had brought home was the coolest thing either of them had seen in real life. They'd seen more impressive things in movies, like chimpanzees who could fly airplanes, for instance, but the parrot was most definitely a star in its own right, and it now had two very enthusiastic fans.

Jeremy was twelve, Lacey eleven. They both took after their father, having dark blond hair and almond-shaped brown eyes, their mother's only noticeable contribution being the dimples in their cheeks. They had only seen their mother twice since the divorce two years ago, but then they hadn't seen her all that often while she was still living with them. She was a singer and did a lot of traveling with her band, Faux Pas, which played the crappy kind of music usually featured on *Saturday Night Live*.

The parrot's cage was sitting in the middle of the coffee table in the living room, on top of some newspapers their father had spread out. They'd all pitched in on cleaning the cage's bottom, which had been incredibly filthy. The old man who'd previously owned the bird probably hadn't cleaned it out in a year. Jeremy was kneeling on one side of the coffee table, Lacey on the other. Their father was sitting on the couch wearing a scowl.

"That's about the tenth time it's repeated that," he grumbled. "Well, it's time for me to head over to the Blue Lady Tavern and ask some people some questions. While I'm gone, I want you to write down everything that bird says. And don't try to teach it anything new. Okay? You'll get five bucks apiece, so be sure to pay attention."

"We will," Jeremy and Lacey chorused.

"We will," Cyrus echoed in his low, gravelly voice.

Hendricks rolled his eyes and got up from the couch with a grunt. At their insistence, he'd started letting the kids stay by themselves for about six months now, and so far so good. They got along fairly well, and they were pretty level-headed kids. They knew not to open the door for anyone while he was gone, and what to say (and not to say) on the phone if someone called, and what to do in the event of an emergency.

He gathered his sport coat and keys and left their eastside house, locking the door on his way out. It was getting close to dusk, and the horizon was aglow with brilliant orange, red, and purple streaks. Since their house sat on the top of a hill, he could look toward his backyard and see the endless spread of the Atlantic Ocean even though it was almost a mile away. The sunset reflected on its slate-gray surface always gave him the impression of a vast bed of diamonds.

He didn't look at it tonight, his mood being far from aesthetic. As he drove toward the Blue Lady Tavern on Danville's seedy southside, he felt a new & improved headache coming on. Its predecessor had arrived with a suitcase full of torture equipment right about the time he'd learned that the unidentified prints they'd lifted in Larry Patton's motel room matched one of the prints found on Rufus Bagget's empty whiskey bottle.

He hadn't really expected it. He probably wouldn't

even have thought to compare the prints if it hadn't been for what had happened on the boat when Deidi Marshall was sighted by the parrot. What would a software salesman from Tennessee have to do with a local fisherman? But obviously they did have at least one thing in common: they'd been killed by the same woman. And it appeared that she'd chosen Patton and Bagget at random, which was going to make her hard as hell to catch without a damn lucky break. He'd already made an attempt to trace her through the knife, only to find that it came from a common set sold in every department store in Danville.

Because of the incident in the boat's cabin, he'd also done a background check on Deidi Marshall, finding it spotless except for a few outstanding parking violations. He hadn't gotten chapped over the fact that she'd never been arrested and fingerprinted; given her background and profession, she was a very unlikely suspect, but the parrot's violent reaction to her presence did make him wonder. Would just any young woman with shoulder-length dark brown hair and brown eyes set him off like that? Hendricks intended to conduct the simple experiment that would answer that question, but first he had to meet the right woman. None of those who worked for the police department fit the suspect's description very well.

The Blue Lady Tavern was nestled between the decrepit Hollander Hotel, where rooms could be rented by the hour, and another eyesore named Bogie's Pawnshop, with its iron antiburglar bars. Ryan Phipps in narcotics had gotten an anonymous tip last week that Bogie was selling more dope than he was anything else. The tip had undoubtedly come from a dissatisfied customer who would henceforth find his drugs elsewhere. But never fear, Bogie, Hendricks thought. Ryan Phipps will be more than happy to take up the slack in your income. What's more, you'll get to be a star on candid camera.

Opening the chipped blue door of the tavern, Hendricks was immediately hit by a fog of pungent smoke: cigar, pipe, cigarette, and marijuana. With the only lights in the place centered on the small stage where the girls danced and on the bar, the tables and booths sat in murky gloom, and all of them were filled, mostly with men. Some were talking and laughing, one-upping each other's stories while they got shitfaced. Others were quietly sipping their drinks, with their eyes glued to the movements of the dancer now on stage, and a few who were sitting on pervert row (the counter that circled the curved stage) gave out loud, obscene suggestions with folded bills between their nicotine-stained fingers.

Hendricks had his mind set on business, on catching the dark-haired woman who'd already killed two men and would probably kill a third if she remained at large. The new & improved headache was living up to its name, and it felt like he was beginning to sprout his first ulcer. But in spite of all that, the sight of the naked girl gyrating up on stage inspired an amazingly rigid hard-on. In less than fifteen seconds his dick went from soft putty to feeling like it could bore a hole through granite. So it had been five months since he'd last had sex. This was rather embarrassing. Even though the room was uncomfortably warm, he was thankful that he'd worn his sport jacket along. He buttoned it to cover the telltale bulge in his pants. Unable to help himself, he stood there watching the girl for a few more minutes. The song she was dancing to was "Night Moves" by Bob Seger, one of his favorite oldies. Her face wasn't pretty, not by a long shot, but she did have one hell of a body: long slender legs, flat stomach, tight buttocks, and full round breasts with tiny brown nipples. Holding on to a pole that ran from the center of the stage to the ceiling, she gracefully lifted her left leg straight up and grabbed the ankle with her left hand, which left no part of her to the imagination. One of the perverts, after jumping up and gawking appreciatively at the girl's splayed genitalia for several moments, inserted his bill into the pink slot, along with one of his fingers. She spun away from him, removing the bill from her cunt as she lowered her leg, and making a full turn around the pole, passed it under his nose so he could get a whiff of her musk. A delirious grin spread over his face.

"Jesus," Hendricks muttered under his breath, pulling his eyes away before they popped out of their sockets. His dick was throbbing now, and he wasn't exactly doing it any favors. Steering his mind back to the matter at hand, he pressed through the thick atmosphere to the bar, where he pulled the composite of his murder suspect out of his shirt pocket. Unfolding it, he handed it to the older woman behind the bar. She had a hard, streetwise look about her, and he couldn't help but wonder if she pandered the girls who danced at the Blue Lady.

"Have you seen this woman in here recently?" he asked her, watching her face intently. People with that hard, streetwise appearance frequently had a policy against helping the police for any reason.

She looked him over first, her expression a mixture of curiosity and distrust. Then her dark, reptilian eyes moved down to the paper he'd handed her. After a few moments she shrugged. "I don't know. This is just a drawing. Could be anybody."

Hendricks took the composite back, folded it and returned it to his pocket with a silent profanity. "Okay, next question. Did you know Rufus Bagget?"

"Hey, Anna, I need two Coors, one bourbon and seven, and three shots of tequila," a harried cocktail waitress said loudly as she slapped a plastic cork-covered tray on the countertop. She gave Hendricks a smile that obviously had nothing to do with the way she really felt. It was something automatic, like a sprinkler system alerted to a fire. She had black hair pulled back into a long ponytail, green eyes heavily made-up, a slight overbite with crooked eyeteeth. Her petite frame was packed into a very skimpy dress made of shiny blue material that just barely covered her ass.

"Yeah, I knew Rufus," the woman behind the bar—Anna—admitted as she began filling the waitress's order, having to almost yell to be heard over the din of the music and boisterous conversation around them. "Read what happened to him in this afternoon's paper. That was too bad, he was a nice old fucker. Good customer, too. So, that drawing you showed me, you think that's who killed him?"

Suddenly a fight broke out in one of the back corners. Two men tumbled over a table to the floor, fists flying. From out of nowhere, or so it seemed, two huge bouncers appeared, with biceps that looked as big around as Hendricks's upper thighs, one set covered with garish tattoos of naked women and roses. They broke up the fight in no time flat and literally pitched the fighters out the door on their asses. It was all right if they killed themselves, but they damn sure weren't going to do it inside the tavern.

Anna let out a bawdy laugh which revealed a long-standing neglect of dental hygiene, shaking her head as she filled the three shot glasses with tequila. "Those dumb fucks! Happens every time they come in here. Don't it, Sheila?"

Sheila, obviously the cocktail waitress with the crooked front teeth, was looking at Hendricks with sudden interest. "Every time," she agreed with the bartender, then leaned against the counter in a seductive pose and said to Hendricks, "So you're a cop, huh?"

"Detective," he amended. "Homicide. I'm investigating the murder of Rufus Bagget. We believe his killer to be a woman in her mid-twenties with dark brown shoulder-length hair and brown eyes, around five feet, six inches tall, weighing approximately a hundred and twenty pounds. Did you notice anyone fitting that description in here last night? I was told

FLESH AND BLOOD

that Rufus was here from nine-thirty until a quarter past eleven with his good friend Zeke Sawyer."

Eyes twinkling, Sheila rose up on her toes and leaned forward. "I have a thing for cops!" she shouted into his ear. Apparently the only thing she'd heard was his affirmative answer to her question. "Do you, like, carry around a pair of handcuffs by any chance?"

"Here, go deliver these drinks," Anna bellowed at the girl with a disapproving glare. Sheila was brazen enough to reflect the same look back, but she took the tray, as she was told, and trotted off to perform her duty, turning once to give Hendricks a sly wink over her bare shoulder. His still-rigid penis started to follow her, but didn't get very far since the rest of him stayed put.

"Last year it was politicians," Anna bellowed with scorn. "Said she scored with one of our state senators. You believe that? 'Course she couldn'ta met him in here, ain't no fuckin' state senator gonna cruise this place for snatch, they'd be too afraid of getting crabs or herpes. And that would be if they were lucky. Nah, I think she just made that up, like it was some big deal. I fucked a city councilman once, but I didn't go around braggin' about it."

Have I walked into the Twilight Zone? Hendricks wondered. He was trying to investigate a murder, and all he was hearing about was sex. Then he immediately felt like an idiot. He was in the Blue Lady Tavern, where men stuck five dollar bills up naked girls' pussies. What did he expect to hear, a discussion on the pros and cons of nuclear energy?

"Can you point me to anybody who knew Rufus Bagget and was in here last night?"

Anna was in the process of getting four drafts for another cocktail waitress with a mop of dark auburn hair and luminous cinnamon eyes, and who looked no older than fifteen. Her skin was free of makeup and her face bore the look of an innocent. She seemed totally out of place, and Hendricks pictured her standing in choir robes, singing from a hymn book instead, which was a much more congruous picture.

A moment later this same girl brayed, "For fuckin' Chrissakes, Anna, take your fuckin' time about it!"

Anna, who had been scouring the smoky darkness for anyone who'd known Bagget and had been in last night, turned to give her a frosty look. "You just cool your heels, Tina, or I'll make you go back to babysittin'. Just 'cause I'm your mama doesn't mean you can talk to me any damn way you please." Turning back to Hendricks, she sneered. "Fuckin' kids these days! Got no damn respect for their elders."

I *am* in the Twilight Zone, Hendricks thought, and then his eyes followed Anna's finger as she pointed to a table near the stage and yelled, "See that guy in the yellow shirt with palm trees on it?"

Hendricks nodded.

"That there's Hank Westering. I think he was in here last night, and he knew Rufus pretty good."

Hendricks thanked her and began moving through the pulsating gloom toward the table where Hank Westering sat with three other greasers. Hendricks was about halfway there when a new dancer came on stage, her body moving in tandem with Billy Idol's "White Wedding."

He stood there gaping for several seconds. She had the biggest tits he'd ever seen in his life, but that wasn't what had him standing there gaping, that or the fact that her pussy was shaved. It was her dark brown shoulder-length hair and brown eyes. Using just a little imagination, her face could fit the composite. Glancing back at Anna behind the bar, he silently thanked her for nothing. "Could be anybody," she'd said, knowing full well that the description fit one of her dancers.

Hendricks didn't know what to make of the boobs, though. It didn't seem likely that the bartender at the Sea Breeze would have missed a detail like that. At

FLESH AND BLOOD

any rate, he'd be very interested in finding out what kind of alibi this woman had for the last two nights.

Moving up behind Hank Westering, Hendricks removed his badge and flashed it discreetly before the man's face. Westering jumped, startled, "What the hell?"

"Homicide detective. I'd like to ask you some questions about Rufus Bagget," Hendricks told him, shoving the badge back into his hip pocket.

Hank's bloodshot eyes widened. "I didn't do it! Swear to God, I never went near his boat. You can ask him"—he pointed to the man sitting across the table—"we left here before Rufus did, and spent the rest of the night next door with a couple of ladies, Scarlet and Bianca. They'll tell you, they'll remember. They should anyway, we paid 'em a hundred bucks each!"

Hendricks noticed that he was being given dirty looks from the other men at the table as well as several men at other tables in that vicinity, which made him uncomfortable. Now that he thought about it, it was pretty stupid of him to come to a place like this without any backup. But he wasn't entirely alone; he was never (except in the shower) without his good friend Mr. .357, and those monoliths with crew cuts were around here somewhere, which was good to know. Probably in back eating roofing nails for a snack.

Pulling up a nearby empty chair, he straddled it, facing Westering. "Don't get excited, I know you didn't kill Rufus Bagget. Evidence indicates that he was murdered by a woman. So what can you tell me about the girl that's up there dancing now?"

The fear left Westering's eyes and they drifted up to the naked young woman cavorting around the pole in a pair of stiletto heels. "She's sure got her a pair of jugs! Bet her titties are bigger'n Dolly Parton's. I been tryin' to figger out if they're real. You think they're real?"

With her legs spread open wide, the dancer was rubbing her shaved cunt up and down the pole. Folded bills were being waved at her from pervert row. The men holding them were practically drooling on the counter, their eyes the windows of sodden minds ruled by dark lust.

Hendricks felt his penis twitch and begin to grow hard again, even though it was fully aware that its efforts were in vain. *Crabs and herpes, and that's if they were lucky.*

He sighed heavily. "That's not exactly what I meant. Did she ever spend any time with Bagget? Do you know of any reason she might have been mad at him?"

Westering laughed. "Bobbi and Rufus? Sheeit. Bobbi's one of them lesbians—what a waste, huh?—and Rufus probably couldn't have got up a boner for Miss Universe. He hardly paid any attention to the girls. All he wanted to do was get three sheets to the wind and talk about his old Navy days. Same old stories over and over again, not that anybody really listened to 'em after the second or third time, and that was way back when."

Keeping his eyes averted from the stage, Hendricks mulled over what Westering had just told him. The girl up on stage, who matched (with two exceptions) the suspect's description, was a lesbian, assuming Westering's information was correct. Was that because she hated men? He'd wondered before what went on inside the women who danced naked for a living, what sort of thoughts they projected, if they really enjoyed what they were doing or if they were just convincing actresses who relied on dope to keep themselves comfortably numb.

Maybe, if the latter was the case, there might come a time when the dope quit doing its numbing job efficiently. In essence these women were prostitutes, being treated as things, as objects, rather than human beings. Resentment, even hate, could certainly flourish in such soil. Maybe it would thrive to the extent that something had to be done to mollify a particularly outraged ego, which had somehow managed to survive in spite of its many degradations. Something like murder, perhaps. And any man would do, since they were all alike.

"Thanks for your help," Hendricks said to Westering as he rose from his chair, nodding and smiling at Westering's companions, even though two of them were still looking at him with expressions that said they'd like to pull off his head and shit down his neck.

He waded through the smoky air back to the bar and waited while Anna filled another order for Sheila, who covertly slipped something into his jacket pocket the moment he got there. He waited until she left the bar with her tray, acting as though she hadn't noticed him, to pull it out. It was a folded piece of paper, and opening it, he found her name, telephone number, and the message "Any time."

He refolded it and put it back in his pocket, planning to dispose of it later. Seeing that he had Anna's attention, he nodded toward the stage where Bobbi, with her head thrown back, was swaying on her widely spaced knees near the edge of the stage, the fat pink lips of her labia spread apart with her fingers. The pervert sitting directly in front of her had his tongue stretched out, moving it rapidly back and forth just inches away. It looked like a huge worm trying frantically to escape his mouth. His fellow pervs laughed and shouted crude encouragements.

"You mind if I borrow her for about an hour when she's finished, uh, dancing? I'd like her to meet a parrot friend of mine." Rather than let the dancer know where he lived, he thought he'd let someone at the station keep an eye on her while he went to his house and got the bird.

Anna shook her head. "I always wondered why you men always had to give it a name. Henry, George, One-Eyed Joe. You ever meet a girl that had a name for her pussy? So what's the deal with your 'parrot'—don't tell me it can talk?" She threw back her head and laughed brashly, again showing Hendricks her rotting teeth. Before he could form a response, she added in a more serious tone, "What these girls do on their own time is none of my business, but I'd advise you to better pick another one. Bobbi sticks strictly to her own sex."

"Never mind," Hendricks grumbled. "Just tell me Bobbi's full name and where I can find her in the daytime."

Anna frowned, her eyes narrowing. "Now, you don't think Bobbi's the one killed old Rufus, do you?"

"She pretty much fits the description. Her name and address, please?"

"Last name's . . . Paulsen," Anna replied hesitantly, her frown deepening. "Stays next door at the Hollander, Room 316. But you're barking up the wrong tree. Bobbi's not the violent type at all."

"The same thing was said about David Berkowitz," Hendricks replied, and turned from the bar, steering his erection toward the door. He followed it outside to find that rain was falling, which was exactly what he needed. A cold shower.

While Harlan was taking a shower in the bathroom off the hallway, Camisa crept into the boys' room to find out if Aaron was really dead. She felt light-headed and dizzy from hyperventilating the past half hour, fearing that her husband would ask her to rouse the children out of bed so he could see them. But he hadn't; he was too road-weary tonight for their boisterous energy. All he wanted was to get clean, fill his stomach, and go to bed, which was fine and dandy with Camisa.

As she leaned over Aaron's side of the bed to touch his forehead, it felt like a hand reached inside her chest and closed its fingers around her heart, giving it a painful squeeze. Because she already knew. She

FLESH AND BLOOD

knew before she touched Aaron's cold forehead and cheeks that he would be dead. And she had killed him. Accidentally, of course, but would that make any difference to a jury? She thought not.

Turning on the small lamp next to the bed, she looked down in horror at the ghostly pallor of his skin. His eyes were still open and rolled back in his head. Dried spittle covered his parched lips, which were parted slightly to reveal a light blue tongue. Camisa felt vomit rise up in her throat, but it went back down, leaving behind an acidic aftertaste.

It was entirely feasible that Harlan would want to at least look in on the kids before he went to bed. Aaron sure as hell couldn't be looking like this if he did. With a trembling hand, Camisa reached out to pull down her dead son's eyelids. She half expected them to keep popping back open, which would be consistent with her luck so far, but they stayed shut. His mouth wouldn't, though. She'd have to sew or glue his lips together.

Hurrying from to room to get her makeup case from the bathroom in the master bedroom, she hoped Harlan took his usual long shower. It was going to take her at least ten or fifteen minutes to make Aaron look like a sleeping boy instead of a corpse, even longer if she couldn't find the spool of clear nylon thread she'd last seen on one of the end tables in the living room, serving as G.I. Joe's fishing reel. The bottle of Elmer's glue, she'd just remembered, had hardened because Aaron had left the cap off, and that was the only glue they'd had. She'd whipped his ass good for doing it, too, and tore up the elaborate Lego castle he'd painstakingly built. But now that he was dead, she felt pretty guilty about the castle.

The water was still running in the main bathroom when Camisa slipped back into Aaron and Michael's room with her makeup case. Working quickly, she rubbed peach-beige foundation into Aaron's cold, lifeless skin, then powdered it lightly and added a touch of blush to his cheeks. When she was finished, she thought he looked much better, in fact without scrutiny he looked quite alive and healthy, except for that blue tongue.

She was in the living room searching for the nylon thread when Harlan came out of the bathroom wrapped in a towel that barely went around his bulging waistline. She'd been so absorbed in her mission that she hadn't noticed the water being turned off. And it was raining outside, a steady patter on the roof that her subconscious had probably mistaken for the continuation of Harlan's shower.

He was coming toward her with a lustful look on his boyish, plump face that was still slightly red from its recent shave. Apparently his shower had revitalized him. Camisa didn't for one minute believe that he went without sex when he was on the road; she'd heard all about the prostitutes and male homosexuals that hung out at rest areas and truck stops. The fags especially went for the he-man macho types, which in their smarmy little minds included truck drivers. Camisa had read an article once that a surprising percentage of perfectly normal heterosexual truck drivers admitted having sex with them, thinking nothing of it. Camisa had wondered where her husband stood on the issue ever since, but hadn't thought it wise to ask him. He'd only hit her once, for calling his mother a big-mouth slut, but the impact of his fist had sent her flying halfway across the room, nearly breaking her jaw. He might have the same reaction to being asked if he got blowjobs from gay men.

"Your supper's ready in the oven," she said, hoping her voice didn't convey the panic she was feeling. "Leftover meatloaf and mashed potatoes. What do you want with it, bean salad or regular salad?"

He smiled, a wet lock of his shaggy brown hair falling down over his forehead as he came closer. "Right now I want you. C'mere."

FLESH AND BLOOD

"Not now, Harlan. Eat your supper first, then we'll go to bed."

"But feel how hard I am." Closing his beefy arms around her, he rubbed up against her, and she could feel his erection pressing against her belly. He took one of her unwilling hands and guided it through the crack in the towel, molding her fingers around his stiff penis. Camisa had always marveled at how a big man like Harlan could have such a skinny prick. After Aaron's birth and the consequent enlargement of her vagina, the only evidence that it had been inside her while he was pumping away on top of her was the sticky mess that came out when she later went to use the bathroom.

"Let's do it on the couch," he said huskily, "for old times' sake." He started guiding her backward, his breath hot and heavy against her neck.

"Harlan, please," she protested, trying to push him away. "I found out some very upsetting news today. My dad died of a heart attack last night, and when I went to the reading of his will this morning, I found out that I had been adopted. And besides that, the bastard didn't leave me a dime, whereas he gave that fucking Sabrina, his natural daughter, ten thousand dollars. If he wasn't already dead, I'd go blow his brains out."

Harlan drew back, his lusty expression replaced by one of shocked disbelief mixed with a trace of anger. Camisa felt his erection begin to wither, and silently praised the Lord.

"Are you shitting me? What an asshole!"

"I hope he's burning in hell," Camisa said, wondering if it was her imagination or if she'd heard a noise down the hallway leading to the bedrooms. All she needed right now was for Michael to wake up and come rushing into the living room squealing "Daddy Daddy!" making Harlan wonder why Aaron didn't do the same. "Anyway, Monday I'm going to find out what I can about my biological parents. Something weird happened to me this morning, I think I might have remembered my real father. Oh well. Did you want bean salad or regular salad with your dinner?"

"That bean salad gives me gas," Harlan replied grumpily, turning to trudge down the hallway to their bedroom for a clean pair of underwear and his robe, his usual Friday night attire, continuing to curse Forrest Murray under his breath. Ten thousand dollars sure would have come in handy with three kids to raise. His earnings as a truck driver hardly kept up with the soaring cost of living.

Camisa watched tensely as he paused at the end of the hallway and peered into the boys' room on the left, but he lingered there for just a few moments before entering the master bedroom on the right. Expelling a breath of relief, she resumed her frantic search for the nylon thread, and found it under the coffee table inside one of Aaron's dirty socks, attached to a dead chameleon. The end of the thread had been tied around the lizard's neck ostensibly as a leash, but its gaping, swollen jaws testified that Aaron had tied it way too tight. Probably on purpose, Camisa thought, remembering the time he'd found a baby bird that had survived the fall from its nest. Wearing a malicious grin from ear to ear, he'd intentionally crushed it under the wheels of his tricycle before she could stop him. Suddenly she didn't feel so bad about the Lego castle.

Five minutes later, with a disgruntled Harlan seated at the dinner table stuffing his face, Camisa slipped back into the boys' bedroom with the nylon thread and a sewing needle to sew Aaron's mouth shut. By pulling the thread through the undersides of his lips, she was able to seal them invisibly, and even managed to create a slight smile that implied he was having sweet dreams. She wondered idly if she'd missed her calling as a mortician.

At any rate, her trouble had been in vain. After

eating his supper, Harlan mixed himself a stiff drink, which had him passed out on the couch half an hour later.

Camisa went to bed wondering what the hell she was going to do about tomorrow. She'd have to get rid of Aaron's body in a way that didn't make the police suspect her of any wrongdoing. She set the alarm for six A.M. and turned off the light, but she remained awake for a long time, eyes open to the oppressive darkness of the room, ears listening to the patter of raindrops on the roof. The darkness seemed to deepen as she continued to stare into it, becoming black as doom. But she was afraid to close her eyes and go to sleep because she might get up again, unaware, and leave the house to commit another heinous crime. Like she really needed the additional stress, on top of the mountain that was already suffocating her.

Eventually she closed her eyes and concentrated on the sound of the rain, which was comforting. One of the reasons she liked Florida was the fact that it rained a lot, almost every day for thirty minutes to an hour, just long enough to wash the air and make it smell clean. When she was a kid, she'd loved nothing more than to play out in the warm rain, and she thought how refreshing it would feel to take a walk out in it now. But she'd better not.

As the minutes slowly passed, the rain finally lulled her into a deep sleep.

Suzanne was dividing her attention between a cable movie and a game of solitaire when Deidi appeared in a Bart Simpson nightshirt, her dark hair a tangled mess, eyes sullen and shadowed underneath by smeared mascara. Only after an all-night finals cram session had Suzanne ever seen her look so bad. She put her cards down on the coffee table.

"Deidi, are you all right?"

Deidi walked past her to the patio door, dragging her feet, and pressed both palms against the glass as she stared out into the night. Rain was dripping from the eaves, and from the broad leaves of Hughman's favorite palm tree, which was illuminated by a pink floodlight.

"I'm fine," she answered without turning. "I think I'll take Hughman for a walk along the beach. You're welcome to come along."

"But it's raining."

"I know," Deidi acknowledged in a flat tone as she slid the glass door open. She looked toward the hearth at Hughman, who was watching her attentively. Requiring no further encouragement, he got to his feet and loped happily toward her, wagging his black stub. Deidi looked at Suzanne. "Well, are you coming or not?" she asked impatiently, and without waiting for a reply, stepped barefoot onto the flagstone patio and followed Hughman into the sultry gloom.

Part of Suzanne wanted to be furious about the way Deidi was treating her. That part of her wanted to grab up her belongings and book it back to Fort Lauderdale, where it would be more than happy to put up with Kurt's suffocating possessiveness rather than take the shit Deidi was dishing out.

But another part of her, a more rational part, told her that Deidi wasn't so fine, something was in fact very wrong, and whatever was bothering her was responsible for her bitchy behavior—and for at least one inexplicable lapse in memory. Suddenly Suzanne was afraid of Deidi being out on the beach alone. Not bothering to slip on her sandals, which would be only be a nuisance in the wet sand, she sprang off the couch and ran out the door Deidi had left open.

By the time Suzanne reached the front of the house, having nearly slipped and broken what was already cracked on the wet stones of the patio, Deidi and Hughman were already near the water's foamy edge, appearing as two indistinct shapes in a world of blue shadows. Away from the protection of the house, the wind was blowing with gusto, flinging cool raindrops

FLESH AND BLOOD

against Suzanne's exposed skin. Wishing she had a raincoat and umbrella (and while she was at it, for a good-looking millionaire husband with a gargantuan cock who lived only to fullfill her every whim), she ran across the moist sand dunes toward the shoreline, which was being continuously lapped by three-foot waves.

When she reached it, she found Hughman investigating a slimy blob that could only be a dead jellyfish. At least he'd better hope it was dead, Suzanne thought. Those motherfuckers could really sting, she knew from personal experience; she'd stepped on one once.

Nearby, Deidi was kneeling in the sand with her knees apart, digging frantically at the sand between them and crying. Every time the tide came in, her hole was refilled with sand and water. But Suzanne didn't think that was why Deidi was crying.

Kneeling down beside her friend, unconscious for the moment of how uncomfortable she felt in wet clothes, Suzanne put her arm around Deidi's shoulder and said in a soothing voice, "Talk to me, Deidi. Tell me what's wrong! I know something's really bothering you."

What Deidi heard was a scathing voice bellowing at her *"What is WRONG with you?"* and she looked down and saw the hole she'd dug, and in it was Mittens, her kitty, with all his guts hanging out of his stomach and little white worms crawling all over them. Deidi's mouth opened to let out a piercing scream, and she was still screaming when she scrambled to her feet and tore off running down the beach, Hughman and Suzanne in close pursuit.

8

It was just after eight the next morning when Judson Hendricks pulled up in front of the seedy Hollander Hotel. He turned off his engine and just sat there for a few minutes looking at the three rough-looking Mexicans lounging on the stoop smoking cigarettes and passing around a paper sack with a bottleneck protruding from it. Their muscle shirts and jean cutoffs were tattered and dirty, feet shod with sandals that looked like they'd been handed down by Moses. All three had been severely whacked in the face with the ugly stick. To Hendricks they looked ready for a hard day of combing the public beaches for unattended wallets.

In the backseat Bagget's parrot piped up from his cage, "Pirate ship dead ahead, Cyrus!"

"You got that right," Hendricks muttered under his breath, beginning to think the bird was more intelligent than he ever would have thought. Five minutes ago when he'd stopped for a red light, a very attractive and skimpily clad young woman had crossed the street right in front of his car, and Cyrus had wolf-whistled. The woman had turned, glaring, and shot Hendricks the finger.

He thought of the two new things the parrot had

FLESH AND BLOOD

said to his kids last night while he was at the Blue Lady. "Hell of a storm brewin' up, Cyrus," and "Catch yourself a mermaid today, oh man," which was probably supposed to be "old man," and also something he might well have picked up from Bagget's killer. More or less convinced that such was the case, Hendricks had a gnawing feeling that there was some significance in that phrase, and of course it would have to hinge on the key word *mermaid*. When he was finished here, he planned to go to his office at the police station and let his fingers do some walking.

The three amigos sitting on the porch stoop had stopped passing the bottle around and were staring back at Hendricks with sneers on their faces that made them even uglier. They were going to give him some shit, no doubt about it. "Fucking wetbacks," he grumbled as he opened his door and stepped out to retrieve Cyrus's cage from the backseat.

As expected, one of them immediately called out to him in his south-of-the-border accent, "Hey, Meester Beesness Suit, you sure you got the right neighborhood, man? Or you here to get some cheap *puta?*"

His companions cackled gleefully, slapping their knees.

Emerging from the backseat of his car with the bird cage, Hendricks shot them the coldest look he could muster, though he doubted his ability to intimidate these desperadoes with anything less than the business end of an M-16. Telling them he was a cop would really be asking for it, so instead he told them that he was delivering a present to Jesus El Durado's favorite niece.

It was apparent on their faces that none of them had ever heard of Jesus El Durado, which was not surprising since Hendricks had just made it up. He was wishing now he'd come with at least two patrol backups, but he didn't think vermin like this crawled out from under their rocks before noon.

"So who's thees Jesus El Durado?" one of them

asked contemptuously, rising up from his perch to stand threateningly between Hendricks and the hotel's graffitied entrance. Having smoked his cigarette down to the butt, he flicked it away with his fingers. Still smoldering, it landed in what had once been a flower bed but now contained nothing but garbage, mostly cigarette butts, crushed beer cans, and broken glass.

Who was Jesus El Durado? Hendricks thought fast as he walked boldly up to the bottom of the cement steps. "Get serious, you don't know who he is? Let me give you a little hint. He runs a very large and powerful operation in Colombia, and anybody who pisses him off gets a free colon exam with a bazooka. *Guaranteed.*"

"Guaranteed," Cyrus confirmed.

"Oh, *that* Jesus El Durado," the Mexican blocking his way said, black eyes widening, the sneer on his lips becoming an amiable smile.

"Yeah, he's one bad dude all right," one of his compadres agreed. "Ain't he the one that like, blew up all them government buildings and shit?"

The one standing nodded thoughtfully. "Yeah, I theen so, man." Looking at Hendricks, he stepped aside and said, "So go on een, man, deleever the present. Who is she, anyway? We know most the people who live in this shithole, but nobody ever told us they were related to Jesus El Durado."

"Maybe she doesn't want you to know," Hendricks said in an ominous tone, taking the first step.

"Fucking wetbacks," Cyrus added.

A second man jumped to his feet, face contorted in anger, and pointed at the bird cage. "Hey, man, that bird just called us fucking wetbacks!"

"You teach heem to say that, gringo?" the one still sitting spat.

Oh shit, Hendricks thought.

The scene that occurred shortly thereafter was

straight from one of his worst nightmares. The three men jumped him at once, their fear of the rich and powerful Colombian drug lord Jesus El Durado completely forgotten. Or perhaps they'd had bazookas rammed up their butts before and liked it.

When all was said and done, the bottom had fallen out of Cyrus's cage and he had taken flight, successfully dodging the rocks one of the Mexicans chucked at him from the ground. They'd managed to get Hendricks's gun away from him while they were busy rearranging his face, finding also the pair of cuffs he'd had in his back pocket for Bobbi Paulsen, should her arrest have been warranted.

After handcuffing him to the porch's iron railing, they'd taken off in his car, laughing and howling and shouting profanities in Spanish.

For the first time since grade school, Hendricks felt like crying.

There was something tugging insistently on her arm. Camisa gradually swam up through the deep, murky waters of sleep to consciousness and opened her eyes to find that the something tugging on her arm was Michael, and he had a very disturbed look on his cherubic face.

"Mama, Airn"—his way of saying Aaron—"won't wake up," he said when he saw that he'd finally succeeded in waking her up.

Camisa gasped, coming fully awake as reality crashed down on her like a ton of bricks. In her dreams she'd had no awareness of Aaron's death; her subconscious had done for her what Calgon bath-oil beads always did for the woman in the commercial, taken her away to a place of fairy-tale perfection where she had absolutely nothing to worry about. There had been no bad dreams (that would later prove to be actual memories of things she'd actually done) involving the killing of some unsuspecting man or the vandalizing of a stranger's corpse, and no humiliating confrontations such as she'd experienced in Wendell Swihart's office.

Bolting upright, she looked at the clock, horrified to see that it was almost eight o'clock. At first she thought the alarm hadn't gone off, then remembered vaguely that it had, but after silencing it she'd promptly gone back to sleep.

The space beside her was empty. Apparently Harlan was still crashed on the couch. Camisa felt her heart thumping madly. What would she have done if Michael had followed his usual routine and gone into the living room to watch the Saturday morning cartoons? He'd have been all over Harlan, yelling and squealing, and she'd have been screwed for sure.

"Mama, Airn won't wake up," Michael repeated firmly, moving his hand to tug on her nightgown. "Airn tick, Mama."

Camisa put a finger to her lips, praying Felicia would hold off on her squalling for just a little bit longer, knowing it was asking a lot. She'd already slept half an hour longer than she usually did. But Camisa still hoped that fate was on her side for once.

"Shhh, you be quiet, Michael," she whispered. "Daddy's here, but he's very very tired from his trip and I don't want you waking him up, you understand?" When he nodded, his chocolate-colored eyes lit up at the mention of his daddy, she continued sternly, "Now we're going for a little outing so Daddy can have some peace and quiet. Go back to your room and wait for me to help you get dressed."

"Is Airn donna go?"

She forced a patient smile. "Yes, Aaron is going to go with us. I know he's kinda sick, but getting out in the sunshine will help him feel lots better. Go on, now," she prodded, lightly patting him on the rear. "And remember, be very quiet and go straight to your room, nowhere else."

Michael pouted. "But I dotta go pee-pee."

FLESH AND BLOOD

"Piss in my bathroom," Camisa whispered harshly, pointing to it. "And don't flush the potty when you're done. That might wake Daddy up, and he'd probably want to beat the living shit out of you."

While Michael crept fearfully into the half bathroom clutching the lower front of his pajama bottoms, Camisa sprang out of bed, stripped out of her nightgown (not caring if Michael saw her naked) and threw on the clothes she'd changed into after getting home from the attorney's office, which was a pair of faded red shorts and a white halter top permanently stained by baby barf, or "spit up," as some mothers affectionately called it, the same mothers who cooed over dirty diapers, referring to the reeking green muck as poo-poo in a goochy-coo voice. To Camisa it was barf and shit and those other mothers were just airheaded Suzie Homemaker bitches. Then she quietly hurried into the kitchen to fix Felicia a bottle of cold milk so that she'd have nothing to complain about while her five-pound wet diaper was being changed. Harlan was still sleeping soundly on the couch, one arm thrown over his face to shield his eyes from the bright morning light glaring through the sheer living room drapes. His mouth was open and he was snoring, the sound reminding Camisa of someone sucking a straw at the bottom of an empty cup. Many a time had she been subjected to that same disgusting noise while she was trying to sleep, and oh how she'd wanted to bash his head in with the handiest heavy object. But this morning his snoring, though still disgusting, was the only thing she wanted to hear until she was safely away from the house with all three kids.

Correction: two kids and the corpse.

Holding Felicia's bottle firmly, she tiptoed back through the living room and down the hallway to the nursery, arriving not a minute too soon. Felicia was waking up, as evidenced by her fussy kicking and preliminary whining. Wearing a motherly smile, Camisa inserted the bottle's nipple into Felicia's pouting mouth, which closed around it and began sucking eagerly. Letting the toddler hold the bottle, Camisa went to work on changing the wet diaper, all the while feeling her heart bang erratically against her chest. All she needed was ten more minutes, at the most, but in her present state of anxiety that seemed like a very long time. From the nursery she could still faintly hear Harlan's snoring, and she clung to the sound as if it were a life raft, which in a way it was.

"I'll be all right, just fine," she whispered to herself consolingly as she reached inside the near-empty box of Huggies for a new diaper. Yes, she would be fine. She knew what she was going to do now, how she was going to take care of her problem, and everything would go smoothly, without a hitch. She wouldn't wind up in some filthy women's prison and be a plaything for a bunch of ugly, smelly dykes.

Then another sound filled her ears, blocking out Harlan's snoring: the whining whoosh of the toilet being flushed in her bedroom. Damn that Michael, he'd forgotten he wasn't supposed to flush after he peed, regardless of the fact that he'd been soundly spanked on countless previous occasions for not doing it like he *was* supposed to.

Every muscle in Camisa's body tensed. She left Felicia undiapered and stepped rigidly out into the hallway just as Michael emerged from her bedroom. He smiled up at her, ignorant of his offense, but his smile fell flat under his mother's scathing glare. When she jabbed a stiff finger toward his bedroom, he hurried into it, shamefaced, without saying a word.

Feeling like her chest could explode any moment, Camisa crept to the head of the hallway and peeked across the living room at the couch and her husband's prone body. Harlan had changed positions; he was no longer lying on his back but on his right side, with his face turned toward the back of the couch. The plumbing noise had quieted, and now she could tell that his snoring had stopped. She didn't like that at all. If he

FLESH AND BLOOD

wasn't snoring and he'd had a fair amount of sleep, any little noise was liable to wake him up. But she could hardly risk turning him back over.

After diapering and putting a clean sundress on Felicia, Camisa carried her into the boys' room and carefully closed the door. Then she put the baby down and helped Michael get dressed in shorts and a T-shirt, resisting the urge to smack him for flushing the toilet because that would only start him crying, and any noise like that she could do without right now. He'd sure get it later, though.

"How tum Airn won't wate up?" he inquired meekly, his big brown eyes staring at his brother's still body. He'd pulled the sheet away, revealing a body of pallid yellowish hue in considerable contrast to a brownish-yellow neck and face. The fingers of both hands were curled up around nothing.

"I'll wake Aaron up in a minute," Camisa hissed through clenched teeth as she jerked up Michael's shorts hard enough to rupture him. "You just be quiet, you hear me? Daddy's still trying to sleep, so while he sleeps we're going to go out and do something fun. But only if you mind me."

"What we donna do?"

Pulling the T-shirt over his head, Camisa answered with an exasperated sigh, "It's a surprise, Michael, in fact I'm going to blindfold you and Aaron so you can't see where we're going. Now will you just please shut up?"

Now that Michael was ready, Camisa sifted through all the toys strewn about the toy chest until she located the two bandannas, one red and one navy-blue, that the boys had worn last Halloween with their outlaw costumes. Sticking them into the waistband of her shorts, she approached the side of the bed on which Aaron's dead body lay, her heart going into a fresh gallop. In the cold light of day his face didn't look so alive and healthy. From the neck down he looked like something from a horror movie, jaundiced fish-belly skin with mottled bruises along the lower areas of his backside.

Aware that Michael was all eyes, Camisa reached down to grasp one of Aaron's cold, curled hands, which she attempted to lift, but he was completely stiff with rigor mortis and the highest it would go without force was a couple of inches. "C'mon, Aaron, time to get up," she said softly, trying her best to act natural. No, nothing wrong here. Just a young mother trying to get her five-year-old son out of bed so she could take him and his siblings on a fun (not to mention educational) trip to Reptile Gardens, Danville's second largest tourist attraction. The main attraction was a preserved pirate ship (or so they said) called the *Aquina*, which was permanently docked at the north end of La Croix harbor and surrounded by a dozen or so concession stands and small souvenir shops.

Turning her face so that Michael couldn't see her lips move, Camisa answered for the dead boy, doing her best to imitate his voice. "I don't want to get up, Mommy, I wanna sleep some more."

"But, Aaron," she replied in her own voice, "we're going to go do something really fun, but don't ask what, because it's going to be a surprise. Now come on, up and at 'em."

As she forced him into sitting position, which took some doing (and made a horrible cracking noise) she responded in his voice, "Oh, goodie!"

She pried his eyes open with her thumbs, and luckily they stayed open. Their surfaces were glazed over, the pupils completely dilated and staring fixedly toward the ceiling, but she didn't think Michael would notice, and of course she had nothing to worry about with Felicia, who couldn't even talk yet. Her main worry at the moment was how she was going to get Aaron into some clothes when he was stiff as a damn board. What the hell did morticians do about this problem?

Camisa didn't know, but she quickly decided what

FLESH AND BLOOD

she would do. She'd just leave Aaron in his pajama bottoms, because he'd have to be nude anyway, later on. If Michael gave her any guff about it, like "I wanna wear my damas, too!" she'd be able to silence him easily enough with threats, beginning with cutting out his tongue if he said another word. But apparently he was so excited about their surprise outing that he was oblivious to all else.

Carrying both a wiggling toddler and a rigid thirty-seven-pound corpse taxed Camisa's strength for all it was worth, but desperation had given her a special reserve; had her freedom depended on it, she could probably have carried them for miles across burning desert sand. And she might have chosen to do that over the alternative of crossing the living room behind Michael, which was by far the most harrowing experience of her life. She just knew Harlan was going to wake up and see her, see Aaron and know. Then the shit would really hit the fan, big-time.

Michael was looking at his father's horizontal bulk longingly, but Camisa kept him going, nudging him along with a knee toward the kitchen. They would go out the sliding patio door, which offered the quietest exit.

She had managed to slide it open about a foot without making any sound at all, which was wide enough for Michael to get through—and he did—when Camisa heard Harlan groan in the living room, and then the couch springs squeaked. Camisa held her breath, wide eyes turned toward the wide archway between the living room and dining area, where she now stood trembling from head to foot listening to the newest sound, that of blood rushing through her ears.

Then she saw him. He moved right into the middle of the open archway and lifted his arms to stretch languidly as he released another groan. Probably had a backache from sleeping on the couch. But all he had to do was look toward the kitchen, turn his head just a little to the right, and he would see her standing in the dining area like an instant mannequin. Felicia must have sensed her panic, for she also grew very still, her little face a mask of nervous anticipation behind her bottle.

As could only happen in Camisa's world, it was the corpse that moved, and Camisa came dangerously close to letting out a bloodcurdling scream. Aaron's body suddenly straightened from the bent position she'd put it in. Of course it was only some sort of muscle contraction; she'd heard of corpses sitting up on the morgue table. Aaron hadn't come back to life, no way. Still, what a hair-raiser! And she knew she couldn't hold him up much longer; her own muscles were being stretched far beyond their limits.

Harlan's stretching session seemed to last five minutes, during which Camisa died a thousand deaths. Then, finally, he began moving toward the hallway in his usual slow, downtrodden lope. Even wearing an expensive three-piece suit complete with power tie and shiny leather shoes, Harlan would still be pegged as the loser he was.

A few seconds later the bathroom door in the hallway closed. Now he'd piss for half a minute, then maybe brush his teeth and use the mouthwash before he went to the master bedroom looking for love.

Camisa dared not waste another second. With her purse hanging around her neck and Aaron's body under one arm like a stack of lumber, Felicia mashed in the other, Camisa hurried around the side of the house, barking softly but vehemently at Michael's heels, "Move it move it move it!"

It wasn't until they were in the car and three blocks from the house that Camisa finally allowed herself to believe that she'd pulled it off. It had been nothing short of a miracle, with Harlan waking up when he had, standing for an interminable length of time where he could have looked over and seen her so easily; and no less than three neighbors had been out

FLESH AND BLOOD

front tending their pet gardens, but they had only given her and her cargo a perfunctory glance, as if there was nothing unusual about a half-naked five-year-old boy who was stiff as a board, though they'd surely have thought otherwise if they'd gotten a peek at his deeply bruised back. But they hadn't, so maybe they thought he was engaged in some sort of tantrum. Then when she'd started her old dilapidated Mercury sedan, she'd thought for sure Harlan would hear and come rushing out on the front porch in his robe to ask where she was going. But he hadn't. And she didn't waste any time speculating on the reason; there were much more important things to worry about, such as how she was going to get through the next ordeal, and the next. At a stop sign, she put the transmission in park and tied the red bandanna over Michael's eyes, afterward only pretending to tie the blue one over Aaron's. What a sight two blindfolded boys would present to passing motorists. Just one wouldn't draw much attention. If they could see Michael at all, they would assume his headband had slipped down, or that he was playing some kind of game. And this was a game, to him. Beneath his bandanna he was smiling widely as he fidgeted anxiously in his seat, periodically clapping his hands and asking if he could see the surprise yet, to which Camisa repeatedly and angrily answered no he could not.

Reptile Gardens was located in the northeast part of Danville among a cluster of other tourist traps, motels, nightclubs, and restaurants. When Camisa was in junior high school, she and a few of her friends had found a way to sneak into Reptile Gardens without having to pay. Following a narrow and winding tree-lined dirt road off North Sunnymeade, she eventually came to a small clearing only a dozen or so yards away from the large bird sanctuary that was part of Reptile Gardens. Farther down, about a quarter mile, the road continued on to the city dump.

The sanctuary was bordered on each side by a tall chain-link fence topped with coils of razor wire, but on the left side the bottom links of the fence had come loose from its metal support. It had been a long time since Camisa had taken advantage of that secret opening, and as she switched off the car's engine she wondered what the hell she was going to do if it had been fixed.

"Mommy, can we see now?" Michael piped up, his chin lifted high in an obvious attempt to peek out from the bottom of the bandanna. Having exhausted the last of her patience long ago, Camisa smacked him on the side of the head and screamed, *"No! Fuck no! Now you just sit there and be still, and no peeking or I'll blister your bottom!"*

Michael's lips curled up and he began to wail, which set Felicia off because her bottle was empty. *Go ahead and take them all,* a voice whispered inside Camisa's head. *Kill three birds with one stone. Think of the freedom. Think how much fun it would be!*

Camisa gripped the steering wheel and shook her head. She had to get ahold of herself, stop thinking such things. Killing Aaron had been an accident; she couldn't cold-bloodedly murder her other two children. A feeling of nausea in her stomach argued that she could indeed—she'd killed two men, hadn't she? —but she absolutely would not murder Michael and Felicia, even if the resulting freedom would be bliss, Heaven on earth. Even if she could, she wouldn't. At least she hoped not.

She opened her car door and stepped out into the blinding sunlight. Taking a few deep breaths, she was reminded that the air around this spot was tinged with a mixture of unsavory scents from Reptile Gardens; lizard and snake musk, bird feathers, tortoise shit, rotting foliage, and of course the muddy cesspools in the gator and crocodile pens. Glancing at her watch, she saw that it was 8:23. The place didn't open until ten, but there would still be maintenance workers to

FLESH AND BLOOD

worry about. And the fence. She'd better go down to check it before getting Aaron's body out of the car.

Wishing she'd worn a pair of long pants, she made her way through brambles and bushes that scraped and scratched her legs, along a forgotten path that was nearly invisible until she reached the rear wall of the bird sanctuary. Following it to her left, she soon came to the chain-link fence. On first sight it did look like it had been fixed, and Camisa felt the world tumbling down around her ears. But she leaned over to tug on it anyway, and to her surprise, the lower end broke free.

Relief washed over her like a pure mountain waterfall, and smiling grimly, she hurried back to the car, ignoring the overgrowth's stinging assault on her legs.

It only took a few minutes to get back to the secret entrance with Aaron's corpse, but during that short time a big problem had developed. A young man dressed in light green sleeveless coveralls was strolling slowly by, hosing off the cement walkway as he went. Camisa hid with the corpse behind the bird sanctuary, gritting her teeth in mental anguish while the Reptile Garden employee passed by with the speed of a tortoise, whistling a maddening tune. She thought anybody that happy should be taken out and shot.

At least a hundred of her hairs had turned gray by the time he was finally gone, or so she believed. After casing the area through the fence and finding the coast clear, she lifted Aaron's stiff body from the ground and pulled it through the opening. It was hard to believe she was doing this in broad daylight, but she really had no choice. Not with Harlan home.

The alligators and crocodiles were kept in two large stone pens a short way down the walk from the bird sanctuary. There were dozens of each species, some partially submerged in their black pools, others drying out in the sun, their scaly, elongated snouts crammed full of sharp teeth, looking dead as shoe leather. But Camisa knew they weren't.

The three-foot wall surrounding the pens was kept

off limits only by a metal guardrail that was easy enough to duck under. Camisa ducked under it, bringing the corpse with her, looking furtively both ways to make sure no one was coming.

"I'm really very sorry about this, Aaron," she whispered to him as she quickly pulled down and removed his pajama bottoms, which she flung over her left shoulder. "You know I'd rather have given you a nice funeral, but I can't without getting myself in a lot of serious trouble. You do understand, don't you?"

She thought she heard him say yes, from wherever he was in the spirit world. Feeling a little better, she then picked his naked body up and tossed it unceremoniously over the wall into the alligator pen.

She hadn't planned to watch the disgusting feast, but she found it impossible to pull her eyes away when the horde of giant lizards converged on Aaron's small white (and purple) body. Several pairs of spiked jaws gaped and closed simultaneously around his limbs and face, initiating a gruesome tug of war in which the distinct cracking of bones could be heard. The largest of them scuttled up and seized him around the middle, its crushing bite, coupled with a savage shaking, literally cutting the corpse in two. The halves parted as the warring gators vied for their portions, stringing in both directions intestines and vital organs which were greedily devoured by the strongest and fastest of their number. At least there was no splattering of red blood, since all of Aaron's had coagulated. The dark, unidentifiable clots that escaped consumption would not arouse suspicion.

A sudden loud cracking noise indicated that his skull had just been crushed by the alligator chomping on his head, which was one thing Camisa had worried about; no identifiable trace of Aaron could be left, otherwise the police would be suspicious when she later told them how he'd been swept out to sea and drowned. She couldn't imagine the pounds of pressure those monstrous jaws could exert, but obviously,

FLESH AND BLOOD

cracking a child's skull was no more a problem for them than eating peanut brittle was for her.

Now there was only one thing left to do. Drive to a secluded beach, and while Michael was still wearing his blindfold, make him think Aaron had gone ahead and jumped into the water. That should be easy enough to do; just find a rock or a shell and throw it in to make a splashing sound, then immediately scold "Aaron" for going out too far.

Then would begin her Oscar-winning performance as the hysterical mother, which really wouldn't require all that much acting, except for the tears. She'd never cried in her life, that she could remember, anyway, unless it was from being in unbearable physical pain, such as labor and childbirth. And of course she'd have to fake the frantic search for Aaron under the water, for Michael's benefit in case the police should want to question him.

That was going to be the hardest part, talking to the police. But she was certain they would believe her. Clinging tenaciously to that thought, she hurried away from the alligator pen before anyone saw her and back through the secret opening in the fence to her Mercury. Michael and Felicia had cried themselves to sleep in the car's muggy interior, Michael in the backseat, curled up in a ball with his blindfold still on, Felicia up front in her car seat with her face squished against the wide padded bar in front of her. Michael woke up when Camisa opened the door and got in.

"Tan I see sprize now, Mommy?" he asked in a small, sleepy voice.

Camisa started the car. "We're not there yet, Michael, and I'll tell you when we are. Aaron, you stop trying to peek under your blindfold or I'll give you a spanking. All right now, here we go. Just five more minutes, boys. See how many times you can count your fingers by then. The one who counts the most times gets to take his blindfold off first."

With Michael annoyingly counting his fingers out

loud (and he could only count to three, corresponding with his age), Camisa drove down the dirt road back to North Sunnymeade and headed east toward the public beaches.

After a few minutes, she became so lost in her own thoughts that Michael's incessant "One-two-fee" no longer registered. It was a wonder she didn't have an accident, for the car was essentially on auto pilot. So it was at least a full minute after she'd done it that she realized she'd gone down the wrong road, and being one she'd never previously explored, realization came with disorientation and a panicked feeling of being lost.

"One-two-fee, one-two-fee . . ."

"Shut up, Michael," Camisa barked, searching desperately for a place to turn around. The asphalt road was narrow, and bordered on either side by steeply sloping ditches. Afraid that if she tried to turn around in the middle of the road she'd get stuck in one of them, which would be nothing short of disastrous, she drove on, and looking ahead could see a spread of sandy shoreline in the distance, with a copse of five-inch palm trees in the foreground.

As she got closer, she could see there was a house behind the palm trees, a large two-story stucco painted light pink. It had a wide upper deck made of redwood, and below that a stone patio with a partially walled courtyard. In a graveled area outside the courtyard, five vehicles were parked in a row.

Camisa felt her heart lurch, and she stomped on the brake so hard that Michael was thrown into the back floorboard. Felicia, jerked rudely awake by the sudden stop, immediately began to wail.

Camisa barely heard her cries, or Michael's either, so stunned was she by the sight of that stucco house up ahead. She knew beyond question that she'd never taken this road before, but she by-God knew that house, she'd seen it at least half a dozen times. She'd

FLESH AND BLOOD

even been inside it, at least part of it. And then she realized where, or more precisely how, she'd gained this familiarity, which filled her with wonder, not to mention a little fear.

She'd dreamed about it. And in those dreams, that was where she lived, just her and a big dog. No husband, no kids.

Her secret life.

A part of her felt compelled to drive right on up to the house and lay all the secrets bare, make real the unreal, plunge consciously into her world of dreams that weren't dreams. But she was too scared of what she might find, of what might happen if she did.

Some thirty feet ahead an intersecting road led to a small cluster of cottages off to the right. Camisa used it to turn around, and sped back to the main road pushing seventy, oblivious to the continuing cries of her two remaining children.

At the moment Camisa was tossing Aaron's body to the alligators, Deidi woke up with a start, a gasp caught in her throat, heart pounding. Eyes darting to her alarm clock, she saw that it was almost a quarter to nine. Swearing softly, she tossed back the covers and leapt out of bed, noting that Hughman was nowhere in sight.

She found him in the living area with Suzanne, both of them sitting on the couch watching cartoons. Their heads turned to look at her when she appeared, Hughman's pointed mug cracking into the closest thing it could come to a smile. Suzanne just stared, as if she was wondering what the hell Deidi was doing there.

"Well, good morning," Deidi mumbled, stretching, feeling her heart begin to slow its pace to normal.

"Good morning," Suzanne responded, her voice sounding a little strange, Deidi thought. What was the matter with her? Was Suzanne pissed at her because she'd gone to bed so early last night? Hells bells, it wasn't as if she'd done it just to be a bitch; she'd been sick, really sick, although she was feeling fine now.

Running her hand through her tousled mane of dark brown hair, Deidi groaned. "I overslept; must have forgotten to set my alarm. Normally I don't have to work on weekends—there's a weekend staff—but Tom told me to make myself Judson Hendricks's shadow. He's convinced there's a female serial killer on the loose in Danville, and he wants me to keep close track of the investigation. Sorry to leave you here by yourself, but Tom said if I let him down he's going to sit on me, and coming from a baby elephant, that's a hell of a threat."

Suzanne shook her head slightly. "You don't remember a thing about last night, do you?"

"Last night?" Deidi's mind whirled. Last night? What was there to remember about last night? She'd gotten sick not too long after Suzanne had arrived, and gone to bed. There was nothing else to remember except maybe the bizarre dreams she'd had after falling asleep, which came back to her now in vivid detail.

"Suzanne, what are you talking about? Remember what?"

Sighing, Suzanne leaned back against the couch, apparently searching for the right words. When she finally spoke, her voice sounded hollow. "You've really got a serious problem, Deidi, whether you know it or not. Last night you came out of your bedroom in your nightshirt and took Hughman out in the rain, for a walk along the beach you said, but when I got down there, you were digging in the sand near the water and crying. Then when I spoke to you, you got up and ran away screaming like the Devil himself was after you. And you don't remember that, do you?"

Deidi felt her face go white. "I thought I just dreamed that."

"Well, it wasn't just a dream. It really happened."

Suddenly feeling as if she might faint, Deidi lowered herself onto the other end of the couch, ignoring Hughman's licks of affection on the back of her hand. Her knees were trembling, as were her hands, and her forehead was breaking out in a cold sweat. It felt like someone had just kicked her in the stomach. "I had other dreams . . . oh God."

Suzanne leaned forward, her face expressing deep concern. "It's okay, Deidi. Nothing else happened. I finally caught up with you and brought you back home, then helped you into bed. You didn't get up again until this morning."

An involuntary shudder ran the length of Deidi's body as her mind replayed the scene of her leaning over a small boy's unconscious body with a couple of live wires. In the dream he had been her son. "Maybe I shouldn't wait until Tuesday to see Dr. Jordan. If I can get him at home, I might be able to talk him into seeing me this evening. Shit, Suzanne, I'm scared. I don't think I've ever been this scared in my life. I feel like I'm losing my mind, and if I am, I'd rather be dead."

"Where's your phone book?" Suzanne asked with grave firmness, rising from the couch. "You're going to call him right now."

Deidi pointed toward the wall end of the kitchen counter, below the telephone, where the tattered directory was buried under a pile of junk mail and bills. While Suzanne thumbed through it for Dr. Jordan's number, Deidi stared at the cartoon action on the television set, but her mind was focused on another scene playing behind her eyes, a scene in which she'd thrown her dream son's dead body into the alligator pen at Reptile Gardens.

"Do you know his first name?" Suzanne called over her shoulder.

"James," Deidi answered flatly as another shudder passed through her. Even in a dream, how could she do such a terrible thing? But maybe her actions in the dream could be interpreted as just a symbolic expression of how much she didn't want to be a mother. Still, how sickening, the idea of throwing a little boy's body into an alligator pen. But damned if she didn't feel slightly ripped-off at not getting to see what happened after the alligators converged, because there the dream had ended. No doubt about it, she was sick in the head. Very much so.

Forty-five minutes later, dressed casually in a white sleeveless blouse, khaki shorts, and tennis shoes, she was on her way to the police station, listening to the radio and puffing away on her fifth cigarette. Little by little she began to relax. Dr. Jordan had agreed to see her this evening at his office, having been convinced that it was an emergency. God bless the man. Of course he never claimed to be a miracle worker, but Deidi believed that he was going to work a miracle tonight. Under hypnosis, all those dark clouds were going to break up, the sunlight of truth was going to come shining through, and it would be a warming, welcome light, not one that burned or blinded her.

She hoped.

Arriving at the police station, she was directed to the booking desk, where she asked to see Detective Hendricks. Notebook and pen in hand, she followed the zigzagging hallway that the aging, potbellied policeman behind the information desk had indicated. Farther down this same hallway, an unseen woman's voice loudly ranted and raved about suing the city for harassment.

When Deidi reached the booking desk, she found standing before it Judson Hendricks, who looked like he'd been used as a tennis birdie in a match between Godzilla and King Kong. The young dark-headed woman doing all the yelling was wearing nothing but a see-through teddy and a G-string, and two uniformed officers were both busy keeping the handcuffed woman in one place and obviously enjoying every second of it.

FLESH AND BLOOD

"I didn't kill anybody!" the woman raved on, struggling against the two men who were holding her. "You stupid fucks! Why would I wanna kill a poor old man? He never bothered me! If I was gonna kill somebody, I know some others that really deserve it!"

After tossing a brief glance at Deidi, which did not include a smile, Hendricks put a hand on his hip and said to the near-naked woman, "I'm not booking you on a murder complaint, so just zip it. I told you, you're under arrest for assaulting an officer. But if you don't start behaving yourself, I'm sure I can come up with a few more charges, like maybe possession of cocaine? I don't think you want me getting too curious about that film of white powder I saw on that mirror on your coffee table. Now let Sergeant Sprigg take your fingerprints or we'll just see how nasty I can get. And after all the shit I've gone through this morning, I bet I can get pretty damn nasty."

The woman suddenly seemed to deflate like a balloon. Her shoulders slumped and the fire went out of her eyes. Hendricks nodded at one of the uniformed officers, who then produced a key and unlocked the handcuffs around the woman's wrist.

Turning to Sergeant Sprigg behind the booking desk, Hendricks said tersely, "As soon as those prints are dry, send them upstairs to the lab for comparison with the ones in files H519 and -20, and tell whoever that I'll be waiting in my office for the results."

Spriggs nodded, seemingly unable to take his eyes off the woman's hardened nipples jutting against the sheer, filmy fabric of her nightie, perhaps wondering if she was cold or sexually aroused by her predicament. "Will do," he said absently.

With a heavy sigh Hendricks skirted the small cluster in front of the desk to head for his office, passing Deidi without so much as looking at her or saying a word. Not knowing what else to do, she followed him, jotting down the numbers H519 and -20 although she had as yet no idea what they meant.

But anything that came out of Hendricks's mouth might turn out to be important.

Hendricks strode purposefully all the way to his office in stony silence, and after letting himself in, started to shut the door in Deidi's face. She stopped it with her hand just in time, her eyes narrowing into slits of anger. He was treating her like she was the one who'd beat him up, and she came close to shooting him with a lethal piece of her mind right then and there. But before she fired the cannon, otherwise known as her big mouth, she reminded herself of the reason she was there, and that getting on his bad side would hardly be productive. Besides, it had to be pretty humiliating for him, getting the shit beat out of him by a woman.

"Hey, am I invisible this morning, or have you gone blind?" she asked with just a touch of irritation as she pushed the door back open for herself. It was the best she could do.

Hendricks had already flopped down in the swivel chair behind his cluttered desk, which was facing the window on the opposite side of the room. "Got any booze on you? I could sure use a drink right now," he said without turning from his sunny view of a rock garden containing several species of cacti, his profiled expression remaining gloomy. Deidi noted that in the wash of sunlight, as opposed to the fluorescent lighting in the hallway, the purple and greenish bruises on his face didn't look quite so bad.

"Sure, I carry a pint with me wherever I go," she quipped, helping herself to one of the two wooden chairs positioned in front of his desk. Crossing her legs, she worked at looking sympathetic. "I take it she's some kind of judo or karate expert?"

Hendricks turned to stare at her. "What?"

"That woman, you know. The one who... assaulted you."

Hendricks stared at her for a few more seconds, uncomprehending. Then what she was implying finally registered with the raising of his eyebrows, and he laughed out loud in spite of himself, though it made his head pound. Gingerly touching the right side of his face, which was not only bruised but slightly swollen, he explained that the woman had only kicked him once in the shin after he told her he was a police officer and wanted to ask her a few questions. "The rest of the damage," he said with sudden grimness, "was the work of three heavily armed Mexicans who also stole my car, which has yet to be found. They left me handcuffed to an iron railing outside the Hollander Hotel, and several minutes later a group of delinquent kids came along and pelted me with rocks and spit. So how's your morning been?"

Deidi didn't want to think about her morning, much less talk about it, although she was tempted to say she would have gladly traded problems with him. But she didn't; unless she could say she'd been shot, knifed, and gang-raped by a bunch of fat, scummy bikers with crabs in their beards and running sores on their dicks, he'd never believe her problems were worse than his. "I had to get up early."

Hendricks snorted. "Must've been rough."

"You've no idea."

"Well, keep your fingers crossed; when I get my call from the lab, your pain and suffering might be compensated, since I gather you're here for some news and not just for another look at my irresistibly handsome face."

"Oh, don't be too sure about that," Deidi responded with pretentious coyness, a little ashamed of herself for using her sex as a means to get what she wanted, but not ashamed enough to stop. Up to a certain point, she'd do whatever it took to further her career, which she hoped would ultimately lead to a television news anchor contract. But exactly where that certain point was, she had no idea, although she suspected she was going to find out with Judson Hendricks.

The detective, apparently disregarding her suggestive remark, leaned back in his chair and turned again to face the cactus garden outside his window. "Actually, I'm not very hopeful that the woman we have in custody will prove to be Patton and Bagget's killer, but I do think I've got a good lead. I can't tell you what it is, though."

Deidi felt the skin on her arms crawl into gooseflesh. The pen she was holding over her notepad trembled. "You're saying the same person definitely murdered both men?"

"Of that I have no doubt," Hendricks confirmed.

It didn't much surprise Deidi that Tom, her boss, had been right; he usually was. Being fat didn't make him stupid. And now she knew for certain that a few inexplicable visions of a mutilated face and a bleeding old man reaching out to her didn't make her a killer. She no longer had to worry about her loss of memory the night Bagget was murdered, or the violent reaction of his stupid parrot when she'd entered the boat's cabin. At least, not as much.

Intrigued by the mention of a lead, Deidi moistened her lips with her tongue and in a sultry voice asked the back of Hendricks's head, "About that good lead you've got . . . care to speak off the record?"

"No. Sorry."

Frustrated, Deidi's eyes roamed the office as she tried to think of another approach. As Tom had said many a time, if you can't get in the front door, slip in through the back. A good interrogator can get the information he (or she) wants without the subject even being aware that the cat had been let out of the bag.

On one corner of Hendricks's desk was a hinged gold picture frame widely parted to show a couple of individual studio portraits of a boy and girl, both looking somewhere around eight or nine. Noting their strong resemblance to Hendricks, she rightly assumed they were his son and daughter, the two kids Carla had told her about. They looked like nice enough kids, if what the camera had captured was true, but she kept her thoughts to herself, since she couldn't imagine how flattering his kids would get her any closer to the information she wanted.

Hendricks began impatiently drumming his fingers on the arms of his chair, and Deidi got the feeling he was wishing she would go away. But as long as he didn't tell her to leave straight out, she wasn't going anywhere. One of the first things a reporter learned was to grow a layer of very thick skin.

After a few minutes of strained silence (except for the occasional drumming of Hendricks's fingers) in which Deidi casually studied the framed diplomas and citations on the wall to her right, Hendricks swiveled his chair around and, completely ignoring her presence, took a phone directory from one of his desk drawers and opened it in his lap. Then, to her dismay, he turned his chair back to the window so that she couldn't see what he was doing. But by quietly rising from her chair, she could see over his shoulder that he was thumbing through the yellow pages. As if that told her anything; she didn't exactly have telescopic eyesight. Acutely aware of her escalating frustration, she sat back down before he could catch her peeking.

He had just stopped turning pages when his telephone rang, the sound giving Deidi a start. Hendricks immediately whirled around and jerked up the receiver. His discolored features, now pinched in agitation, demanded the reward of some good news. "Hendricks here."

As he listened intently to whatever was being said, Deidi came up with an idea that should get her at least a glimpse of the phone book pages in which he had a mysterious interest. Accidentally on purpose dropping her pen on the floor, she slid off her chair to retrieve it, then rising to her full height, pretended to see something of interest through the window, which required her to lean slightly over his desk to get a better angle.

"You're positive?" Hendricks muttered, glancing up at Deidi with a look that suggested she might soon find herself down at the police academy, being used as a target on the firing range. At the same time, he moved his legs underneath the desk to hide the open telephone book, but not before Deidi's eyes caught sight of the quarter-page advertisement for Merfeld Plumbing and Heating.

Shrugging sheepishly, she retreated back to her chair, silently gloating.

Hendricks muttered an insincere thanks into the receiver and dropped it abruptly into its cradle, his almond eyes fixed glaringly at a small cobweb in the southwest corner of the ceiling. "Well, that's that," he said, as if to himself, then his gaze fell on Deidi's face. "The lesbian's definitely not our girl. So, you've got all the big news there is to be had. Sorry I couldn't give you a juicier scoop, but that's just how it is. Check back with me on Monday, I might have something more to tell you then."

"But my boss told me to be your shadow," Deidi said, pouting. "If he finds out I let you run me off when you were working a hot lead, I'm going to get flattened, and I mean that literally. Come on, have a heart. I swear I won't print anything until you say it's okay. Besides, I saw what pages you'd turned to in the phone book—one had Merfeld Plumbing's ad on it. You want me going around to all those places asking my own questions?"

For a few seconds Deidi was sure that Hendricks was going to explode with anger, fiercely as his eyes glowed. But surprisingly, a slow smile began to spread on his lips. She smiled back, confident that a partnership had just been established between them.

FLESH AND BLOOD

"You're under arrest," he said amiably, still smiling.

It was almost six-thirty that evening before Deidi was finally released from the holding cell she'd shared all that day with an older woman who'd been arrested for shoplifting at a grocery store. All she'd done was eat a few grapes, the woman had complained to Deidi about six hundred times. Everybody did it, and what could a few lousy grapes cost? From now on, she'd do her grocery shopping elsewhere, and so would all of her friends.

Deidi couldn't have cared less if the woman had eaten every piece of fruit in the store, or for that matter, set off a bomb at the YMCA. All she could think about was how badly she wanted a cigarette, and how she was going to get even with Judson Hendricks for doing this to her. That son of a bitch! When he'd said she was under arrest, she thought he was kidding, of course, and had even laughed. So had he. All the way down to the booking desk where he charged her with interfering with a police investigation.

She'd thought she would be sitting there, cruelly deprived of her much-needed nicotine and other "luxuries" of life such as freedom, privacy, and Cottonelle toilet tissue (the jail provided rolled sandpaper) through the whole weekend, since arraignments were only scheduled Monday through Friday, when she would be allowed to post bond. But apparently Hendricks had only wanted to get her out of his way for today, leaving instructions for her to be released that evening, with the single piddly-ass charge on her dropped.

As she drove to Dr. Jordan's office for her seven o'clock appointment, she was still so mad she could hardly see straight. Puffing vigorously on a cigarette, which was making her feel a little dizzy, she determined to find out just what that asshole Judson

Hendricks had gone to such shitty lengths to hide from her. Her resolution was followed by a series of tortures she'd like to put him through, beginning with staking him naked over a fire anthill.

Then suddenly she winced as if she'd been slapped.

Less than a mile away from the street on which Deidi was traveling, standing in the living room of her messy home, Camisa Collins cringed, her right hand automatically flying up to cover the cheek Harlan had just smacked with the back of his hand. Fresh tears sprang to her eyes.

"God, Harlan, you act like it was my fault! I almost drown myself, looking for him!"

His eyes narrowed, mouth formed in a drunken sneer. "It *was* your fuckin' fault! You should've been watching him closer; you know he never had no swimming lessons. And I still wanna know why you snuck the kids out of here this morning like you did. You're holding something back, Camisa, I know it and the cops know it, too! Why'd you think they were asking you all them questions about your family, so they could send 'em Christmas cards? They're gonna check you out!" He lifted his near-empty bottle of Jim Beam and took another long swig, wiping his mouth on the back of his hairy wrist, his reddened eyes blazing with fury. "So out with the fucking truth! If I have to beat it out of you, I will!"

"I told the truth," Camisa whimpered, still caressing her throbbing cheek in the hope that the gesture would evoke some sympathy from her enraged husband. She couldn't believe the way he was acting, after all the bawling he did in front of the cops. And besides, hadn't he himself said on several occasions when Aaron had done something shockingly sadistic, such as squash that poor baby bird, that he would probably end up in prison? Couldn't Harlan see that this "tragedy" was really a blessing in disguise?

Harlan growled and backhanded her on the other

cheek. "Bull*shit!* You know what I think? I think you probably held him under the water! I must've heard you threaten to kill him a hunnerd times!"

"And you never did?" Camisa shot back.

Harlan struck her again, this time hard enough to knock her into the television set. Finishing off his bottle, he stomped over to the front door. "I'm going over to Smiley's," he said with a hateful sneer, throwing the empty bottle to the floor. "Don't expect me back anytime soon."

Then he slammed out, rattling the windows.

"Get a life, Harlan," Camisa hissed at his lingering image.

Pulling up in front of the V-shaped stone building on Palm Drive and West Boulevard where Dr. Jordan had his offices, Deidi wondered why her heart was pounding so. She was definitely apprehensive about the regressive hypnosis she was soon to undergo, but not enough to account for such an intense arousal of her parasympathetic nervous system. Maybe it had something to do with the three cigarettes she'd smoked in the last ten minutes.

Dr. Jordan had already arrived, although it was only six-fifty. His red Porsche gleamed a few spaces away under the parking lot's mercury vapor lamp, and hints of light peeked through the beige Levelor blinds over the two windows of his offices.

"Well, here we go," Deidi muttered under her breath, flicking her finished cigarette into the shadows as she emerged from her car. Taking a deep breath, she headed for the building's entrance in the crook of the vee.

As always, Dr. Jordan greeted her warmly. "Deidi! Come on in and pull up a couch," he said when he looked up from his desk and saw her standing timidly in the doorway. It was a well-worn salutation, but he still seemed to think it was amusing. He was a slightly built man in his late forties who reminded her of

Woody Allen, with his receding hairline and black-framed glasses which had gone out of style eons ago, as had the blue and yellow plaid sport jacket he always wore.

"Hello, Dr. Jordan," Deidi sighed, shuffling into the dark paneled room and sitting slump-shouldered on the beige contoured couch. Jordan wasn't strictly a psychoanalyst; in his own terms he was an "eclectic," but he did believe in the couch, preaching that a relaxed patient was an open patient.

Leaning back in his chair and clasping his hands together at his waist in the classic headshrinker pose, he gave her a benevolent smile. "So, would you like to tell me what's going on?"

Deidi reluctantly told him all of it, starting with the minor revelation of Larry Patton's body being found nude. He interrupted her once, telling her to lie down on the couch and take it easy when she became visibly distressed describing the bloody vision of the old man. Concluding with Suzanne's account of what she'd done the night before on the beach, and that she still had no memory of it, Deidi closed her eyes and issued a long sigh. "I'm really losing it, aren't I?"

Jordan said nothing for a few moments; he was too busy scribbling notes. When he was finished, he got up from his chair and turned the lights down low. "I'm sure it's not all that serious," he said in his soft Southern accent, easing himself into the plump leather armchair between the couch and built-in shelves, stuffed mostly with leather-bound books, which constituted the rear wall. "I don't know what to tell you about the ESP experiences you've been having lately, except that they belong to the realm of parapsychology, and in that field I'm hardly an expert. About the other matter—we already knew about your tendency to block out what you don't want to remember. But I can certainly understand your wanting to see me as soon as possible. We've been scratching at the surface of this thing for a long time now, Deidi, and I think we're finally hitting paydirt. I told you it wasn't going to be pleasant. Of course, that's exactly why you've been resisting the excavation. But perhaps not as effectively as you think, which may explain these two occasions of memory loss. I suspect that on these occasions you were confronted by the demons arising from your past, but unable to cope with what you saw, your mind blotted out the entire time frame. But believe me, under the guidance of hypnosis you'll be able to look squarely at those repressed memories, and they won't blow you away. I promise."

Deidi sighed again, her eyes remaining closed. "Just get on with it before I chicken out, okay?"

Dr. Jordan reached over to one of the shelves and switched on a reel-to-reel tape recorder, then cleared his throat and began speaking in a soothing lilt, going first through a rote of relaxation techniques that included suggestions that Deidi's body was becoming heavier as she sank further and further down, down, down.

She could feel herself sinking continually deeper into a muddy darkness in which Dr. Jordan's voice alone existed. His voice washed all cares and worries away as it took her into the deepest recesses of her mind, and then he began to take her back in time. During their many previous sessions it had become obvious that the culprit memories lurked somewhere in her childhood years, below the age of ten.

In his soothing, rhythmic voice, Dr. Jordan told her that she was back at her ninth birthday party, then asked what she saw.

Deidi gazed into the blackness, and soon brightly colored ribbons and balloons began to appear. She told him about them, then went on to describe the rest of the scene as it unfolded.

There was a table, and on the center of the table was her birthday cake. Festive paper plates, napkins, and matching cups surrounded the cake, and behind each setting stood a child. They had just finished singing

Happy Birthday to her, and she leaned over to blow out the burning candles on the cake, but one remained lit, meaning that she wouldn't get her wish to be a movie star when she grew up. She was furious. One of the other children, a boy with red hair and freckles, impudently bent and blew out the last candle.

"Too bad, you don't get your wish!" a kid on her right taunted, and all of them laughed.

She wanted to kill them, even if they had brought her presents.

Her mother began cutting the chocolate cake into portions and putting them on the paper plates. Deidi looked across the table at Crystal Britton, whom she hadn't even wanted to invite but her mother had insisted, since she and Crystal's mother were good friends. Crystal was nothing but a fat little pig, and she was always doing gross stuff like picking her nose and putting her hand down inside her underwear to scratch her rear because she was always getting pinworms. This Deidi had overheard Mrs. Britton tell her mother in an exasperated tone, and Deidi had wasted no time spreading the news all over school— an action that quickly backfired. When Crystal began getting teased unmercifully about it, she'd gone home crying to her mama, who was pretty good at putting two and two together. Under an intense interrogation by her mother, Deidi finally confessed to the crime and was not allowed to watch television for a whole month.

Now she said to her mother, "Don't give Crystal any cake, she's too fat already!"

All the other kids howled. Crystal's lower lip began to tremble, and she burst into tears.

Deidi's mother gaped at her in shock. "Deidi! You apologize to Crystal this instant!"

But instead Deidi looked directly at the weeping fat girl and said, "Besides, I think she likes boogers better!"

Dr. Jordan interrupted Deidi at this point, asking

FLESH AND BLOOD

her if she was aware of anything oppressing her at this point in her life, to which she languidly answered no.

"All right," he said gently, "we're going to go back a little further. You're getting younger, drifting peacefully backward through time . . . now you're eight years old, and still going back further, further, relaxed and at peace, back to the age of seven. You're seven years old, Deidi. Tell me what you see and feel."

She looked again into the blackness, and this time a frightening image emerged and she felt like running away but couldn't. She was sitting in a padded pew between her mother and father, and she knew they wouldn't let her get past them. She was supposed to sit very still and very quietly while the man standing in front of the room said words that held no meaning for her.

Also in front of the large room, which she now recognized as a church chapel, was a long elevated wooden box with flowers draped over it. She knew that it was a casket and that inside the casket lay the body of her maternal grandmother. Deidi was having a hard time sitting still. An overwhelming fear had seized her, and she squirmed in the pew, whimpering. Her mother hissed at her to straighten up or else.

Noting that Deidi was squirming on the couch with a distressed look on her face, Dr. Jordan interjected some calming words. "It's all right, Deidi. You're completely safe; no harm is going to come to you. Relax, breathe deeply. It's all right." The anxiety gradually melted from her face along with the tension in her muscles. He went on, "Now I want you to tell me why you're so afraid. Do you understand your feelings?"

Deidi was still looking at the casket. The man had finished speaking now, and he and another man removed the flowers from it, putting them aside. Then they opened one of the casket lids, and she could see the pale, wrinkled face lifted on a satin pillow, surrounded by a halo of white hair.

"I don't wanna kiss Grammy," she wailed softly.

"Is that what your parents made you do?" Jordan inquired.

Deidi's hands balled into fists. Her mother had taken one hand, her father the other, and they'd dragged her up the aisle to say good-bye to Grammy. The closer they got to the casket, the more her fear increased, and accompanying the fear was an inexplicable feeling of guilt. Her mind was repeatedly screaming the word no, but nothing came out of her mouth other than gasping breaths.

Her mother, tears wetting her cheeks, leaned over the casket and planted a gentle kiss on Grammy's pallid, waxy forehead. Then it was Deidi's turn, but when she was forcibly brought before the display of death, something inside her snapped. Instead of kissing her Grammy's corpse, she began to pummel the dead face with her fists. Before she could be stopped, she had flattened the nose and separated the sealed lips to reveal Grammy's stained dentures.

Her mother fainted on the spot; it was her father who'd jerked her away from the casket with such force it was a wonder her arms hadn't been pulled out of their sockets. And just before he did, for just an instant, Deidi had seen someone else lying in that coffin. Another woman, one much younger. The sight had shocked her into unconsciousness as well.

Jordan saw that Deidi was hyperventilating, and spent another few minutes getting her calmed back down. He was quite pleased with the way this session was going; it looked like they were finally getting somewhere. He would bet anything that the other woman Deidi had visualized in the coffin was the key to her dungeon door.

When she was breathing normally again, and seemed relaxed, he took her back a couple of years further, to the age of five, and again asked her what she saw and how she felt.

She said nothing for a few minutes, but he knew she

FLESH AND BLOOD

was seeing something by the way her eyes moved behind their lids. He was about to repeat his question when she giggled. "Froggy guts," she said in a little-girl voice.

"What about froggy guts?" Dr. Jordan prodded.

"Froggy guts squished out of his mouth," she replied. She was standing by the curb in front of her house, looking down at a squashed toad in the street. It wasn't completely flattened, so it must have been run over by a bicycle instead of a car. A mass of greenish entrails, swarming with ants, protruded from its open mouth.

Wearing a mischievous smile, she picked it up by one of its hind legs and carried it away from her person to the house. Letting herself in with her free hand, she took the dead frog into the kitchen. Her mommy was elsewhere in the house. Deidi opened the refrigerator and placed the frog inside a covered dish which contained leftover casserole. Giggling, she ran back outside to play.

After several moments of silence, Dr. Jordan asked her why she'd done this, to which Deidi replied, "Don't like Mommy."

"And why don't you like her?"

Deidi said nothing. She watched apprehensively as new images drifted into focus. A charred baby doll with its arms and legs missing. Grass on fire. A plucked, headless chicken tumbling round and round in the clothes dryer.

She was no longer five years old, she was four now, having reeled back another a year without Jordan instructing her to do so. She wasn't alone, either, but whenever she tried to see who was with her, she found herself looking in a mirror.

They were biting the chubby little boy next door, biting him all over and as hard as they could, which was sufficient to break the skin and draw blood. He was howling his head off, and pretty soon his mother came running out of the house, screaming at them to get away from him. Seeing what they'd done, she gave them the most hateful look possible, then promptly marched them along with her wailing son over to their house so she could show the damage to their mother.

Their mother? That couldn't be right. She was an only child. But she was far more concerned with what she'd been doing to the little boy than the source of that errant thought. She was certain it hadn't been her idea to attack him, but she'd certainly followed the leader. And what was worse, once she'd gotten started, she'd actually enjoyed biting the boy, sinking her teeth into his meaty flesh.

Dr. Jordan's voice came lilting through, "Tell me what's going on now, Deidi."

They were standing out on the porch, waiting. The boy's mother had angrily pushed the doorbell three times, and now she was telling them what horrible little girls they were, and that they ought to get spanked with a belt until their bottoms were raw. About half a minute later the front door opened and a young woman appeared with a baby in her arms.

Deidi reluctantly looked up at the woman's face, her eyes then darting to the baby's.

A split second later she began to scream.

Dr. Jordan jumped up from his chair to restrain her flailing arms, his efforts earning him a painful punch in the face that knocked his glasses askew. Deidi continued to scream, fighting him with the strength of a maniac, so it took him a few minutes and all of his muscle power to subdue her. When at last she lay still, she burst into sobs.

We've found the mother lode, he thought grimly.

"Deidi." He spoke softly, relaxing his grip on her arms. "Can you hear me?"

Tears streaming down both sides of her face, Deidi nodded.

"What did you see, Deidi? Can you tell me about it?"

Suddenly, as if an invisible faucet had been turned

off, Deidi stopped crying, becoming calm and emotionless. "I don't know what I saw. I can't remember."

"Then can you tell me the last thing you do remember?" Jordan persisted, letting go of her entirely so he could readjust his glasses.

"My ninth birthday party. I told my mother not to give Crystal Britton any cake because she was already too fat."

Jordan sighed. "All right, Deidi, I think we've gone far enough for tonight; I'm going to bring you up now. At the count of ten, when you open your eyes, you will feel calm and refreshed . . ."

When Deidi opened her eyes, she indeed felt calm and refreshed, but the feeling didn't last. Nightmarish shadows of memories began to press in on her almost at once, filling her with a consummate dread. The more she tried to shove them away, the larger and more sinister they became.

Sitting back in his chair, Dr. Jordan switched off the tape recorder, then turned to look at Deidi for several moments, rubbing his chin. There was a red mark on his nose where the bridge of his glasses had been mashed into his skin. "As I said earlier, I believe that these blackouts of yours are simply your mind's way of protecting itself from its personal demons. Cognitively you want to see and deal with them, but emotionally you want to just hide yourself away in a dark place where they can't find you, which is exactly what you've been doing. We're almost there, Deidi, and that emotional part of you doesn't like it a bit. Maybe by Tuesday you'll be able to look at them good and hard, which is all you need to do to rob them of their power over you."

"I need a cigarette," Deidi muttered, rising to a sitting position. Hateful images continued to flash behind her eyes, not long enough to leave a lasting impression, just an emotional bruise. Rummaging through her purse with a trembling hand, she realized she'd left her cigarettes in the car.

"Well, sounds good, Doc. Guess I'll see you Tuesday, then. And thanks a lot for seeing me tonight, but I'm sure I'll make it up to you on your bill, right?" Forcing a smile and clutching her purse, she rose to a standing position. Dr. Jordan followed suit, a slightly worried expression on his Woody Allen face.

"Are you all right? I don't have a license to write prescriptions, but I've got a friend in psychiatry who'd be more than happy to get you some mild sedatives tonight."

"Thanks, but I don't need them," Deidi said, not knowing why she said that, because she did need them, she needed one right this minute. Giving him another false smile, she turned and strode quickly from his office.

Outside in the parking lot, the demons pressed ever closer.

9

In bright pink fluorescent tubing with script-style lettering were the words *Merry Mermaid*. Below that, blue fluorescent tubes in slightly smaller script glowed with the words: *Massage Parlor*.

Turning off the engine of his borrowed Malibu Classic, Judson Hendricks sighed. After his embarrassing experience at the Blue Lady, he really didn't want to go in there, but duty demanded that he do so. That morning, after booking Deidi Marshall for interfering with his investigation (the memory brought a smile to his still-swollen lips), he'd left the station with a list of all the businesses in Danville whose name contained the word Mermaid. There were five: Little Mermaid Daycare Center, All Mermaid's Health Spa, Mermaid Village Apartments, Mermaid Inn, and Merry Mermaid Massage Parlor. The daycare center was closed until Monday, he'd discovered, so he'd gone on to the health spa. There he'd spent the rest of the morning going through the employee files and membership list with the spa's director, leaving with four names and addresses to check out after having lunch at home with his kids. Of course, they'd been greatly dismayed by his beat-up condition, but it seemed they'd been much more disturbed by the news that the parrot had flown away. Typical.

It had taken him most of the afternoon to track down and question the four women from the spa, only to find that he'd wasted a lot of time. But that was also typical. In his line of work, one often had to sift through tons of sand to find a single gem.

And sometimes that sand was more like dirt, he thought as he stepped from his car and headed toward the recessed entrance to the massage parlor, wondering if the woman he sought was on the other side. After cooking dinner and giving the kids a little more of his time than he'd spared them at noon, he'd set off again, promising to return no later than eight. He'd planned on going to the Mermaid Inn, which was closest to his house, but changed his mind en route and drove to the massage parlor instead, with the same reasoning he'd applied to Bobbi Paulsen.

As he well knew, most if not all of the "massages" given in this place "accidentally" triggered seminal ejaculations. It had been busted half a dozen times, but always the next day they'd be back to business as usual. Where there is a demand, come hell or high water, there will be a supply, and maybe one of those suppliers had developed a bad attitude.

Loosening his tie a little, he opened the pink door on which a seductively smiling mermaid with flowing black hair and huge breasts had been painted, and walked in.

She wasn't all that surprised to find herself across the road from the large pink stucco house. Wasn't that where she lived part-time, cloaked in her other identity? The sight of it and who or what she might find within didn't frighten her now; the coin of her psyche had again been turned by a mysterious inner hand, unveiling the secrets kept from her primary self. Still, she didn't want to go inside. She had an irrepressible urge to do something *bad*.

FLESH AND BLOOD

Darkness had fallen, and a gentle wind carrying the smell of the ocean toyed with her hair. She was looking at the upper windows of the house, which were all ablaze with light, and thinking about the gross fat woman who lived in the apartment with the upper balcony. Having killed two men, she was in the mood for something a little different. Hatred for many things roiled turbulently inside her, men certainly being chief among them, but there was a special poisonous place in her heart for fat people, then came stupid people, and shitheads who took more than the specified number of items to the express line of the supermarket, or drove around with their heads shoved up their asses . . .

She began walking casually across the road, her eyes fixed on the upstairs windows, wondering how the fat woman was spending the last minutes of her life. Probably stuffing her fat ugly face. She hadn't gained the ability to seesaw with a Volkswagen by sticking to three meals a day.

Her footsteps were silent on the redwood staircase leading up to the second-floor balcony. Trailing her right hand lightly along the guardrail, she encountered a splinter that almost made her cry out in pain. Gritting her teeth, she plucked the tiny sliver of wood out from beneath her fingernail and flicked it away. Examining the wound in the moonlight, she could see a pregnant dot of dark blood growing bigger. She placed the bleeding tip of the finger in her mouth and sucked on it gently.

At the top of the staircase, she took a few deep breaths to calm her excitement, then knocked three times on the sliding glass door over which green drapes had been drawn. It took a small eternity for the woman to answer. Maybe she'd gotten stuck in her chair. But at last the drapes parted slightly and the fat moon of a face peered out, its eyes widening with pleasure at what they saw. The door was quickly unlocked and slid across its track to permit entry.

"Well, hello there! What a nice surprise. Come in, come in." Smiling widely, the fat woman shuffled back to give her room. She was wearing a floral-print housedress that, if cut, could probably cover a king-sized bed. Her gray head was full of pink sponge curlers, which was a laugh. Why would such a grotesque woman waste any time curling her hair? Was that really supposed to make a difference in her appearance?

She accepted the invitation, also smiling, aware of a nervous flutter of butterflies in her stomach. There was absolutely no guessing what sort of strength rested beneath those huge flabby arms. Big was not necessarily synonymous with strong, but there could be a surprise in store.

"Have a seat. Can I get'cha glass of tea? Or I've got a few cans of pop, if you don't mind diet."

She looked into the woman's pale blue eyes, which were seeing their last sights. A light shining from the dining area reflected in them, and she saw the twin white dots as two tiny skulls. "I'll take a cup of coffee, if you have some."

"Oh, surely," the aging blimp said, her round, pocked cheeks lifted by another eager-to-please smile. "It'll just take me a minute to heat the water. You go on and sit down, make yourself comfortable."

The upstairs apartment was much like the one downstairs, except for the furnishings, which looked old enough to have belonged to Whistler's mother. The walls were covered with framed embroidery, apparently the woman's hobby when she wasn't eating. Judging offhand, there was at least a thousand hours' worth of work hanging on the walls; clearly the woman's fingers were a lot more nimble than her feet.

The sofa was a light pink, the sloping, curled arms draped with embroidered lace, the back with a large patchwork afghan. Looking at the large braided rug on which all the living room furniture sat, she wondered if the woman had made that, too. Besides the sofa,

FLESH AND BLOOD

there were two mismatched easy chairs to choose from, their arms also adorned with embroidered lace. It was easy to tell which one the woman usually sat in: the one with the caved-in seat.

In the kitchen, the woman began rambling about all the aches and pains she'd suffered that day, not knowing how soon she was going to be put out of her misery. Her major complaint was that her legs kept going numb, and sitting in the plump-cushioned easy chair, she thought to herself that it was hardly a wonder, with all the weight they had to carry around, and as hard as her heart was having to work to disperse blood over such a vast area, poor circulation was to be expected. So was cardiac arrest, but Baby Shamu wasn't going to go that way. Then again, maybe she would, when the true purpose of this visit became apparent.

There was a small color television on a stand against the wall to her left, and it was turned on, tuned to a religious station. A middle-aged man with a used car salesman's face and a thousand-dollar tailored suit was striding up and down a stage with a big microphone in one hand, sputtering in a madman's cadence that Jesus was coming back any day now, any minute, and if any were harboring secret sins—at this point he listed a few examples, which included cheating God on his tithes—they'd better make it right, not next week or even tomorrow, for just an hour from now it could be too late.

A smile came to her lips as she wondered how much of God's money he'd paid for the diamond ring flashing on his pinky finger, how many hungry children could have been fed instead. Not that she cared, but she bet God was sure going to have something to say about it when this guy's ass was hauled up before the throne of Judgment. She already knew she was going to Hell; she'd always known that. But obviously the abomination with the diamond pinky ring thought he had it made in Heaven's shade.

The fat woman appeared with her cup of coffee in a saucer. "Careful now, it's mighty hot."

She could see that was true; there was steam rising from the dark brown surface.

"Oh, I forgot to ask," her hostess said, moving her bulk over to the television set to turn it off. "Do you take cream or sugar?"

"Black is fine." She smiled, holding the cup and saucer in her lap. She wasn't planning to drink it, or she would have answered differently. She watched the woman ease herself into her favorite chair with eyes that were as cold as the coffee was hot.

"I see you got comp'ny staying with you. She any relation or just a friend?"

"Just a friend."

"Well, why didn't you bring her up with you? Or has she left?"

Leaving the question unanswered, she carefully rose with the cup and saucer to her feet, her heart pounding. The steaming surface of the coffee rippled with her unsteady hand. Looking down at the upturned moon face, she felt a shiver of anticipation go through her. Oh, but this was going to be fun. *Tons* of fun.

The woman's mouth opened in prelude to speech, but whatever she was going to say never got out. At that moment the entire scalding cup of coffee was splashed in her face, in her open eyes.

On contact, her mouth gaped wide as a loud, shocked gasp of air was sucked into her lungs, and before it could be released as a shattering scream, the embroidered coverlets on the arms of her chair were stuffed into her mouth. Her eyeballs blistered instantly, turning deep red along with the rest of her face. Her beefy, liver-spotted hands fought desperately to pull the cloths from her mouth as muffled screams continually burst from her lungs in spite of them. But as it turned out, she wasn't strong at all, certainly no match for her attacker, who had very little trouble keeping

FLESH AND BLOOD

the cloths in place and her nose pinched at the same time.

It took two or three minutes for the oxygen deprivation to take its toll, rendering Flora unconscious. Or she might just have fainted, but an erratic pulse indicated she had not yet gone to that big smorgasbord in the sky. That was good. Blisters were appearing all over her face, which was now as red as a lobster's shell.

Leaving Flora Bushbaum slumped in her favorite chair, she hurried into the kitchen and started pulling out cabinet drawers. In the third she found what she was looking for—the silverware and knives. Taking from it the largest butcher knife, which had a metal handle, she held it up for a moment and gazed at her reflection in the two-inch-wide mirrored surface. Her eyes had a wild, maniacal look, round and glassy. Her nostrils were flaring slightly, lips pressed together in a straight line that was almost a smile.

Holding the knife's handle firmly, she rummaged around in a few more drawers until she found something for binding her victim's hands, finally coming across a long extension cord that would do nicely.

The job was finished only seconds before the scalded face returned to life and the muffled screams started up again. The woman's hands had been tied tightly together, then tethered to one of her fat legs, making it impossible for her to lift them. Her eyes were obviously blind, and moving out of sync with one another, though the pale blue irises were hardly distinguishable in their bubbled, crimson surroundings.

Tapping the knife's blade against one of Flora's blistered red cheeks, she asked in a malicious tone, "What's the matter, old woman? Are you hungry?"

The pink curlers were tossed violently from side to side.

"No? I thought people like you were always hungry.

Well, why don't we just have a little peek inside your stomach and see whether or not it's empty."

Flora Bushbaum escalated her futile attempt to free her hands from the extension cord, crying now, the salty tears bringing fresh pain to her inflamed eye tissue and scalded skin. Without the use of her hands, there was no way in hell she was going to get out of that chair, but she tried anyway, pushing her upper body forward again and again. The effort accomplished nothing. Behind the rags stuffed in her mouth, her screams mellowed into racking sobs.

Then she became aware that her house dress was being unbuttoned, and ultimate terror seized her by the throat. Deidi was really going to do it! She was going to cut open her stomach to see what was inside! Flora couldn't believe this was really happening. What in God's name had she ever done to her neighbor to make her want to do this? Had Deidi gone mad?

Oh, but her face burned, it felt like it was on fire, and she was blind! Blind as a bat! But why sweat the small stuff—she was going to be dead soon, if Deidi actually went through with what she'd threatened. Flora felt like she was about to pass out again, and prayed fervently that she would. She didn't want to be aware of what happened after this. Her enlarged old heart was pounding frantically, painfully in her chest, and she expected it to arrest just any second now. It couldn't take this kind of stress. But that would be all right, too. If she had to die tonight, she would much rather have a heart attack than get butchered to death by Deidi, who'd always seemed like such a nice girl.

Flora did not faint, nor did she suffer a heart attack, but at least she was spared the sight of the butcher knife slicing across her soft middle, and the gush of blood that sprayed from the wound. She could certainly feel the slicing, though, and it didn't feel very good. Nerve endings screamed in white-hot pain, and Flora's bladder released, but she was too preoccupied

FLESH AND BLOOD

with terror to feel any shame. She could also feel the warm blood cascading down to her lap, which was mostly hidden under the grotesque protrusion of her tiered, bumpy abdomen. A mountain climber's dream, if he was only an inch tall.

Again the knife blade was thrust in about half an inch, this time cutting downward from the left end of the bloody and somewhat jagged horizontal line. The thick layer of fat, which resembled chicken skin, separated widely in the blade's wake, tiny drops of blood spraying the air while the rest of it made a glistening red stream for the blade to follow. Flora didn't think there was this much pain in the whole world, but there was, and she was suffering it. And though she directed her screams to God, begging Him to take her now or at least render her unconscious, she remained alive and fully aware of the atrocity that was being committed on her body.

When the "door" was completed, it was opened, which required a fair amount of tugging. And like a child's jack-in-the-box, out came Flora Bushbaum's guts. She who had made and opened the door jumped back in horror, totally surprised by this. Though she'd been prepared to see something gross, what had popped out at her and now lay dangling between the woman's parted legs went far beyond gross. And talk about a stink! She felt as though she might vomit, but she didn't.

Staring in horrified wonder at the glistening tangle of entrails, she decided she didn't really want to know what was in the old woman's stomach, which looked like a python's underbelly smeared with blood. She'd had enough fun for one night, she supposed. Looking up at her victim's agonized face, she could see that the old woman was still alive, although she'd stopped making noises behind her gag. Amazing.

"Well, thanks for your hospitality, but I think I'll be on my way now," she said, bringing the knife down one more time to leave it sticking up in the woman's left thigh. As Flora thrashed and screamed, she looked down in disgust at her own clothes; they were completely splattered with blood, as were her bare arms, so it was probably on her face as well.

Frowning, she headed for Flora's bathroom to take a shower.

10

The next day, Sunday, Judson Hendricks took his two children to Rainbow Park to play Frisbee. What he really wanted to do was work, especially since he thought he was on to something at the Merry Mermaid massage parlor, but since he was both father and mother to Jeremy and Lacey, he had an obligation to give them some quality time.

They had been at the park for perhaps half an hour when Hendricks noticed two women sitting at a cement picnic table shaded by a towering poplar tree about a hundred yards away. One was smoking a cigarette and staring off into space while the other talked. A few feet away lay a black and tan Doberman pinscher who seemed very interested in the Hendricks's Frisbee game.

He thought the dark-haired woman smoking the cigarette was Deidi Marshall, but he wasn't sure. He was going to find out, though. Tossing the fluorescent yellow Frisbee to his son, he called out, "You two go ahead, I've got to go over there and talk to those women a minute."

Jeremy smirked. "Sure, Dad. Cruise all you want."

"I'm not cruising," his father replied with a dour

expression as he headed in the direction of the shaded picnic table.

"Go for the blonde!" Lacey encouraged teasingly, and giggled. Her comment was ignored.

The closer Hendricks got, the more convinced he became that the dark-haired woman was, in fact, his little jailbird. He normally wasn't one to rub things in, but today he was feeling ornery. Behind the orneriness was a very active sexual frustration, and he knew it, but how could there not be after all the explicit sexuality he'd witnessed the past couple of days? If he didn't feel frustrated, he'd have to assume he'd croaked without knowing it.

He was almost to the table before Deidi noticed him, and she only did then because Hughman started to growl. Hendricks smiled at her. She glared at him.

"This dog attacks on command, Detective Hendricks," she warned in a voice as vicious as the dog's growl. "I wouldn't come any closer if I were you. Go away. I came here to try and relax, and the sight of you makes me want to smash something."

Not knowing for sure whether she was mad enough to sic the dog on him, Hendricks stopped in his tracks, eyeing the Doberman warily. It had clambered to its feet, guarding its mistress with an impressive display of sharp teeth behind its curled black lips.

"I take it you didn't enjoy your stay at the Iron Bar Motel?"

"Very funny, Hendricks," Deidi snarled.

"Hi, I'm Suzanne Weiss," Suzanne said, beaming a friendly smile at Hendricks, which earned her a scathing look from Deidi.

"Don't be nice to him, he's a class-A jerk. I didn't deserve to go to jail. I was only trying to do my job. I even promised him I wouldn't report a thing until he gave me the okay."

"But you know you would have anyway," Suzanne accused.

Deidi shrugged, taking another drag from her cigarette, unwilling to admit it aloud even if it was the truth. Turning her icy gaze back on Hendricks, she exhaled the smoke and asked in a sarcastic tone, "So, did you catch the killer? Or are you at least hot on her heels?"

"Make your dog stop looking at me like I'm a juicy steak and I'll tell you," Hendricks muttered.

Deidi reached out and stroked Hughman's head. "It's okay, boy, settle down. I know how much you'd like to tear his throat out with those nice sharp teeth of yours, but then he wouldn't be able to tell me what I unfortunately need to hear. So hush, now, and sit down."

The Doberman obediently stopped growling and sat, but his ears remained at attention and his black eyes never left Hendricks's face. Deidi looked back up at the detective, still wearing a hateful expression.

"You were saying?"

He cleared his throat, feeling just a little less like a baby jackrabbit facing a hungry coyote. "I haven't caught her yet, but I believe I am definitely hot on her heels, as you say. I should be making an arrest early next week, maybe even tomorrow."

Deidi crushed her cigarette out on the table, a disdainful smile appearing on her lips. "That's all I get? I spent the whole day in jail and that's all I get? Sounds like the standard bullshit to me."

Hendricks looked thoughtful for a moment. "That's right, you did spend the whole day in jail, didn't you? Well . . . in that case I might be persuaded to divulge a little bit more, but only if you'll agree to have dinner with me tonight." His muscles involuntarily tensed again, prepared for flight should Deidi dispatch her dog to deliver her answer.

She looked at him incredulously, ignoring Suzanne's whispered, "Ooh-la-la," although she did wonder if Suzanne was going blind. Hendricks still looked like he'd gone ten rounds with the Tasmanian Devil.

Many things ran through Deidi's mind in the space of a few seconds, many colorful adjectives sandwiched between "You" and "jerk." Too many, in fact, for her mind to decide on, so all she could do was laugh. Tossing her head back, she let it fly. Hughman looked at her with his ears pricked and a question mark in his black marble eyes. He'd never heard her laugh like this before. With a groan, Suzanne slumped over the table with her eyes rolled skyward.

Hearing the laughter of others never failed to infect Hendricks, making him the perfect sit-com patsy, but Deidi's present mirth was breaking him out in a sweat. He just knew that when it died, it was going to be followed by a verbal typhoon. But he was in for a surprise.

When Deidi finally got her laughter under control, she looked at him with only a slightly mischievous expression and said evenly, "I would be supremely delighted to have dinner with you, as long as you're picking up the tab, and you take me to the Cyprus Gourmet."

Before his quirky emotions could be intercepted, Hendricks found himself grinning like a moonstruck pubescent, an obvious clue that he was much more interested in Deidi Marshall than he'd realized. Either that or he was receiving some very strong signals from his "parrot," who had in fact been unmercifully tormented lately. Embarrassed, he quickly wiped the grin away and pretended to weigh the proposal, although the Cyprus Gourmet was exactly the place he'd had in mind. Deidi had claimed to be allergic to seafood, but they also served the best steaks in town. And as for picking up the tab, he never went on a dutch date with a woman anyway.

"I don't suppose you're allergic to prime rib," he said after several moments, eyeing her with suspicion.

She smiled wickedly. "I *love* prime rib. And I bet I can eat ten pounds of it."

"She probably really can," Suzanne warned. "You

should have seen her at this one dorm party back in college, she must have eaten—"

"Shut up, Suzanne." Deidi glared at her friend, marveling at how some people never changed. Several times during their college years, in social situations similar to this, Suzanne had competed for the guy's attention by trying to make her look bad. Not that she would give two cents to save Hendricks's life—she'd just like to see how much she could cost him for putting her in jail—but the old shit was not going to fly anymore. Or it was going to fly in both directions.

"I'm sure he'd much rather hear about the contest you had with Lisa Jablonski and Christie Letterman," she continued in a conversational tone. "You know, to see which one of you could screw the most guys in a week's time?"

Suzanne's cheeks instantly blossomed with color. Sitting up rigidly, her fists clenched, she muttered through her teeth, "That's a lie and you know it! What's wrong with you?"

What is WRONG with you, what is WRONG with YOU?

The words echoed in Deidi's head, and suddenly she felt extremely dizzy and nauseous. A horrid vision flashed before her eyes, an undefinable mass of bloody gore jumping out at her face. She almost fell backward off the bench.

Hendricks rushed forward to help her, but he only got a few steps when Hughman warned with a toothy snarl that he'd better not come any closer, if he valued his windpipe. But Deidi managed—barely—to catch herself by clutching the edge of the table, and when she pulled herself back up into a sitting position, her face was white as a sheet.

Forfeiting her anger, Suzanne placed a concerned hand on Deidi's arm. "Are you okay? Are you going to faint? Put your head down between your knees—"

"I'm all right," Deidi grumbled, but it was obvious by her pallor and her shaking hands that she was not all right. She fumbled another cigarette out of her purse and lit it, having to use both hands to hold the lighter steady.

Suzanne leaned closer and asked in a softer, motherly voice, "Are you sure? You don't look all right."

"If you're not feeling up to it, I can give you a rain check for those ten pounds of prime rib," Hendricks offered, taking a few careful steps backward under Hughman's glowering stare.

"I said I'm all right," Deidi responded hotly, making it two glowering stares in the detective's direction. "Pick me up at seven sharp, and I do mean sharp." After telling him where she lived, her eyes ticked to his left, remaining riveted on something behind him. Hendricks turned to find both his children shyly standing about ten feet away, Jeremy holding the Frisbee.

He smiled at them with a waving gesture that invited them to come forward and join him. "Don't worry about the dog," he said with as much conviction as he could muster. "He doesn't bite unless she tells him to, and she's a very nice lady who wouldn't dream of telling him to bite anybody, unless maybe her life depended on it."

"Baloney. Sometimes I do it just for fun," Deidi teased, giving the children a wink to let them know she was only kidding. Drawing deeply on her cigarette, her shaking began to subside, the vision of leaping gore safely tucked away in her subconscious, like a caged tiger.

Jeremy and Lacey timidly stepped forward, both giving their father knowing looks. Hendricks introduced them to Deidi and Suzanne, and after the proper amenities were exchanged, raised his right wrist to check the time. "Well, I guess we'll get back to our Frisbee game now. You ladies have a nice afternoon, and I'll see you at seven sharp, Miss Marshall."

Deidi gave him a tight-lipped smile that said he'd damn sure better.

FLESH AND BLOOD

When they were out of earshot, Jeremy ribbed his father and said, "Way to go, Dad. Up close, the dark-headed one's a lot prettier than the blonde. Too bad she's a smoker, though. But I guess nobody's perfect." He spun the Frisbee around on one finger, a sly grin on his face.

"But why did she fall backward like that?" Lacey asked, glancing back toward the picnic table. The two women were getting up from it, and they appeared to be engaged in a heated argument. "It was like something hit her in the face, only nothing did. Unless a bug flew up her nose, but I didn't see one. Did you?"

Jeremy gave his sister a disparaging look. "If a bug flew up her nose, don't you think she would've sneezed, or tried to honk it out? I'm really sure she'd let it just crawl right up to her brain."

The same question was nagging Hendricks, but by the time they left the park two hours later, he'd forgotten all about it.

In spite of her concerted efforts to sit down and relax, Camisa could not stop herself from bouncing back up and pacing from room to room. She felt like climbing the walls, and for the first time in over two years she was craving a cigarette. But that was no surprise. She'd already started smoking again, in her secret life. Different personality, same body. The addiction to nicotine naturally transcended the chasm, and the image of the fat woman's scalded face springing to mind every ten seconds wasn't exactly helping matters, especially when it was followed by the sight of those bloody intestines leaping out at her. Memories like that she could well do without, but thinking about it served it right up again. She shuddered, then the term "gutless wonder" voiced itself and she released a nervous giggle.

Harlan had still not come home, and she was beginning to wonder if he ever would. But of course he would have to some time; all his clothes were here, as well as some other personal possessions that meant a great deal to him, such as the big yellow yield sign he'd ripped off as a teenager. It was nailed up over the headboard of their bed as a commandment to her, and if seen by the wrong person might get them in trouble. But she felt no compulsion to hide it. Compared to multiple murders, why sweat something as insignificant as theft of city property?

Felicia and Michael were taking their naps, and the house was quiet as a mausoleum, which was why the sudden sound of the telephone ringing nearly made her jump out of her skin. Her heart began pounding erratically, a block of ice settling in the pit of her stomach. Walking on rubbery legs, wringing her hands, she reluctantly went to the kitchen and answered it on the fifth ring, her voice sounding tremulous when she spoke into the receiver.

"Hello?"

A male voice responded. "Hello, Camisa? It's Uncle Lance."

Ex-uncle, she thought, her heart slowing its rhythm as she waited impatiently for him to go on.

"You have my deepest sympathy for the loss of your son," he finally continued when it was clear she wasn't going to say anything. "And for what it's worth, I'm appalled at what my dear departed brother did to you. As far as I'm concerned, you're still family, and you're welcome to call or drop by anytime you feel like it."

She had a picture of Lance Murray in her mind, a considerably more attractive version of her "departed" (dead as a doorknob and roasting in Hell) father, with deep-set hazel eyes and a cleft chin, ski-jump nose and wavy chestnut hair. "That's very good of you, Lance. Was there a story in today's paper? I haven't looked."

He cleared his throat. "Well, there is a story in the paper, but I didn't read it until after . . . after the police left, which was about fifteen minutes ago."

FLESH AND BLOOD

Camisa's heart revved up again, her throat constricting as if someone had her in a choke hold. "What? The police came to your house? What did they want?" Although she knew very well what they wanted—to prove that Aaron hadn't really been pulled away in an undertow and drowned like she'd said.

"Well, they, ah,"—another throat-clearing—"they were asking a lot of questions about you, like what kind of mother you were, if you ever abused your kids. I'm afraid it slipped out that Aaron wasn't with you when you came to the will reading, though your other two children were. They seemed, ah, rather interested in that fact. By the way, where was he that day?"

I'm dying, Camisa thought. Dying right here and now. And she believed it, the violent way her nervous system was reacting to this information. She had to sit down in one of the kitchen chairs and hang her head down to keep from fainting. She was going to get caught, oh indeed she was, she could fucking bet on it. Dyke City, here I come. She couldn't say that a neighbor had been watching Aaron; they would want to know which neighbor, and they'd sure as hell check it out.

"He . . . wasn't feeling too well," she said in a breathy voice as she slowly rose up. Her head felt like a block of ice now, numb and completely drained of blood. "Nothing serious, just a little upset stomach, but it was bothering him enough to make him want to stay in bed. I know I probably shouldn't have left him here alone, but I knew I wouldn't be gone very long."

"I see."

His response was repeated in her brain, but this time another man was saying it, a certain police captain named William Tarpley, and he was looking at her with piercing, knowing eyes. He could see, all right. He could see right through her, and knew that she was lying her ass off. And just leaving a five-year-old boy at home alone was probably sufficient grounds to put her in jail, where she would be fingerprinted and photographed and body-searched by a mean, ugly matron who moonlighted as a mud wrestler.

"Are you all right, Camisa?" Lance Murray asked the dead silence on the other end of the line.

She quickly covered her mouth to suppress a hysterical burst of laughter. Was she all right? Was an armadillo who'd just been run over by nine of an eighteen wheeler's gargantuan tires all right? It had just occurred to her that if she was fingerprinted, they'd be able to hang those other murders on her, Mr. Accountant Face, the old fisherman, the gross fat woman. After putting those puzzle pieces together, who the hell would care if she did something terrible to her little boy? After all, one can only be fried once in the electric chair, or shot up full of lethal drugs, however they killed condemned prisoners these days.

"Well, of course I'm still very upset, Uncle Lance," she managed to say calmly. Rising from the wobbly kitchen chair, she slumped over to the counter. "But I'm bearing up. Thanks for caring, it means a lot. Listen, I have to go now, I think I hear Felicia crying." Before he had a chance to say good-bye, she replaced the receiver in the wall cache and flopped her upper body across the counter, moaning, "Woe is me."

Then suddenly she straightened, jerked up by the invisible strings of a brilliant idea. All she had to do was get rid of her fingerprints, and then they would have nothing, no evidence whatsoever that would convict her. Maybe the bartender and that slutty barmaid could identify her, but so what? They only saw her leave the club with Patton; that didn't necessarily mean she'd killed him. That alone did not constitute a case.

She looked down at her fingertips, which were now her greatest enemies. The only question was, how to do it? She didn't think she could use one of Harlan's

FLESH AND BLOOD

razor blades to slice off the pads of her fingers. Maybe there was some rough-grade sandpaper in the garage ... no, that wouldn't be quick enough, and she wanted to do both hands at once.

Slowly, her eyes turned to the stovetop, specifically to the large cast-iron skillet sitting on the right front burner. Yes, that was the way to do it. Burn the suckers off. And if the police wanted to know why she had Band-Aids on all her fingers, she could claim the burns were accidental; silly her, forgetting to use her padded mitts while taking a hot baking dish from the oven.

Pushing down her fear, she forced herself to approach the stove. God, but this was going to hurt. But it would be nothing compared to dying, especially getting juiced in the electric chair. She turned on the right front burner and placed the setting on High. While she was waiting for the iron to get as hot as possible, Michael stumbled into the kitchen, rubbing his eyes sleepily.

"I wate up, Mommy."

"I can see that," she snapped. "But you go on back to your room, and you stay there until I say you can come out. I'm busy right now."

He stopped rubbing his eyes and looked up at her wearing a slight pout. "But I hun-gy, Mommy."

"I'll hun-gy you," Camisa said venomously, putting her hands on her hips and taking a threatening step forward. If he knew what was good for him, he'd run back to his room like the wind. That skillet was probably hot enough to burn already, and in her present mood, if Michael pushed her any further he might have a little accident of his own.

But apparently he could sense that he was in danger, because he did turn and run, not as fast as the wind, but certainly as fast as his little legs could carry him, and a few seconds later his bedroom door slammed. Camisa gritted her teeth, barely containing the scream that wanted to burst from her lungs. And just as she expected, a few seconds after that Felicia began to cry from the nursery.

Fucking kids!

Breathing heavily, she turned back to the stove, determined that the baby's crying was not going to bother her. She didn't feel like changing a shitty diaper at the moment; a far more pressing concern needed attention.

The small bits of hamburger left in the bottom of the greasy skillet were turning black and smoking. Now that she was thinking in terms of infection, it would have been prudent of her to wash the skillet first. Oh well. She would just have to use hydrogen peroxide afterward.

On the count of three, she told herself silently, poising her fingers over the skillet. In spite of her determination, Felicia's crying was getting on her nerves, as if she needed any additional stress. Her heart began beating faster, and suddenly her bowels felt loose and hot. What a riot it would be if she filled her own pants when she mashed her fingers down on the skillet's surface, which was now sending up ominous radiations of heat. Who would clean her up? If she cried, would her real mother hear and come running? Camisa didn't think so.

One . . . *Oh God, it's going to hurt so so so much . . .*
Two . . . *But it's gotta be done, absolutely has to be done . . .*
Three . . . !

Squeezing her eyes shut, Camisa pushed her fingers down on the bottom of the skillet as hard as she could, and an instant volcano erupted in her brain, pain beyond comprehension, and the scream she'd held back a few minutes earlier now came out in full force. In spite of its volume and the volcano's deafening roar she could hear the sizzle of her meat frying, could smell the sickening odor of charred flesh. Instinctively she tried to jerk her hands away, but they were stuck!

FLESH AND BLOOD

The skillet came off the burner about half an inch, melded to her fingers as one. Camisa's eyes bulged in horror as another scream tore from her throat, and another and another as the unbearable pain electrified every fiber of her being.

A mere second before blackness claimed her and temporarily cut her off from the excruciating pain, the skillet dropped back onto the burner, and with it ten blackened pieces of skin.

The argument that had started at the park was a full-blown war by the time Deidi and Suzanne got back to Deidi's apartment. Out had come all the resentments Deidi had repressed in college, and in defending herself Suzanne had planted a sizable crop of new ones. Chief among them was the accusation that Deidi was a complete fraud, that hidden behind her benign facade was a malevolent demon. Although Deidi greatly feared that it might be true, coming from Suzanne's mouth at this particular time the statement added gasoline to a fire already burning out of control. They had just entered the apartment when Suzanne said it. Deidi flung her purse on the couch and whirled around to face her friend-turned-enemy with raging flames dancing in her eyes.

"Oh, so now you're a fucking psychologist, too?"

"No, but I can see your evil aura!" Suzanne shot back with equal venom.

That sounded so ridiculous to Deidi that she couldn't help but burst out laughing. "My *evil aura?* Jesus Christ, give me a break! I've known some dingbats in my time, but you're their queen! So what's it look like, Madam Zooka? Is it black? Maybe black with glowing red eyes floating in it?"

"Stare in a mirror hard enough, maybe you'll see for yourself. I'm leaving," Suzanne snapped, heading for Deidi's bedroom to collect her things. Hughman, standing on the living room side of the kitchen counter, watched her go by with a slight snarl on his lips. He'd been listening to her verbally attack his mistress for approximately fifteen minutes now, and he could sense the distress it was causing her. Suzanne was slowly but surely going down in his personal popularity poll.

Deidi followed her, wanting to vent as much of her anger as possible while she had the chance, for she knew with certainty that once Suzanne left, they would never speak to each other again.

"You're expecting me to break down and beg you to stay, aren't you? I know you are, it's just like you to revert to such juvenile tactics. Well don't hold your breath, Suzanne, because I really don't give a flying fuck. I want you out of here, and if I never see you again, it'll be too soon for me!"

Suzanne paused from packing her suitcase and smirked. "Just listen to your mouth. 'Flying fuck,' 'fucking psychologist.' It only proves what I said is true. This is the *real* you. What next, are you going to beat me up? I wouldn't put it past you. I wouldn't put *anything* past you."

Deidi took a threatening step closer, her hands balled into fists. Hughman was right behind her. "Don't tempt me too much, you filthy lowlife slut."

A hint of fear came into Suzanne's blue eyes, and her hands trembled slightly as she finished folding a blouse and putting it in the suitcase. In a relatively calm voice she answered without looking up, "Okay, you get the last word. Just let me finish packing, and I'll be out of here. Out of your life."

It is written that "a soft word turneth away wrath"; not so in this case. Deidi's anger was a runaway train, and it was looking to mangle something. Presently Suzanne Weiss was the only something in its path. Deidi took another step forward and practically shouted, "What's the matter, *slut,* are you *scared?* Scared of *me?* Come on, where's your spunk? You started this, dammit, I'm not going to let you pussy out of it! You've made me too fucking mad!"

FLESH AND BLOOD

Behind her, Hughman growled deep in his throat.

Suzanne tensed, seeing from the corner of her eye that the Doberman was looking straight at her. Grabbing another blouse to fold, she said in a tremulous voice, "If you're going to keep yelling at me, at least get your dog out of here. Please. He's making me nervous."

Deidi smiled, gleefully seizing the opportunity to scare the piss out of her ex-best friend for getting her this upset. "I'll bet he is. You've seen his teeth, and I'm sure you can imagine the damage they could do. You should have seen him in training school, when I gave the command to attack the instructor in the padded suit. I think Hughman must have been a Bengal tiger in his previous life. Even the instructor was impressed, and he's trained plenty of attack dogs."

Suzanne could feel the pulse beating in her throat, and her knees suddenly felt weak. She was scared, all right; very much so. But in her heart of hearts she still couldn't bring herself to believe that Deidi would actually turn the dog on her, not even when she was this mad. Maybe there was a dark side to Deidi (wasn't there a dark side to everyone?), but there was also a rational side that was surely stronger. A rational side that understood terms like "lawsuit" and "jail." And there existed a strong chance that in the aftermath of an unwarranted attack, Hughman would be put to sleep. Deidi would never pay that high a price for revenge.

But she had not yet sent the dog away, and he was growling steadily now, attuned to his mistress's highly charged emotional state. Suzanne was getting so nervous she thought she might vomit. "Please send Hughman into the living room," she said meekly, thinking to hell with folding her garments. She carelessly stuffed the remaining few into the suitcase, closing and locking the lid with careful deliberation.

"It's his house," Deidi said hatefully, crossing her

arms. "He can be wherever the hell he wants to be. And that's usually with me."

"Deidi, can't you hear the way he's growling at me?" Suzanne implored, too afraid to pick up her suitcase and attempt to pass the agitated and dangerous dog, who was standing between her and the doorway. "Look, if you're wanting an apology, okay, I apologize. I didn't really mean the things I said, I just had to say something to counter your jabs."

Deidi snickered. "Right. And later on I'll get a phone call from you, taking that back. You're not sorry in the least. You're just scared."

Actively fighting now to keep her lunch down, beads of cold sweat forming on her brow, Suzanne raised her hands in supplication. "What do you want me to do, get down on my knees and beg? Would that satisfy you?" Her voice was laced with panic.

Quickly deciding that was a sight she'd really like to see, Deidi nodded, her smile widening. "It might. Try it and see."

Bitch, Suzanne thought as she slowly lowered herself to her knees in front of Deidi, at the moment feeling much more humiliated than frightened. What next, was she going to have to bend down and kiss Deidi's feet?

Hughman slowly came forward a couple of feet, like a stalking predator, his taut shoulder muscles working visibly beneath his sleek black coat. The growl died in his throat, but that was hardly a consolation in view of the way he was looking at her with his ears pressed forward, eyes black with malice. Suddenly Suzanne's humiliation was eclipsed by terror. A primal instinct made her aware that he was only a hair's breadth away from attacking her.

Though Deidi hadn't really expected it to, the sight of Suzanne kneeling there so humbly on the floor began to soften her heart. The raging fire of her anger was quickly reduced to a low simmer, and she even started thinking how stupid this all was. From a

FLESH AND BLOOD

calmer perspective, she couldn't imagine how it had gotten this far out of hand. But she supposed it was too late to salvage the friendship. Too many hateful words had been exchanged.

"You can get up," she said very softly, now feeling rather ashamed of herself.

She spoke a little *too* softly. What the Doberman heard was *Hugh, cut 'em up,* the very words he'd been anxiously waiting to hear.

Like a streak of black lightning, the dog lunged at Suzanne, knocking her over on her back, snarling and snapping with deadly ferocity, a savage demon out of control. Deidi was so shocked, she just stood there gaping for a few seconds, unable to believe what was happening.

Suzanne could believe. She could feel the sharp canine teeth sinking into and tearing at her flesh with the feral force of a mountain lion, and she knew beyond a doubt that this animal intended to kill her. Screams tore from her throat as she tried to fight back with her fists, the only weapons she had. But the demon was relentless, and its teeth and muzzle were now coated with her blood.

"No! Hughman, stop it!!" Deidi screamed, her heart thundering as she tried to pull him off Suzanne, but the Doberman continued his savage attack, the terrible, bone-chilling sound of his growls and snarls filling the room. In her fevered frenzy Deidi remembered that only a certain countercommand would make him stop, and she shouted it at him now, tears streaming down her face.

"Take a break!! Take a break!!"

And just as if she'd turned off a light switch, the dog backed off in silence, licking the blood around his mouth and looking very pleased with himself.

Deidi looked down in horror at his handiwork. Suzanne was bleeding profusely from the many deep puncture wounds Hughman's wickedly sharp teeth had made, mostly about her face and throat. Or what *had* been her face and throat. Both Suzanne's cheeks had been torn open, revealing bloody teeth and gums through the jagged holes, and on the left side even her jaw was visible. Her nose was almost completely gone; all that remained was a bloody stump of cartilage. But her throat was the worst. Veins and muscle tissue were exposed, and an alarming amount of blood was spurting rhythmically like a little fountain from the severed jugular vein.

Deidi felt as if all the blood had suddenly been drained from her own body. "Oh my God," she whispered, an acute wave of dizziness rolling over her. Certain that she was two seconds away from fainting, she stumbled over to the bed and sat down at the foot, hanging her cold and tingling head between her knees. She promptly vomited, then fell back and passed out anyway.

Hughman sniffed the carpet where she'd blown her lunch, then started to lick it up. His appetite primed, he moved over to Suzanne's body and began to lap her blood. She was still alive and conscious, but she couldn't talk—she could just barely breathe, and every time she released a breath, red bubbles formed in the crimson carnage of her throat. She knew she was dying, could feel her life ebbing away with each beat of her heart. But that didn't bother her as much as the thought of this black death machine lapping up her blood. With all the strength that remained in her, which wasn't very much, she reached up her left hand and tried to push the dog's muzzle away.

With a snarl and a snap, half of her index finger was gone.

Still lying unconscious on the kitchen floor, Camisa was having a dream. In it she was dressed up like a little girl with a petticoat under her blue velvet smock, which was frilled at the collar and sleeves with lace. A matching ribbon tied her hair into a ponytail, except for her bangs.

FLESH AND BLOOD

She was searching all over a strange neighborhood for her mother, her real mother, but she was nowhere to be found. And she kept hearing a baby crying, when there was no baby to be seen.

From their porches, strangers watched her with narrowed eyes, staring at her as if she'd done something wrong. And then she remembered—she *had* done something wrong, very wrong, so that it was no wonder people would stare at her like that. But she couldn't remember exactly what her crime was, only that she wasn't entirely to blame. Someone had coaxed her into doing it. Who that someone was she didn't know.

Suddenly she heard a man's voice behind her, calling her name. She turned around, fingers held to her lips, eyes wide and frightened. The voice had sounded authoritative and angry.

There was a man standing on the cracked sidewalk with his hands on his hips. He was grossly overweight, his swollen face supported by three chins. She knew who *he* was. He was her father. Her real one.

"Camisa, you're coming home with me right now," he said, thrusting a beefy hand out toward her. "You've got some explaining to do."

She wanted to run away and hide. She didn't want to go home, and certainly didn't want to have to explain anything. He was talking about her crime, she knew he was. And whatever it was, she didn't want to face it. Not now or ever.

He snapped his fingers impatiently. "Come now, Camisa. Right now."

But her feet wouldn't move. Not even when he charged forward to grab her by the arm, though she could easily have taken off and gotten away from him. He began dragging her down the tree-shaded sidewalk, and the people on their porches looked on approvingly.

Halfway down the block he turned up the driveway of a white clapboard house with a colorful flower bed out front. At that point she began trying to get away from him, kicking and biting and tugging her arm back, but he seemed made of steel, oblivious to the pain she was inflicting upon him. She started to scream, but of course that had no effect, either. He pulled her up on the cement porch, opened the front door, and dragged her inside.

There was no furniture in the house; the living room was completely bare, and so was the dining room beyond it. Cobwebs were draped all over the ceiling, and bits of trash littered the green pile carpeting. The air had a musty, dank smell, but underneath that, Camisa could smell something worse. It reminded her of the wounded mouse she'd got and put in a jar, to keep as a pet. But she forgot to punch holes in the lid, and the mouse soon died from lack of air. She'd kept him anyway, as a "conversation piece." But she didn't keep him for very long, because of the bad smell that began to emanate from the jar after a few days, even though the lid was screwed on tight.

Her father pulled her through the dining room into the kitchen. It was also bare; no pots or pans hung from the hooks suspended over the butcher block; no pictures or calendars hung on the walls, nothing sat on the counter's Formica surface or on top of the appliances, except dust and mouse turds.

As soon as they entered the kitchen, the baby's cries started up again, this time very loud. She looked about frantically but couldn't see the baby. Still, its cries rapidly escalated in volume until they were deafening, and Camisa thought her eardrums were going to burst. She started screaming again herself, telling it to shut up shut up *SHUT UP!!!*

Her father jerked her along toward the pantry closet door inside the utility room. Seeing it, Camisa's heart flooded with dread. She began shaking her head, begging and pleading for her father to let her go. On and on and on the baby cried, a horrible cry filled with

FLESH AND BLOOD

fear and pain. Her father reached for the pantry door's knob and twisted it, twisting her arm at the same time hard enough to make her yelp. She didn't want to look, didn't didn't, but her eyes wouldn't shut.

He opened the door, and the sight beyond it slammed an invisible fist into her stomach. There was her mother, her real mother, dangling limply from a length of clothesline, her feet hanging about two feet off the floor. Her eyes were bulged sightlessly out of their sockets, and her tongue protruded obscenely from her mouth. Her face was so purple it was almost black.

"Take a good look!" her father roared.

With an earth-shattering scream pressing for release, Camisa's eyes sprang open, and she found herself looking up at her kitchen ceiling. She was hyperventilating, and her heart was slamming against her chest. Consciousness brought with it intense awareness of the throbbing pain in her fingers. It still felt like they were mashed down on the searing-hot skillet.

From the nursery, Felicia was crying her head off. That explained the unseen baby's cries in her awful dream. Turning her pounding head to the left, she saw Michael standing a few feet away, looking down on her with wide, inquiring eyes. She was a little angry at him for disobeying her order to stay in his room until she told him to come out, but she'd let it slide this time. Undoubtedly he'd heard her scream, which would certainly foster an irresistible curiosity about what had happened to her.

He was looking at her hands, at her brownish-red fingertips which were oozing blood. "Mommy dot hurt," he commented.

That was the understatement of the century. She doubted even morphine could do much for the pain she was in, much less extra-strength Excedrin, which was all the painkiller she had on hand. But to look on the bright side, she no longer had fingerprints to worry about. The police could suspect all they wanted. They wouldn't be able to hang anything on her.

"Get me some ice out of the freezer, Michael," she croaked, gritting her teeth, wishing like hell Felicia would shut up her damn crying. Michael obediently pulled a chair up to the refrigerator, crawled up on it, and stood to reach the freezer. But when he attempted to pull open the freezer door, his chair toppled over and sent him crashing to the floor, the back of his head cracking against the hard linoleum. He immediately began to howl and scream, making Camisa wonder if there was any rope in the garage. She had just about reached the end of hers.

Deidi wakened to the sound of smacking, chewing noises and for several moments felt totally disoriented, not knowing what time it was or even what day of the week it was. All she knew for certain was that she'd just had the most terrible dream she'd ever had in her whole life. She'd dreamed that Hughman had attacked and killed Suzanne right here in her bedroom.

Feeling sick to her stomach, she sat up to see what Hughman was doing, suspecting he'd gotten hold of one of her good shoes again and was chewing it to pieces. A few seconds later, when she saw what he was really munching on, it seemed a ton of bricks had suddenly fallen on her.

It hadn't been a dream!

Suzanne's body was lying crumpled on the floor and from the shoulders up was drenched in blood. Hearing her sharp intake of breath, Hughman looked up at her, his stub wagging gleefully, stringy red tendons dangling from his wet, gore-caked mouth. Although Deidi's mind screamed for her to look away, her eyes disobediently locked on the ruined mess of Suzanne's face, which Hughman's lowered head had been blocking. If that had been all there was to see, she would

FLESH AND BLOOD

never have guessed it had once been a woman's face; it looked more like a large raw meatball with blond hair. Deidi clamped a hand over her mouth to suppress a scream.

Hughman was looking at her with a quizzical expression on his face, as if to ask her, *Aren't you pleased? Isn't this what you wanted me to do?*

Deidi thought she was going to throw up again, but there was nothing left in her stomach to eject except some foul-tasting bile, which she forced herself to swallow and retain. Her heart was thumping like mad. How was she supposed to deal with something like this? Suzanne was dead. There was no way she could look like that and still be alive.

With tears standing in her eyes, Deidi looked up at Hughman, who was now busy working the dangling tendons into his mouth. Her beloved pet. Her companion and guardian. She'd had him since he was six weeks old, and now he was almost four. She was more attached to him than she'd ever been to a person, including her own parents. If she called the police and reported this, they would take him away, and more than likely an order would be issued for him to be destroyed. The thought of that happening was totally unbearable. And it wouldn't bring Suzanne back.

Deidi decided then and there that she wasn't going to call the police. Hughman had been her faithful guardian for a long time; now she would be his, even if it meant committing a felony. Over her dead body would they destroy her beloved Hughman.

A cold calmness began to settle over her as the rational part of her brain took charge. There were plans to be made, things to do, evidence to erase. And a fucking detective would be over at seven to take her out to dinner. Talk about bad timing!

The first order of business was getting rid of the body, and then cleaning up the blood (thank God she didn't have carpet), and lastly getting rid of Suzanne's possessions, which included her car. That was going to be a tricky number, but as they say, necessity is the mother of invention.

Hughman lowered his head to nibble some more at his kill.

"No!" Deidi shouted, grimacing. In a stern voice she continued. "No, Hughman, you did a *bad* thing! I did not tell you to cut her up. I wasn't even talking to you, I was talking to Suzanne and I said 'You can get up.' God, how could you have done this? This is serious, Hughman! As serious as it gets! I could go to prison for covering up your crime, did you know that? And what do you think will happen to you if I go to prison?"

Of course Hughman had nothing to say for himself, but suddenly he looked ashamed. The tone of her voice informed him that he'd definitely screwed up somewhere.

Twisting inwardly in emotional agony, Deidi dropped her head in her hands and began to think of ways to get rid of the body. The first and most logical thing that popped into her mind was the ocean, which happened to be very convenient as well. Suzanne would decide to go for a midnight swim tonight, and drown. When and if the body was found, the damage to it would be attributed to sea creatures. And that would eliminate the need to get rid of her possessions.

But of course the deed would have to be done after dark; there were neighbors to consider. The blood should be cleaned up as soon as possible, though, before it soaked into the wood. So she'd put the body in the bathtub for now, wrapped in the shower curtain, then she could work on cleaning up the mess. As she numbly went about carrying out her plans, she kept praying that she would wake up to find that this had all been a nightmare after all. But she never did.

11

Promptly at seven a knock came at the door, and Deidi tensed. She'd been hoping he would stand her up, but no such luck. What a nerve-racking experience, knowing a detective was at the door when there was a dead and ravaged body in the bathtub.

Her black and tan bodyguard followed her to the door, and when Deidi pulled the drape aside, he emitted a low growl.

"You stop that," she hissed at him, then said to Hendricks through the glass, "Just a second, I need to grab my purse."

Half a minute later they were walking through the courtyard toward his car, she at a much faster clip. Glancing back over his shoulder, he said, "If you'd like to invite your girlfriend to come along with us, it would—"

"Suzanne doesn't want to come," she cut in as her mind scrambled for an explanation. "There's a movie starting in half an hour that she doesn't want to miss."

Inside the green-over-white Malibu Classic with the doors closed, Deidi could smell the cologne he was wearing. She couldn't name the scent but it was very sensual. The bruises on his face looked so much better that she wondered if he'd used makeup. He was wearing dark blue jeans and a light yellow jacket over a white shirt, unbuttoned to the center of his fuzzy chest. A single gold chain hung around his neck.

He likes me, she thought. He'd obviously put care into his appearance, certainly more than she had. So maybe she had one ace in the hole, if worse came to worse. She'd better be nice to him.

"So, did you have a nice day at the park with your kids?"

He glanced at her with obvious surprise at her friendly tone. "Yes, as a matter of fact I did. We had a great time there, then we went through Reptile Gardens for the umpteenth time, and afterward we caught a movie."

Deidi nodded, a slight tremor running through her at the mention of Reptile Gardens. "So where are they now?"

"Spending the night with friends." After a pregnant pause, he went on, "Still think you're going to be able to put away ten pounds of prime rib?"

Deidi thought it was going to be a miracle if she could get a single bite of anything down her throat. "Hardly. I'm really not very hungry at all, but I could sure use a drink."

"I take it your day wasn't so great."

If only he knew. "I've had better ones."

At the restaurant he insisted that she order the prime rib dinner, saying that what she didn't eat now she could take home and eat later. Deidi relented without much argument, being in no mood to argue about anything. The seams of her world were being strained enough as it was, threatening at any moment to burst apart. It had seemed that way even before the crowning catastrophe of Suzanne's violent death.

When their cocktails arrived, Hendricks gave her an odd look. "I can't believe you haven't said one word about my lead on the killer yet. Isn't that the only reason you agreed to have dinner with me?"

FLESH AND BLOOD

"I've got a lot of other things on my mind," she admitted with a contrived half smile, lifting her glass and taking a hefty swallow of her Long Island tea. Conscious of the trembling in her hands, she reached inside her purse for her package of Virginia Slims. "But now that you mention it, I'm all ears. Go ahead, spill your guts." The moment those last words left her mouth, a vision of Suzanne's carnage flashed, turning her stomach over. The acrid bile rose again in her throat, and she washed it back down with another swallow of her bittersweet drink.

"You have to make me a promise first," he said in a no-nonsense voice. "What I tell you now stays under your hat until I've made an arrest. Is that a deal?"

"Deal," Deidi muttered.

Hendricks leaned over the table slightly, resting his chin on an upturned palm. "I believe our lady works at one of the massage parlors here in Danville. She's a prostitute."

Deidi's eyebrows rose. This was certainly interesting. "Which one? You know I know which of the yellow pages you were looking at, I could figure it out on my own. But it would be nice if you'd save me the trouble." With her mind centered on a different subject, Deidi felt herself begin to relax a little.

Hendricks sighed, but a tiny smile played on his lips. "You are a reporter, aren't you?"

"I was born with a foot-long nose. My parents had it bobbed."

"The plastic surgeon did a nice job."

"Thank you." Deidi took a long drag on her cigarette and exhaled the smoke over his head, her eyes fastened on his like a hawk's. "Now quit trying to change the subject. Which massage parlor?"

Remembering his experience inside the Merry Mermaid, Hendricks felt a stirring deep in his groin. Mistaking him for a customer, the madam, a short, plump woman of about thirty with a blond wedge, who introduced herself as Melanie, called out the troupe of merry mermaids for his inspection. Seeing firsthand how she operated, it was no wonder the place had been busted so many times.

Four girls came out, ranging in ages from fourteen to forty, in his estimation. All of them were wearing extremely revealing costumes whose fabric was covered with imitation fish scales, though Hendricks was sure he'd detected a very real fishy smell. In spite of that, their appearance had given him an instant erection which had not gone unnoticed, making his consequent interrogation quite uncomfortable.

"The Merry Mermaid," he admitted after his brief rumination. "I showed the composite to the owner, Melanie Graff, and four of her girls, and all of them said the picture looked almost exactly like another girl who works there, but she wasn't working last night. Nor did she work the nights the murders were committed."

"So why didn't you go pick her up?"

"Nobody knew where she lives, or anything else about her other than the first name she works under, Starla, which is probably an alias. But she's supposed to be there tomorrow night. I'm going to start staking the place out at six o'clock."

Deidi took a sip of her Long Island tea and thought to herself that his enthusiasm was a castle made of sand. Composite drawings were so unreliable, and so what if this "Starla" didn't work the nights of the murders? This sounded more like a long shot to her, but long shots sometimes made it in. And Tom would want her to go along no matter what.

"Mind if I go with you, just in case?"

When he started to protest, she said firmly, "You owe me, buster. Your Iron Bar Motel isn't exactly a pleasure palace."

Hendricks found himself wondering what Deidi would look like in one of those little mermaid costumes, and tried to visualize it over the veto of his higher, more gentlemanly self. But he couldn't help it.

FLESH AND BLOOD

The erotic image of her near-naked body was formed, and she looked *damn* good.

He shrugged. "Okay, what the hell. But after that, my debt is clear."

Deidi wasn't sure it was all that fair an exchange, as likely as it was for an ocean wave to come along and wipe out his little sand castle, but she wasn't about to play hardball with him. She'd have to figure out other ways to make him feel obliged. And seeing the obvious desire in his eyes, she had a good idea what those ways might be. It was devious and deplorable, but so fucking what. There was a lot at stake.

Their dinners arrived, and they ate in relative silence. Deidi did little more than pick at her food, with unwanted visions of Suzanne's chopped hamburger face slipping through the mental barrier she'd tried to erect. She ordered two more Long Island teas, and by the time she finished the third one, she felt like she'd just gotten off a merry-go-round that had been spinning her for hours.

A short while later she found herself entering Judson Hendricks's bedroom and trying desperately to remember how the hell she'd gotten there. Hendricks turned on a small bedside lamp, which cast off a soft, warm glow. The furniture was heavy dark wood and very masculine, the effect enhanced by a huge framed poster of a maned lion over the headboard. Deidi detected the scent of lemon furniture polish, and that along with the room's immaculate appearance made her suspicious that he'd had every intention of bringing her here after dinner. Or maybe he'd just been hopeful. Not that it really mattered; she was using him, too.

He came toward her now with a tender look on his face and began to undress her. Deidi assumed she must have said something that indicated he had her permission to do this. Well, he'd have to do it on the bed; she was having a hell of a time staying upright. Wordlessly, she moved away from him and stretched out on the black velvet spread draped over his king-sized bed. Wordlessly, he followed.

When he had her completely undressed, he began gently rubbing her up and down, over her breasts with a light squeeze, down between her thighs almost to her knees. Deidi closed her eyes, drowning in the delicious sensations. She was surprised that he didn't hurriedly chuck off his clothes and jump right on her bones, as was typical of most men. Lo and behold, a sensuous cop. Or maybe he was making up in advance for a disappointingly small dick. It didn't really matter.

A minute later Deidi passed out.

The sound of the doorbell made Camisa's heart leap up into her throat. Certain it was the police, she wondered frantically how she was going to hide the blackened, crusty tips of her fingers which were, even after several hours, still in considerable agony.

After his chair accident, she'd given Michael some baby aspirin and put him to bed, but after several hours he was still in pain, too, crying over and over that his head hurt. An hour earlier, totally fed up with his complaining, Camisa had finally checked the back of his head and was horrified to find that it was very swollen and squishy. He'd gone and fractured his damn skull! She had felt like screaming her head off, so she buried her face in Aaron's pillow and did just that. Of all fucking things to happen now! She couldn't take Michael to the hospital with a fractured skull when the police suspected her of doing away with Aaron. They would think she was responsible for the skull fracture, too. She just had to pray like hell that Michael didn't slip into a coma and die. God only knew what she'd do then.

Felicia was on the living room floor playing with her plastic blocks, seeing how far she could throw them, which was about a foot. Camisa decided she could hide her telltale wounds underneath the baby's cloth-

FLESH AND BLOOD

ing. A light blanket would be even better. She rushed to the nursery to get one just as the doorbell sounded again.

Sabrina Murray had turned to leave when the front door opened behind her. Looking back, she saw her adopted older sister framed in the doorway. In her arms Felicia was nestled in a light yellow blanket.

Seeing that the caller was Sabrina, Camisa's eyes filled with contempt. "What the hell are you doing here?"

"Well, I was here on a goodwill mission, but if you're going to speak to me that way, just forget it." She started walking toward her car in the driveway, but she'd taken only a few steps when Camisa called her back, her voice considerably less hostile.

"Come on in," Camisa said with a forced smile when Sabrina turned around again, hoping that the "goodwill mission" was an offer to split the ten thousand dollar inheritance Sabrina had gotten. "I'm sorry I was rude, but after what happened in that lawyer's office, and now Aaron . . ." She let her voice drift off wistfully.

Sabrina approached her and put a comforting hand on her shoulder. "I understand." Giving Felicia's cheek a gentle caress, she walked past Camisa into the disorderly living room. The mess was no surprise to Sabrina; she couldn't remember a time that she'd come over and it hadn't been disorderly. She'd often wondered how two sisters could be so opposite in character and personality. Now she knew that in their case, at least, it was because they really weren't related at all.

Camisa followed her and closed the door, which sent an intense flare of pain from her fingertips up the entire length of her arm. She barely managed to keep from crying out, but she could do nothing about the automatic grimace that appeared on her face, and Sabrina, who had just perched herself on the edge of the couch, noticed it.

"What's wrong, Camisa? Did you step on something?"

That was as good an excuse as any. Camisa nodded, still grimacing, and lifted her right foot, pretending to look for the offending object. "I don't see anything . . . must have been a tiny sliver of glass." She hobbled over to the other end of the couch and sat down with Felicia in her lap, looking at Sabrina expectantly.

The younger woman cleared her throat, her eyes averted. "Well, I know you'd like to find your real family, but I also know that the agency which handled your adoption would only give you general information, such as your medical history and where you were born, that sort of thing. Nothing that would lead you to your real father, because he wanted to remain anonymous. But I know who he is. Mom told me after church today, while we were out having lunch. She found out by accident a long time ago, overhearing a conversation at a restaurant one night. Your real father's name is George Gaston."

Understanding that no offer to split the inheritance money was forthcoming, Camisa felt her suppressed animosity rising again to the surface. A question rose with it, one that she really didn't want to ask, but she had to know. "What about my mother?" she asked tersely.

Sabrina sighed, wringing her hands together in her lap. "From what Mother gathered, it seems that your real mother is dead."

Remembering the terrible dream she'd had while lying on the kitchen floor, Camisa felt her chest tighten. Holding tightly to her squirming toddler, she asked in a voice now ripe with spite, "How did she die? Did she commit suicide by hanging herself in the pantry?"

For the first time since Camisa had sat down, Sabrina looked at her squarely in the face, blue eyes wide with surprise. "What makes you say a thing like that?"

FLESH AND BLOOD

"Just answer my question," Camisa growled. From down the hallway, Michael began whimpering again. The sound made Camisa's tension increase tenfold.

Sabrina averted her eyes before answering. "I don't know how she died. But I'm truly sorry, Camisa. I know we haven't always gotten along, but I don't bear any grudges against you. And of course I'm very sorry about Aaron. I can't imagine the sense of loss you must be feeling, even if he did sort of drive you crazy sometimes."

Michael's whimpering was steadily growing louder. Camisa tried to ignore it, hoping Sabrina would do the same. "Have the police been around, asking you questions about me?"

After a few moments' hesitation, Sabrina nodded.

"And you said those very words to them, didn't you? That Aaron 'sort of drove me crazy sometimes.' You did, didn't you?"

Sabrina swallowed, giving her a brief, nervous glance. "Well, it's the truth, isn't it? And you know I refuse to tell lies. The detective's questions were very direct, leaving no room for ambiguous answers. Incidentally, his visit was a big part of the reason I came. I thought that if, well, if you were going to be investigated and all, you would probably appreciate the moral support of your true family."

Camisa stared coldly at Sabrina for an interminable length of time in which she mentally stabbed the blue-eyed blonde with a large butcher knife until nothing but bloody pulp was visible. If only she could do it for real. Absolutely nothing would give her more pleasure.

"It sounds like Michael's crying," Sabrina said, shifting uncomfortably as she directed her gaze toward the shadowy hallway.

"I'm not deaf," Camisa snapped. "I'm not blind, either, and the sight of you is making me extremely sick. So if you would be so kind as to get the hell out of my house before I throw up, I'd be very grateful."

Sabrina quickly rose to her feet, her blue eyes flaring with indignation. "Camisa Collins, you're the most hateful person I've ever known. God only knows what's wrong with you, but at least it's not my problem anymore, or Mother's."

"Get the fuck out of my house!" Camisa screamed, now completely consumed by rage. If it hadn't been for her wounded fingers, she would have tossed Felicia aside and gone after Sabrina to tear her limb from limb with her bare hands.

Sabrina apparently picked up on this, because she practically ran from the house, not bothering to shut the door behind her. On the front porch she collided with Harlan, who'd just arrived reeking of sweat and liquor, his reddened eyes smoldering.

Deidi bolted upright in the darkness, her heart thudding against her rib cage, her head swimming. At first she didn't know where she was, but then a body lying next to her shifted, and she remembered. She was at Judson Hendricks's house, in his masculine bedroom with the framed lion poster over the bed. Christ! She couldn't stay here. She had to get home and drag Suzanne's body down to the beach, where hopefully the outgoing tide would carry it far, far out to sea before pulling it down into its dark, icy depths.

On a cabineted wooden nightstand to her right, small red digital numbers glowed, announcing that the time was now 10:42. That was something of a relief; she'd awakened with the impression it was near dawn. Shivering, she pulled the covers back around her shoulders, wondering where her clothes were; she was completely nude. Had she and Hendricks . . . ? She couldn't remember, but she didn't think they had, since there was no indication of stickiness between her thighs.

Peering into the darkness at the foot of the bed, she thought she saw her white nylon bra, and very slowly reached down for it, being careful not to awaken

FLESH AND BLOOD

Hendricks. After she was dressed, she'd go to the kitchen or wherever she could find a telephone and call for a cab to take her home.

But she had no sooner closed her fingers around one of the bra straps when the detective's voice piped up groggily, "Brenda?"

Deidi shot him a dirty look he couldn't see. "Guess again."

Hendricks sat up, his chest naked, and probed the shadows with one hand until he located her face, his thumb almost poking into her right eye. "Deidi?"

"Bingo," she said dryly, pulling away from his touch. Letting the covers fall from her shoulders, she began putting on her bra. Not that she really cared, but she couldn't help but wonder who Brenda was. Maybe his ex-wife. Or maybe some girl he'd brought here the night before.

"What are you doing?"

"I'm getting dressed, that's what. I have to get home."

He let out a light groan. "Don't go. I really wish you'd spend the night."

Deidi forced her voice to remain calm in spite of the panic she was beginning to feel. "Sorry, but my dog can't open the door for himself when he needs out."

"Won't Suzanne let him out?" Hendricks asked protestingly, reaching out to caress her upper arm.

Deidi's last memory of Suzanne sprang up in technicolor detail, and no, she would not be letting Hughman outside to potty. Not hardly. "No. She's afraid he'll run off if I'm not there, and I think she's right. He probably would try to find me, attached to me as he is. Maybe some other time, Judson."

Hendricks yawned and stretched, and afterward rubbed his eyes with the palms of his hands. "Well, guess I can't argue with that, much as I'd like to." He threw back his covers with a deep sigh, preparing to get dressed himself.

"You don't have to get up; I'll call a cab," Deidi said quickly, praying he couldn't argue with that, either. But on that point he definitely could.

"Oh, no, you won't. I picked you up and I'll take you home. I may be a real sonofabitch at times, but I'm never a cad."

Deidi suspected he might be ultimately hoping for an invitation to spend the night at her place. Oh sure, definitely. *But only if you'll promise to stay out of the bathroom, Judson darling, there's a rather nasty little mess in there. If you need to pee, you'll have to go outside and water Hughman's favorite palm tree. Otherwise, you can go for a little swim down at the beach, just be sure to keep moving.*

"Okay, I'll let you pay for the cab. That would leave your gentleman's honor intact."

"I don't mind at all, really," he insisted as he picked his shirt up off the floor and thrust his arms into the sleeves.

Deidi decided this was one of those times he could be a real sonofabitch. What did she have to do, scream at the top of her voice that she didn't want him to take her home? But if she did that, it would undoubtedly make him curious, and then he might only pretend to leave, fully intending to sneak back and spy on her. As she finished dressing, a simple solution presented itself. She could just say that Suzanne was sleeping in the bedroom. That only left the couch, and it was hardly wide enough to comfortably accommodate two adults.

As Hendricks was leading the way through the darkened living room, Deidi suddenly suffered an acute anxiety attack accompanied by an irrational paranoia that Hendricks was going to turn around and try to strangle her. But of course he did no such thing; he opened the front door and stepped out onto the porch, and a few seconds later Deidi heard him exclaim, "Well, I'll be damned!"

When she'd closed the door behind her and joined

FLESH AND BLOOD

him out on the porch, he pointed to a mimosa tree in the small patch of his yard across the driveway, which was well-illuminated by a nearby street lamp. Perched on one of the lower branches was a green parrot with blue-feathered wings. Deidi's heart skipped a beat when she sighted it. Was it the same one who'd gone nuts when she had entered the deplorable cabin of that fishing boat?

"Pirate ship dead ahead, Cyrus!" the bird squawked.

"I'll be damned," Hendricks repeated, slowly going down the porch steps with a big smile on his face. "The little fart must be part homing pigeon! I kept him here for a little while, then lost him clear down by the old Hollander Hotel. I can't believe he found his way back."

Deidi eyed the bird contemptuously. It *was* the same one. Great, this was just what she needed right now, a feathered, talking lizard who seemed to think she'd murdered its master. At least Hendricks was no longer looking at her as a suspect. "If he's that damn smart," she said with obvious spite as she followed Hendricks across the yard, "I wonder why he didn't go back to that old man's fishing boat."

Hendricks stopped, turned, and looked at her, his features deadpan. "Maybe because he's smart enough to know the old man's dead."

Now that Deidi had emerged from the shadows of the house into the bluish-white glow of the street lamp, the bird was able to get a good look at her, and the moment it did, it launched upward from the branch, unclipped wings furiously beating the air, its screeching and squawking filling the night.

There was no doubt in Camisa's mind that Harlan intended to strangle her. He'd already gotten his hands around her throat once, screaming: "You killed my son! You bitch, you killed my son!" and squeezing so hard she'd almost blacked out. Only by kneeing him in the groin had she been able to get away from him.

Now they were playing ring-around-the-dining-room-table, and Harlan looked like an absolute maniac, his eyes virtually radiating madness. Too much alcohol and probably some other drugs as well, too little sleep, a severe overdose of grief turned into anger. Added together, it was a recipe for second-degree murder. Hers.

According to Camisa's electrified brain, she had three options: One was to get the hell out of the house if possible. In the open, she was sure she could outrun him. Or she could use psychology, try to calm him down with words. Then there was always the "fight fire with fire" option. Attempt to knock him out, kill him if it became necessary. She decided to try the second option first as she danced around the table's rim, wondering how long it would take him to figure out he could simply toss it aside. He was certainly strong enough.

"Harlan, get hold of yourself! Think what would happen to Michael and Felicia if you killed me and went to prison! My so-called family certainly wouldn't take them, and you know what yours would do! Do you want them growing up in moral straitjackets? Getting severe whippings just because a deck of playing cards was found in one of their dresser drawers?"

"At least they'd grow up," he snarled, continuing the chase.

"I swear, Harlan, I swear to God that what happened with Aaron was an accident. You have to believe me!"

"Because you swear to God?" Harlan brayed malicious laughter. "Shit, Camisa, you'd lie right to God's face. Nothing's sacred to you. And I know you don't give a damn about Michael and Felicia. You wouldn't care if they grew up on the streets, eating out of garbage cans and sleeping in cardboard boxes. You let

FLESH AND BLOOD

Aaron die and you know it! And I've got an idea he was dead even before you left the house yesterday morning!"

Fuck option number two, Camisa thought, her eyes frantically scanning the kitchen for something to use as a weapon. If she bolted for the front door, Harlan would surely catch her. Michael was wailing from his bedroom, Felicia was crying in the living room, and her fingertips were sending up their own silent screams of agony, but her nervous system was in hyperdrive, muting all other stimuli but what was imperative for survival. In his highly aggravated state, Harlan hadn't even noticed the blackened, grisly pads of her fingertips. Three of them had began oozing blood again, which was getting smeared on the backs of the kitchen chairs, but Harlan didn't seem to notice that, either.

"Tell me the truth, you bitch!" Harlan raged, darting to the left. Camisa quickly compensated by sprinting to the right, which aligned her back with the open kitchen area. If her memory served correctly, her two-pronged cooking fork was among the dirty dishes in the sink. It had a black plastic handle around a sturdy steel rod about a foot long, ending in two three-inch prongs. Of course, if her memory did not serve correctly, she was probably dead meat. In the kitchen she would be utterly trapped, and no way would she have enough time to rummage through the silverware drawer for a sharp knife.

Just then her enraged husband overturned the kitchen table, sending it crashing on its side far enough toward the living room so that its protruding legs did not obstruct his path. All that stood between Camisa and his wrath now was the chair Michael had fallen from earlier. A picture flashed in Camisa's mind, a lion tamer warding off a dozen man-eating beasts with only a bullwhip and a chair. At that moment she'd have gladly traded Harlan for a ferocious lion.

In a thundering heartbeat she spun around and dashed for the kitchen sink. Harlan charged forward, flinging the chair behind him, where it splintered against the wall.

To Camisa, the single second it took to locate the black handle of the cooking fork seemed to last a century in which Harlan murdered her a thousand times. She only had time to grab it firmly with both hands, which caused a great deal of pain, and turn back to face the human locomotive bearing down on her.

The prongs of the fork entered Harlan's thick middle, just below the sternum, disappearing along with three-fourths of the metal rod. His sweat-stained T-shirt immediately began to turn bright red where the fork had gone in.

Initially a look of complete surprise claimed Harlan's features. He gaped down at the few inches of shiny rod and black handle protruding from his stomach as if seeing some kind of miracle. Camisa's hands had flown to her mouth, her eyes bulging in horror at the rapidly spreading bloodstain. She'd only intended to keep him at bay with the fork until she could get out of the house.

Realization finally soaked into Harlan's alcohol-muddled brain, and with it the awareness that he was in a world of hurt. Not even the worst whipping he'd received as a boy from his authoritarian, fanatically religious parents compared to the pain he was experiencing now. A deafening howl erupted from his lungs as he tried to pull the offending object out, but it would not come easily. He staggered back and forth, the sight of so much of his own blood making him feel faint.

"Help me!" he screamed at Camisa, his face twisting into a mask of dire agony as he continued to pull at the black handle. Now the whole front lower half of his T-shirt was soaked with blood, and it was beginning to drip onto the floor and his shoes.

FLESH AND BLOOD

Instead of helping him, Camisa inched away from him until the back counter stopped her from going any farther, his recriminating words swirling in her fevered brain. *You killed my son! You bitch, you killed my son! Nothing's sacred to you! You let Aaron die and you know it! I've got an idea he was dead even before you left the house yesterday morning! You'd lie right to God's face! Tell me the truth, you bitch!*

So instead of helping him, she stood there hoping that he would die. It would serve the bastard right for trying to choke her to death.

When at last Harlan succeeded in pulling the cooking fork free of his stomach, blood began gushing from the wound like an open spigot.

"Oh my God," he breathed, his face turning a pasty white. Trying to stanch the crimson flow with one hand, he reached out with the other to the telephone as he stumbled toward it to call 911 for help.

The cast-iron frying pan Camisa had used to obliterate her fingerprints had been returned to the front right stove burner. When Harlan picked up the telephone with his free bloody hand, Camisa very casually crossed the linoleum floor to the stove and picked up the frying pan by its thick needle-eye handle. And before Harlan could push the third and final digit, she swung the pan bottom against the back of his head with every ounce of strength her arms possessed.

12

Early Monday morning Deidi was wakened by the insistent ringing of the telephone. She had a horrendous hangover, but she was extremely glad to be awake and removed from the nightmare she'd been having. Suzanne's body had risen from the sea, covered with seaweed, and was walking slowly up the sandy incline toward the house, wanting revenge.

Feeling like shit on a stick, she gave Hughman a halfhearted pat on the head and dragged herself out of bed, tromping heavily to the slender wall of the dividing counter where the instrument hung. This morning its shrill rings seemed loud enough to burst her eardrums.

Picking it up, she answered with a groggy hello.

It was Kurt, Suzanne's estranged boyfriend. He had a very distinctive voice that Deidi recognized immediately when he asked to speak with Suzanne, declaring fiercely that he knew she was there. Deidi swallowed a sudden lump in her throat, staring at the empty couch.

"Well, uh, she doesn't seem to be here right now, Kurt. She must have gone out for a walk on the beach or something. But I'll tell her you called as soon as she gets back."

FLESH AND BLOOD

"And tell her that if she doesn't call back by noon, I'm driving down there. If she thinks I'm going to let her go so easily, she'd better think again. I'll *never* let her go."

But if you could see her now, Deidi thought grimly, you'd have a few second thoughts of your own. You wouldn't want to touch her with a ten-foot pole. "Kurt, my house is off-limits to you. I don't need or want this crap between you and Suzanne happening around me. If you so much as show your face, I'll call the police."

"Cops don't scare me," came his sneering reply. "You'd just better make sure Suzanne calls me before noon. And tell her I don't want to hear any more of this 'we're through' shit, because we're not through unless *I* say so. Got that?"

Deidi dropped the receiver back into its cradle. "Yeah, I got it, asshole." What a jerk. Apparently this was an acute case of wounded male ego, its severity a result of Kurt's ego's extraordinarily inflated condition. It was really a little frightening. Kurt was just the sort who would resort to violence and even murder if nothing else worked. And sometimes they didn't just waste the object of their obsessions (though in this case, unbeknownst to the antagonist, said object was already wasted), but anyone else who happened to be around.

Deidi looked across the living area at Hughman, who was waiting near the sliding door to be let out. If it weren't for him, she'd probably be scared shitless, because no way was Suzanne going to be calling Kurt back by noon, or for that matter, ever again.

At least Judson Hendricks was capable of taking no for an answer. As she shuffled barefoot across the parquet floor, she remembered the look of disappointment on his face when she'd shot down his last hope of spending the night with her. Then something on the ceiling caught her eye, and she looked up to see an irregular-shaped, light brown stain over the left end of the couch. Her brows knitted together in confusion. What the hell was that?

She continued to study it as she unlocked the sliding door and pushed it along its track to let Hughman outside. Come to think of it, she hadn't seen Baby Shamu lately, nor had she heard any of the usual sounds from upstairs—creaking floorboards, the sound of the toilet flushing, the faint din of a television program.

A possible identification for the light brown stain came to mind, making Deidi feel sicker than ever. Blood? Was that a bloodstain? Several years ago she'd read about a man dying in his upstairs apartment, and his death wasn't discovered until his decomposing body began leaking through the ceiling of the apartment below. Of course Flora Bushbaum couldn't have been dead that long, but the idea that she might be up there, bled to death, wouldn't leave Deidi's mind.

Leaving the sliding door open for Hughman, she hurried back toward her bedroom to get dressed, but first had to make a pit stop in the bathroom to throw up.

Ten minutes later Deidi was scanning the beach with an old pair of binoculars for any sign of Suzanne's body, fearing that her nightmare was a psychic warning that it had washed ashore. But much to her relief, she saw nothing that might have been a body.

Hoping the three aspirins she'd just taken would quickly cure her pounding head, she turned back to the house with Hughman on her heels, now preparing herself for what she might find in Flora Bushbaum's second-floor apartment. Her mind refused to speculate on what course of action she should take if the worst-case scenario was realized, which was going up to discover a murder scene. The chances of that being the case were far too remote anyway.

Just as she rounded the corner of the house, the

twenty-year-old college student named Cindy Fidelman who occupied the other downstairs apartment was crossing the flagstone patio wearing a McDonald's uniform. She smiled brightly at Deidi, her eyes appearing owlish behind the thick lenses she wore. Her scraggly dishwater-blond hair, banded in a ponytail above the adjustable strap of her uniform visor, hung straight as an arrow to her waist.

"What's with the binoculars?" she asked Deidi cheerfully.

Deidi wanted to tell her to mind her own damn business, and to quit being so frigging cheerful before someone with a bad hangover threw a brick at her, but she forced herself to be civil. After all, Miss Smiley Butt had just become a *witness*.

"I was looking for my friend Suzanne," Deidi answered with just a hint of concern in her voice. "When I woke up this morning she was gone, but her car is here, so I thought she might have taken a walk along the beach. I was trying to see if I could spot her because she had an urgent telephone call."

Cindy flashed her another dazzling smile. "Oh. Well, guess I'll see ya later. If I don't hurry I'm going to be late, and my supervisor can be a real gritch about stuff like that."

Unaware that she was gritting her teeth, Deidi stepped back into her own apartment, tossing the binoculars onto the couch. Then she waited behind the drape for Cindy's dilapidated VW Beetle to putter off down the road. As soon as it disappeared from sight, Deidi stepped back onto the patio and looked apprehensively at the redwood staircase leading to Flora Bushbaum's apartment. Beside her, Hughman lifted his head and sniffed curiously at the air. Deidi could smell nothing out of the ordinary.

"What is it, boy? An armadillo? Maybe a stray cat hiding somewhere?"

He couldn't tell her what he smelled, but he could certainly lead her to its source, and a few moments later he trotted to the bottom of the staircase and began lumbering up.

Oh God, Deidi thought, feeling her stomach twist into a tight knot as she tentatively followed him. When she reached the landing, Hughman was standing at attention in front of the sliding glass door, his long pointed nose poking through the foot-wide opening.

The pounding in Deidi's head increased as she drew closer to the opening. The aspirins were doing no good at all, but it was no wonder. She knew she was going to see something really horrible when she looked through that open space, she knew it now with absolute certainty. And she had the most dreadful feeling she'd already caught a glimpse of it at the park the day before, that unimaginable horror jumping out at her face. God only knew what it had been, but she was probably about to find out.

Hughman issued a low growl, and from within the apartment Deidi could hear a mass fluttering of wings accompanied by the unmistakable cawing of several crows. Subconsciously holding her breath, she stepped up beside Hughman and forced herself to look inside.

Several crows? It looked more like a hundred of them, all massed around an old-fashioned armchair that sat facing the door. And unless the birds were piled high on top of one another, there was something else in the chair beneath them, a large unidentifiable lump. Whatever it was, the crows were busy eating it, picking at it greedily with their yellow beaks, and apparently they weren't about to let anyone or anything frighten them away from it.

Deidi clasped a hand over her mouth, fighting an acute wave of nausea. There was really only one thing that large lump could be. Backing away, she leaned against the glass and took several deep breaths in a vain attempt to calm her racing heart. She wasn't about to do any measuring, but she judged the location of that armchair to be just about directly over the left end of her couch, meaning that in all likelihood, the light brown stain on her ceiling was indeed blood that had seeped through the floor.

Only one way to find out for sure. Looking down at Hughman with a deeply perturbed expression, she pulled the door open another foot and uttered the magic words. *"Hugh, cut 'em up!"*

At once the dog lunged inside, snarling and barking ferociously at the thick congregation of large black birds. Dispersing with a nerve-jarring cacophony of caws and screeches, the spacious room immediately filled with desperately flapping wings and stray feathers. Hughman caught one bird after another in his powerful jaws and crunched them into silence, flinging the broken and bleeding bodies aside to go for the next one. Some of them flew toward the glass door, crashing into the unseen barrier and breaking their necks. But several made it safely through the opening, and of those, two began pecking viciously at Deidi, reminding her of the old Hitchcock movie *The Birds*. She screamed and swung at them, knocking the largest one into Flora's barbecue grill, breaking one of its wings. It fell and flopped about helplessly on the redwood deck. The other was not so easily defeated. It was bound and determined to have a chunk or two of Deidi's face, and continued to dive at her, skillfully eluding her frantic swats. Having never experienced a bird attack before, she was absolutely terrified, afraid that it might succeed in putting out one of her eyes. But mainly she was afraid because she felt trapped. If she tried to go down the stairs, the bird might land on her head or something and make her fall, and she shuddered to think what would happen if she was knocked unconscious. And she couldn't go into Flora's apartment, where dozens more of the black demons were stirred up.

The guerrilla crow swooped down on her again, this time managing to tear a small piece of flesh from the back of her left hand. At that same moment, three others made it through the two-foot opening and flew quickly out of sight. With a cry of rage, Deidi yanked the door all the way back, and seconds later the remaining survivors of Hughman's crushing jaws darted from the apartment in a fluttering black stream. Deidi crouched with her face against her knees and covered the back of her head with her hands, the wound on her left leaking blood into her hair. Fucking birds were getting *way* down low on her own popularity poll.

But there were no more attacks; the one who'd bitten her merged in flight with the last birds to escape the apartment.

Now that they were gone, the silence was roaring. Slowly Deidi stood up, wincing at the sight of her bloody hand. Inside, brittle crunching noises informed her that in the aftermath of the excitement, Hughman had decided to snack on one of his feathered victims, even though she must have told him a hundred times that bird bones could be very hazardous to his health.

Stepping inside to scold him, she instead gasped at the terrible scene that greeted her eyes. The mysterious lump had been Baby Shamu, all right. And what remained of her was a vision straight out of the Devil's worst nightmare. Both eyes had been pecked out and the lids torn away, leaving dark, mournful caverns from which nerves and stringy tissue dangled. Some of the original pocks in her face had been turned into grand canyons, giving the impression of brownish-red Swiss cheese that rats had been gnawing. Her lips had been eaten, giving her an obscene toothy grin. Above it, her nose now resembled a pig's snout. But worst of all was the sight between her enormous, chalky breasts.

Dried intestines and organs, or what was left of them after the birds' feast, was spilled from a squarish hole in her abdomen, stretching all the way past her parted knees. At first Deidi's mind was too paralyzed by shock to have a single coherent thought, but when the first came, it was that she sure as hell did have of vision of this, the literal spilling of Flora Bushbaum's guts. But how could she have? And for God's sake *why?* Surely she hadn't done this atrocious thing in a fugue state! Pressing her temples, she fought against the madness pressing in on her. *What is WRONG with you, what is WRONG with you, what is WROOONG WITH YOOOU???*

Repressing a scream, she strode purposefully into Flora Bushbaum's kitchen and, careful not to leave any fingerprints, located a large trash bag and began to gather up the crows Hughman had killed, starting with the one he had in his mouth. After scolding him mildly, she told him as she methodically tossed the others into the bag, "We didn't see this, Hughman. Didn't see a damn thing, do you hear? Didn't see anything or hear anything and it has nothing to do with us. You got that straight? As far as we're concerned, *this did not—fucking—happen!*"

When all the dead birds were in the bag, Deidi led Hughman out onto the redwood deck and pushed the door closed behind them with her elbow. The bird she had injured herself was still flopping around beneath the barbecue grill. Deidi stooped to pick it up by its broken wing and toss it into the bag with its dead comrades, but when she did, it tried to bite her. She almost gave Hughman the kill command, but instead took the matter into her own hands—or foot, rather. Very quickly she stomped on the crow's shiny black head, hearing the crunch of its fragile skull beneath her sandal. Served the little bastard right, for trying to bite her.

After disposing of the bag in the community trash Dumpster located at the far end of the small parking lot, she went back to her own apartment to treat the nasty wound on her left hand. When that was done, she called the *Chronicle* to give Tom an update on the

Patton/Bagget homicide investigation, telling him only that the detective on the case had a strong lead, and a stakeout was planned for six that evening, which would probably result in an arrest. Not knowing that he was being cheated out of some much juicier facts, Tom was elated by the information, and ordered her to stick with Hendricks for the duration, not to worry about her regular duties, which had been divided among her coworkers. They were bitching to high heaven about it, but that was just tough cookies.

"Stories like this one are what it's all about," he told her with firm conviction.

"You're just a ghoul, Tom," Deidi responded with equal conviction, and hung up. Slumping against the counter, she looked down at her faithful Hughman. "Well, boy, looks like I've got to play reporter today, much as I'd like to crawl back in bed and sleep for a thousand years."

Hughman cocked his head, ears bent forward, his chocolate eyes questioning. *Is that supposed to mean something to me?*

Deidi supposed it would be a good idea to take Suzanne's car, in case Kurt made good his threat to drive down. If he saw that her car wasn't here, surely he wouldn't stick around. But most definitely he would if her car was here; in fact, if his knocks went unanswered, he'd probably try to break in. And as they say, where there's a will, there's a way, regardless of the fact he'd be very sorry when he saw who was inside to greet him. Hughman felt free to attack prowlers without being told.

In a kitchen drawer she removed a sheet of stationery and a pen. Since she was supposed to be unaware of Suzanne's death, it would make sense to leave her a note. After a few moments' thought, Deidi wrote that the Corvette wouldn't start this morning, so she had taken the liberty of borrowing Suzanne's Z-28. She also warned that her crazy boyfriend had threatened to drive down if he didn't hear from her by noon.

FLESH AND BLOOD

Of course, that might make Kurt look extremely suspicious in the light of Suzanne's disappearance, but Deidi didn't care. He was such an asshole, richly deserving of any shit that might fly into his fan.

Thinking of the grueling ordeal he would undoubtedly be put through at the police station, she smiled, having already completely blocked from her consciousness the horror in the armchair. Such total repression was truly an art, and she was exceptionally good at it.

Sprawled sideways across her disheveled bed, Camisa was still asleep, and she was dreaming. She was watching herself laboriously drag Harlan's considerable weight out to the garage, just as she had really done the night before. The blow to the back of his head with the iron skillet hadn't killed him; she'd checked his neck for a pulse and found one. But he was certainly out cold, and seemed to weigh a ton.

After several minutes of tugging, she finally got him out there, her back aching miserably by the time she was finished. Straightening up slowly, wondering with a grimace how she could possibly be so out of shape at her relatively young age, she closed the door to the kitchen, then shuffled over to the shelves where Harlan kept most of his tools.

Reaching up to the center shelf, she carefully lifted down his twelve-inch Echo chain saw. Cute little thing, but oh, it could saw through just about anything. Hearing a low moan, she turned and looked down at Harlan's sprawled body. Blood was still gushing freely from the hole in his gut, and had already formed a dark pool on the cement floor. His head was lolling from side to side; he was coming around.

Camisa yanked the pull handle, and the gas-powered sawing machine roared to life, the menacing sound of a bumblebee in flight amplified a thousand times as the hooked steel teeth of its circular blade became a single blur. She carried it over to where Harlan lay, feeling its vibrations throughout her entire body. They were good vibrations, good and powerful. With this thing in her hands, she could really kick some ass.

She kicked Harlan in the middle, making him vomit something that looked like mashed sardines in mustard sauce. Camisa had seen worse vomit, such as the time Aaron barfed up a little toad one of his friends had dared him to swallow—it was still alive, kicking its legs in a pool of creamed corn and bits of hot dog—but the sight of Harlan's mess was certainly gross enough to earn her disgust. And for making it, she kicked him again, very hard, but this time in the leg.

He yelped in pain as his eyes fluttered open out of focus. Try as he might, he could not straighten his vision; there was three of everything. Of course, what he noticed most was the three Camisas standing over him holding three activated chain saws.

"You sonofabitch," they said simultaneously, glaring down at him. "You tried to kill me. And I didn't much appreciate your accusations, either, or your other cutting remarks. I think you owe me an apology, don't you?"

He most certainly did. Continuing his attempts to consolidate his triple vision, apologies began to flow profusely from his lips, along with a few excuses, all spoken loud enough to be heard over the noise of the chain saw. He'd come home so drunk he hadn't known what he was doing, and honestly couldn't remember trying to kill her. But yes oh yes, he was sorry with a capital S! Sorry and ashamed as a man could possibly be. Couldn't she understand, though, how crazy with grief he was over the loss of his firstborn? (Not that she wasn't as deeply affected, no, she just hid her grief a little better is all.) Even so, he was utterly contrite, and begged her to forgive him for all he'd said and done.

FLESH AND BLOOD

The three Camisas smiled at him. "I thought you'd be sorry, now that I obviously have the upper hand. But I wonder how long you'd stay sorry if I put this away and got you to the hospital? Would you tell the attending physician the truth, that your stabbing was an accident, or would you try to get me arrested?"

He'd been stabbed? Lifting his six hands and seeing all the blood on them, he felt a jolting stab of pain in his chest. Suddenly the lost memories came slamming into his head, all that had transpired from the time he and Sabrina had collided on the front porch to him picking up the telephone in the kitchen to call 911.

He did need to get to a hospital, and fast. "Camisa, I said I was sorry, and I meant it. I'll still mean it a week from now, a year from now. Just please for God's sake call me an ambulance before I bleed to death!"

Camisa heard his words, but she detected no sincerity behind them. What she detected was desperate fear; he'd promise anything that would get him an ambulance. To prove it, she asked him tauntingly, "If I do, will you buy me a new sports car like I've always wanted, and you've always told me we couldn't afford?"

Pressing against his wound with his blood-crusted hands, his face contorted in agony, Harlan nodded vigorously. "Yes, yes! Now go call!"

"And how about hiring a nanny for Michael and Felicia so I can go to modeling school?"

"Okay, *fine!* Just please—"

"Wait, one more thing. I'd like to take a nice long trip to Europe without you or the kids."

"*All right, all right!* Now would you please call the *fucking ambulance!*"

"Just tell me this," the three Camisas hissed in response, bending toward him with the three loudly buzzing chain saws, the rounded ends of their whirring blades held dangerously close to his throat. "How the hell are you going to afford all that, my dear truck-driving husband? Have you got a pile of money stashed away that I don't know about?"

He opened his mouth to say more, but Camisa had heard quite enough of his lies. Nor was she going to give him a chance to have her arrested on a charge of attempted murder. Clenching her jaws, she plunged the whirring end of the chain saw into Harlan's throat. A gurgling scream escaped his widely gaping mouth as his eyes crossed at a comical angle.

At the same moment, a thick spray of blood spattered across Camisa's face, some of it getting into her eyes. Temporarily blinded, she dropped the droning saw on Harlan's chest, where the blade began digging a deep rut into his well-padded flesh, spraying blood as high as the ceiling and all over the walls. His hands instinctively came up for the saw, but his shocked and reeling brain misguided them to the blade instead of the handle, and in a blink all eight of his fingers were severed, tossed and flung in every direction with a fresh spattering of blood. Camisa got her vision cleared just in time to witness it, and surprised herself by tossing back her head and barking out a demented laugh.

Now the dream fast-forwarded several minutes, and she was using the saw to cut off his legs. By this time he was dead, nothing but a slab of meat, and before the night was through, the hungry alligators and crocodiles at Reptile Gardens would see to it that the meat no longer existed, either.

The gory, blood-smeared body parts took up two Hefty thirty-gallon trash bags. Camisa was tempted to cut off the head and keep it for a souvenir; very tempted. She could curse Harlan right to his face whenever she felt like it. But that would really be a stupid move, and besides, the head would soon start to stink with rot.

Then she was at Reptile Gardens, wearing clean clothes, lugging the second and heaviest Hefty bag along the shadowed walk. Her scabbed and still

FLESH AND BLOOD

painfully sore fingertips were bleeding again, making the green plastic slick and even more difficult to hold on to.

She'd not seen one sign of a security guard, but that didn't surprise her. Night guards were notorious for sleeping on the job. Pulling the bag up to the crocodile pit, she hoisted it with great effort upon the top of the wall, uncinched the end, and dumped out Harlan's torso, head, and arms. At once she heard the rough slithering of a dozen or more scaly bellies on the concrete below, which was quickly followed by the sounds of tearing and chewing. This time she didn't watch; she was in a hurry to get back home and hose down the garage. She didn't think there was a square inch of wall or floor space that didn't have some of Harlan's blood on it.

She turned to head back for the secret entrance, but had taken only a few steps when she froze in her tracks, eyes widening with fright.

The walkway, the grass, the wire front of the bird sanctuary, the fence, the wall of the alligator pit, and the overhead utility cables were thick with huge black birds. They were crows, and she'd never in her life seen so many gathered together. Their presence in such massive numbers was ominous to say the least, and there was no way she could get by them. Except for an occasional fluttering of wings, they were preternaturally silent.

Feeling her heart pounding against her rib cage, Camisa wondered where the hell they had come from, what they were doing here, why they were staring at her with countless glowing yellow eyes like a congregation of vultures.

Then one of them perched on the utility cable directly above her suddenly took flight, made a U-turn in midair and dived straight down at her like a guided missile, issuing a battle cry that stirred all the others into action. The next thing she knew, they were all flying at her, pecking her with their sharp beaks, claws getting caught in her hair, raking at her face. She screamed at the top of her lungs as she tried in vain to protect herself, but the guard was asleep and didn't hear.

Her scream was cut off when one flew into her mouth. She reflexively bit down hard, severing the bird's neck. A rancid taste filled her mouth as she spat out the head, its yellow beak opening and closing spasmodically on the ground between her feet. Wildly batting against the other relentless bombardiers with her fists, she drew breath for another scream when a crow atop her head craned its neck downward and plucked out her right eyeball.

It was then that Camisa jerked herself awake and bolted upright in bed, her skin damp with cold sweat, her breath coming in fast and shallow gasps. The nightmare had seemed so real, she had to feel her right eyelid to make sure the eyeball was still there. Finding that it was, she began to breathe more normally, and as she gathered her composure, she looked down and noted the dried blood caked under her fingernails. Up until the appearance of the crows, the nightmare *had* been real. She'd sure enough killed that lying bastard Harlan with his Echo chain saw, then cut up his body and taken it to Reptile Gardens, where she'd fed it to the alligators and crocodiles. And she wasn't a bit sorry, either; he'd never been anything but a ball and chain. So, two down, two to go.

The house was totally quiet. Maybe it was three down, one to go. She climbed out of bed and crept to the room directly across the hall. The door was open. Stepping inside, she studied Michael's still, prone form. He'd kicked away his covers. His pajama bottoms, which was all he wore, were twisted around. At first she thought he was dead, but then he took a hitching breath and rolled over.

Seeing that he'd survived through the night, Camisa thought it would be safe to assume he was going to be all right, which was truly a miracle considering that

FLESH AND BLOOD

the rest of her life was being governed by Murphy's Law. But not for long. Her life as Camisa Collins was moving toward a swift end.

Moving down the hall quietly so she wouldn't waken Felicia, Camisa went to the kitchen and removed the telephone book from the top of the refrigerator. Sitting down at the table she'd righted after hosing down the garage last night, she began thumbing through the residence section looking for a listing for George Gaston. When she found it, another dose of adrenaline flooded her bloodstream, making her heart pound.

She stared at the name, address, and number for what seemed to her a long time, her mind filling with questions that only this man George Gaston, her real father, could answer. But she wasn't so sure she wanted any answers—what difference would knowledge of the past make now? She really only wanted him to take in his grandchildren, Michael and Felicia, so she could go live in her house by the sea, completely submerged in her other identity.

After memorizing the number, she closed the directory and timidly approached the telephone, which was still smeared with Harlan's blood; a little detail she'd overlooked. What the hell was she going to say? No matter what she said, he was in for a real shock.

She picked up the receiver and pushed the correct series of digits with the knuckle of her right index finger, feeling her hands become suddenly sweaty as the other line began to ring. A variety of opening lines skittered across her mind. Guess who this is, *Dad!* . . . Are you sitting down? I think you'd better, because you're about to be hit by quite a *blast* from the *past!* . . . Does the name *Camisa* mean anything to you, Mr. George Gaston?

On the third ring, a woman's voice answered.

Totally thrown off by this, Camisa quickly hung up. A few seconds later, Felicia began to whimper from the nursery.

13

Six o'clock found Deidi Marshall and Judson Hendricks sitting covertly in his borrowed car about half a block from the Merry Mermaid massage parlor. Hendricks's own car had still not been found, and he was pretty sure it never would be. Undoubtedly those three scumbags had driven it straight to a professional chop shop.

With Deidi tagging along faithfully if not cheerfully, Hendricks had spent the day checking out boardinghouses, motels, and apartment complexes in hopes of locating his prime suspect, "Starla," just in case she decided not to show up at the massage parlor tonight. It wouldn't surprise him in the least to find out that one of her fellow "mermaids" had lied to him about not knowing where she lived, and had rushed right over there to warn her. But his intensive search had been in vain, so he had no choice but to sit and wait and hope like hell she showed. His captain was beginning to breath down his neck on this.

Deidi was also quietly watching the sidewalk in front of the massage parlor, her face serene, but internally she was having a royal spaz worrying that Kurt had driven down as he had threatened. At least fifty times now her mind had conjured an image of

FLESH AND BLOOD

him breaking into her apartment—at the cost of his face and his life. And since her imagination was prone to extremes, in it Hughman then escaped the apartment to go on a city-wide killing spree, concentrating mostly on bent old ladies and small children, since they were the easiest to catch.

"This your first stakeout?" Hendricks asked her, still keeping his eyes glued to the front of the massage parlor. Two bearded men with the brawn and dirtiness of dockworkers were standing outside it, apparently checking their cash supply.

Grateful for the distraction from her horrible daydream, Deidi shook her head. "No, this is my third, actually, but my first with a cop. Remember the infamous Mayor Sebastian Ludwig? It was yours truly who got the goods on him, and I did it by practically living in my car for a solid week. I had so little food and sleep those days that I almost checked into the hospital when it was over, although I looked like I belonged in the morgue. But it was worth it. At least to my fat-ass boss it was." She reached into her purse for a cigarette, discovering to her dismay that she'd already smoked the last one without knowing it.

Hendricks tore his gaze from the two burly men who were still counting their money to look at her appreciatively. "I'm impressed. I'd always suspected that guy was a snake, but I never gave any thought to actually investigating him. Were you surprised to find out about the drugs, or was that why you were dogging him in the first place?"

"The drugs were a complete surprise," Deidi admitted. "Originally I was checking out a rumor that he was taking kickbacks from one of the city contractors in the form of thrice-weekly visits from his twelve-year-old daughter—which turned out to be false. But what the hey. We got our money's worth."

The two men standing outside the massage parlor finally went inside. Hendricks and Deidi continued talking as they kept their vigil, sharing their on-the-job war stories. When there were no more of those to tell, they moved on to exchange information about their personal lives. Hendricks talked at length about his marriage and divorce, glancing often at his watch, thinking five minutes had passed, finding instead that it was more like ten or fifteen. Time was flying; it was now almost seven o'clock, and he felt tension creeping back into his muscles. Starla was due to appear on the scene any second now. There was a rear door, but Madame Melanie had assured him it was used only for emergencies, for instance, irate wives storming in through the front demanding to know if their husbands were there.

Deciding that she'd rather not go into her disastrous past relationships with men, Deidi steered the conversation back to the matter at hand. "Do you plan to slap the cuffs on her and ask questions down at the station later?"

Tapping the steering wheel nervously with the band of his wristwatch, Hendricks made a face and shrugged. "Oh, I might give the murdering little psychotic a chance to talk first, if she wants to after she's been Mirandized. Then I'll slap on the cuffs, tight as they'll go, and on the way to the station we can do a brake check on the expressway. Wait, that won't work. We'd need a car with a cage."

Deidi quickly got the picture: Thrown forward from the backseat, the handcuffed Starla has a face-on collision with the sturdy wire mesh, receiving a long-lasting waffle imprint on one of her cheeks, either that or a squashed nose. "That's really sick," she said to Hendricks in a reproving tone, although her sincerity was betrayed by a slightly lifted corner of her mouth.

"Yeah, but it's fun."

"And besides, it only happens to the prisoners who really deserve it, right?"

"Oh, of course. Some of them get back there and think they can just spit away, or call us dirty names or say disgusting things about our mothers. You'd be

FLESH AND BLOOD

surprised at how fast a brake check improves their attitude. Or a screen test, as it's sometimes called."

Deidi laughed, and then her breath caught so that she almost choked. "That's got to be her," she said, her eyes fastened on the passenger-side rearview mirror. A woman framed in it was striding purposefully up the sidewalk against which they were parked, her stiletto heels clicking smartly on the pavement, a smoldering cigarette dangling from the side of her ruby lips. Besides the stilettos, she was wearing a lightweight ivory overcoat which was fully buttoned. A small beaded purse swung from her right shoulder. She was looking straight at the car in which they were sitting.

Deidi was amazed at how much the woman resembled her; they could have been sisters. Their hair and coloring was exactly the same, and though the overcoat made it difficult to judge, the woman also appeared to be the same height and weight. Even their facial features were similar, except that her own nose was somewhat narrower, her cheekbones a little higher, and the other woman's eyes were deep-set and more widely spaced. But they could have traded lips and not even their parents would have noticed.

"That's her, allright," Hendricks said tersely, looking at the approaching woman in the rearview mirror on the windshield. Taking a deep breath, he added, "Well, let's rock and roll." He jerked up his door handle and out he flew, confronting the woman just as she was about to step off the sidewalk to cross the street. In the mirror, Deidi saw him flash his badge. The woman glared at it with obvious scorn.

"Rock and roll," Deidi repeated under her breath as she got out on her side. Closing the heavy door as unobtrusively as haste would allow, she hurried to join Hendricks and the woman on the sidewalk, all ears.

"Yeah, I'm Starla, so what? Get out of my way, asshole, you're gonna make me late for work."

"If you refuse to answer my questions here and now," Hendricks growled, "then I have no choice but to go ahead and arrest you on suspicion and take you downtown. And my name's not Asshole, by the way, it's Hendricks. You'd better remember that, too; I'm not in a very jolly mood at the moment. Now I want to know where were you last Wednesday and Thursday nights."

Starla gave Deidi a scathing glance as she drew deeply on her cigarette, obviously mistaking her for a plainclothes policewoman. Deidi, eyeing the cigarette longingly, was wondering uneasily if the woman might possibly be a cousin or some other black-sheep relative never mentioned at the family reunions.

"If you must know," the woman spat, blowing her smoke in the detective's face, "I was at the motherfucking hospital those two nights *and* days watching my mother die of colon cancer! And if you don't believe me, just call up those ignorant fuckwad doctors and nurses on the terminal wing and ask them! They'll tell you I didn't leave that room once for fifty-two hours! So *fuck you, asshole,* get your *stupidshit* self out of my *face!*"

Her words certainly had the biting ring of truth, and suddenly Hendricks felt like a total jerk, regardless of the profanities and belligerence being hurled at him. If what she said was true, and his gut told him that it was, then he could give her a little slack without suffering any damage to his ego. In a soft, magnanimous voice, he responded, "I'm sorry to hear about your mother, I know that had to be really rough. But I'm working on two homicide cases, and I'd very much appreciate your cooperation."

Taking one last drag of her cigarette before flicking it into the street, Starla placed one hand on her hip and stared at Hendricks contemptuously. "So what the fuck do you want?"

A cigarette, Deidi pleaded silently.

"You have any ID on you? I believe what you told

me, but I still have to verify the information. You know the system."

Surprisingly, a slight smile appeared on the woman's face. "Yeah, I know the fucking system, all right." Reaching into her small purse, she produced three forms of ID. Glancing at the laminated cards as Hendricks made notes, Deidi saw that Starla's real name was Paulina Raye Little, and she was coming up on her twenty-ninth birthday. Before too many more years, she was going to have to find herself another line of work.

Deidi wasn't very surprised that Hendricks's "hot lead" had led him straight to another dead end. This whole mermaid thing was of the wild hair persuasion in her opinion, based on nothing more solid than the utterances of that stupid parrot. But Tom was certainly going to be disappointed. He'd have to console himself with a couple of lemon meringue or chocolate pies. Maybe a couple of each.

After Paulina Raye Little was permitted to continue on her way, Hendricks and Deidi got back in the Malibu Classic and headed for the police station, where Deidi had left Suzanne's car.

Silence rode with them most of the way, Hendricks brooding about the evening's turn of events, which for him had been a major disappointment. He'd been so sure he'd found Patton and Bagget's killer. Right now he didn't feel like he could find his own ass with both hands and a flashlight. Of course there was still the Mermaid Village Apartments to check out, and the Mermaid Inn (nixing the Little Mermaid daycare center), but in the last half hour enthusiasm for his theory had waned considerably.

A few blocks from the police station, while they were waiting at a red light, he turned to Deidi with a hangdog expression. "You wanna follow me over to the house? I'm grilling steaks for dinner. Big juicy T-bones."

"Sounds tempting," Deidi said, smiling, "but I'll have to pass. I've got—"

"I know, I know," Hendricks sighed, lifting his hand. "You've got to go home and let your dog out before he turns your living room into a lake."

Not to mention an abattoir, unless he's already done so, Deidi thought uncomfortably. "Sorry."

"Can't Suzanne put him on a leash to keep him from running off?"

"Actually, I should spend some time with Suzanne tonight; she's going back to Fort Lauderdale tomorrow and I probably won't see her again for another six months."

Hendricks pulled into the near-empty station lot and parked along the back fence next to Suzanne's red Z. Switching off the engine, he turned sideways in his bucket seat, elbow slung over the back rest. His eyes appeared darker in the waning daylight. "If you'd rather keep this a professional relationship, just say so. It won't hurt my feelings."

Deidi knew that what she would or would rather not do no longer counted. Circumstances dictated that intimacy was required, and in the heart of the man who now so nonchalantly awaited her answer, feelings capable of being hurt had to be cultivated. Wordlessly, she reached over and took his left hand, which was draped over the steering wheel, and guided it to her breast.

"What do you think?"

Needing no further encouragement, he leaned over to give her a lingering kiss, his tongue probing hers sensuously. Deidi felt her breath quicken as unexpected desire began to race like wildfire through her body. Hendricks gently kneaded one breast, then the other, and as his lips trailed down to nuzzle the hollow of her neck, his hand inched its way down between her thighs.

"For God's sake, we're in the parking lot of the

FLESH AND BLOOD

police department, and it's still daylight!" Deidi protested breathlessly.

Hendricks ignored her, continuing to rhythmically pump her crotch with the palm of his hand, his tongue and teeth on her neck sending tingling thrills of pleasure down the length of her body. A minute later Deidi didn't care if they were stopping traffic on the Brooklyn Bridge at high noon.

Reaching for his lap almost shyly, she discovered what might easily have been mistaken for a thick steel pipe capped with a mushroom. A soft moan escaped her throat as lust completely overtook her mind and body. For the last several months, her sexual energy had been channeled into her career, or so she'd thought, but now it seemed much of it had simply been dammed up, and now the dam was breaking. Her body was all but screaming for satisfaction. It didn't matter what she'd always heard about girls or women who did it in cars, that they were cheap sluts. Right now she'd have CHEAP SLUT tattooed on her forehead if only Hendricks would put out the consuming fire between her legs.

Just then he pulled away from her and said, "You're right; this is hardly the time or place. Well, give my regards to Suzanne. Guess I'll see you back here tomorrow morning, if your boss still wants you to shadow me."

Still breathing heavily, Deidi glared at him fiercely. "You shit. You're just getting back at me for passing out on you last night, aren't you? Getting me all hot and bothered, then suddenly it's, Well, thank-you-ma'am, but you don't even get the slam-bam."

Hendricks gazed back at her with genuine surprise. In truth he wasn't just surprised, but even a little shocked by Deidi's explosive response. It wasn't so much what she'd said or the way she had said it, but the look in her eyes that chilled him to the bone. He'd seen that very same look three years ago, in the eyes of a drunken biker who had intended to give him a free appendectomy with a broken glass bottle. It was a look that could damn near kill on its own. He was truly thankful she didn't have a weapon handy, because the demon glaring at him through her eyes guaranteed that she would use it. But surely that was just his paranoid occupational imagination talking. Maybe she'd want to, didn't everybody at one time or another? But like most people, Deidi Marshall had self-control; she was a lady, a very nice lady who obviously couldn't take what she dished out. She'd nearly driven him out of his mind the night before with the things she said and did on the way over to his house. And then what does she do?

"Okay, I confess, that was a childish act of revenge," he said with a tentative smile. His previous suspicion of her tried to resurface, but he quickly pushed it back down. What the hell did a stupid parrot know?

"I'm sorry," he added, looking as contrite as possible, but he could tell that he was appealing to a stone wall.

"You most certainly are," Deidi quipped, reaching for her door handle. Her need for a cigarette had just surpassed her need for sex, and no way was Judson Hendricks going to get a second chance tonight. "Now would you like to apologize?"

He leaned forward in hopes of breaking down the wall with kisses, but Deidi was out of the car before he could get his arms around her. "See you in the morning," she snapped just before slamming the door shut again.

Puffing furiously on a newly purchased cigarette, Deidi turned off North Sunnymeade onto the winding gravel road that would take her home. Her dread mounted as the distance closed. She had no idea what Kurt drove, but she had no doubt that as soon as the house came into view, she'd see an unfamiliar vehicle parked in the lot, and it would have to be Kurt's. But maybe, just maybe, he would be sitting in it, waiting, not foolish enough to break into the apartment.

Though it was a powerless, asinine gesture, Deidi crossed her fingers.

Topping the last rise, her eyes scoured the small lot while she held her breath. Moments later she released it with a light moan of relief. There were no unfamiliar cars to be seen; only those belonging to her and the other tenants. Still an edge of tension hung on. That didn't mean he wasn't in town, maybe grabbing something to eat with the intention of coming by later to see if Suzanne had returned.

After letting Hughman out to do his thing, Deidi climbed wearily onto one of the studded leather counter stools and stared at the telephone. It was drawing close to eight o'clock, and she'd last seen her friend around eleven-thirty the night before. No sign of her since. No indication that she'd come back to the apartment during the day. So there was cause for concern, but it wouldn't be unreasonable for her to wait until bedtime to become truly alarmed. She would call the police then.

Hughman nudged her bare calf with his nose, a plea for affection. Leaning over, Deidi scratched behind his ears. "You know what I feel like doing, boy? Just packing up and running away, getting a new set of IDs made, starting over from scratch. I've got almost eight thousand dollars saved. What do you think?"

Hughman whined softly.

"You're right," Deidi sighed, rubbing under his uplifted chin. "Stupid idea. Well, I'm hungry. How about you?"

He followed her around the counter into the kitchen area, where she first opened a can of his favorite dog food and plopped it into his dish. Then she began making herself a lettuce and cheese sandwich, and while she was spreading the mayonnaise on the bread, she again had the unnerving feeling that someone was watching her every move. The drapes over the sliding door were completely closed, so it simply wasn't possible. Yet the feeling persisted, and Deidi quickly lost her appetite.

Was this place haunted or something? Was Suzanne or Flora Bushbaum looking at her from the spirit world? But neither of them had been dead the first time she'd felt this way. Hands shaking visibly, she removed the new pack of cigarettes from her purse, took one out and lit it, her narrowed eyes exploring the large room suspiciously, except for the brown stain on the ceiling, which was studiously avoided.

For about half a minute the only sound was that of Hughman wolfing down his Alpo. Then Deidi began to hear another, altogether different sound. At first it was very faint and seemed to be coming from inside her head. The sound of a baby crying.

She couldn't stand it, and immediately clamped her hands over her ears, but that did no good; she could still hear the baby's cries, becoming louder and louder until Deidi was certain she was losing her mind, and then all at once it stopped, leaving her in the vacuum of a deafening silence which was broken a few seconds later by an insistent knock on the door.

What is WRONG WRONG WRONG?

Growling softly, Hughman immediately loped toward the door and nosed the drape aside, giving Deidi a glimpse of blue jean and cowboy boot. Kurt, had to be. That damn jerk, she thought, drawing on the misshapen butt of her cigarette. Did he think he had a golden dick or something? From the way Suzanne had described it, sex with Kurt was more like masturbation, only a lot messier. He would just lay there on his back and expect her to do all the work.

Why was that baby crying, Deidi? Why why why?

Tapping her ashes into a nearby crystal tray, she walked rigidly across the living area to join Hughman at the door. Ignoring Kurt was not going to make him go away.

FLESH AND BLOOD

Pulling back the drape, she glared at him through the glass. It had been almost two years since she'd seen him, and in that time he'd put on a lot of weight, which Suzanne had mentioned, now that she thought of it. Most of it had settled around his middle, the result of his love affair with beer.

"Get lost, Kurt. Suzanne's not here."

"Don't give me that bullshit," he shot back, pounding the glass with his fist. "Her car's parked right over there."

"Yes it is, but she is *not* here. In fact I haven't seen her all day, and frankly I'm beginning to get a little worried, especially since you're around and I know what guys like you are capable of doing."

His face twisting into an ugly snarl, Kurt hit the door again, this time igniting Hughman's temper. He jumped at the glass to his full height, emitting savage snarls. Were the glass to suddenly dissolve, Kurt would have just cause to worry about his vulnerable throat.

He must have realized this, must have realized also how easy it would be for Deidi to slide that door back, which she was already tempted to do, just to scare him. It was so fun to watch egotistical Rambo types fall to pieces and cry like little girls.

But he knew when it was best not to push his luck; he wasn't about to provoke her or the dog any further. Shaking a finger at Deidi, he departed with the words, "You tell her this little game of hers is pissing me off bad! *Real* bad! And the longer she plays it, the sorrier she's gonna be when she loses! That's *when,* not *if!* So if she wants to cut her losses, she'd better get her ass up to the Mermaid Inn tonight, room seventeen."

"Dickhead," Deidi muttered, letting the drape fall back into place. Hughman's snarls mellowed to a simmering growl that gradually died on the way back to his unfinished dinner.

Deidi finished her cigarette, then stretched out on the couch to watch some television, desperate to keep herself from thinking. Halfway through the first program, she drifted into a fitful sleep filled with unspeakable nightmares. In one of them she went to the Mermaid Inn, to Room 17, with a steak knife concealed behind her purse.

The green metal door opened about a foot and Kurt looked out with a cigarette hanging out of his mouth. He squinted at her through a spiral of smoke for several moments, the expression on his face indicating that he couldn't decide whether to slam the door in her face or let her in. Finally he stepped back, pulling the door with him, and left it standing open while he crossed to the desk to flick his cigarette over a full ashtray. He was wearing only a towel, his clothes lying crumpled on the foot of the bed. She would have assumed he had just come out of the shower, but his hair wasn't wet. She'd caught him right before he got in, apparently.

The only light in the room was coming from the television set, its volume turned low. Closing the door behind her, she caught a glimpse of actress Glenn Close on the screen. *Fatal Attraction.*

Squeezing the knife handle, she stepped closer to him, noting the rigid muscles in his back. There would be no playing around this time. Too dangerous.

"So what did Suzanne tell you to say?" he asked tersely without turning around, and she raised the knife, thrusting the entire length of the blade into the side of his throat as she answered between clenched teeth, *"She said to tell you it's* over, *asshole!"*

After she was finished with him, she took a leisurely shower to wash his blood from her hands, face, and hair. There was quite a lot of it, for Kurt, now lying stretched out on the floor beside the bed, no longer resembled anything even remotely human.

14

On Tuesday afternoon, after much internal debate, Camisa finally decided to forget about making the phone call, thinking it would be best to just take the kids over there without warning. Seeing them and knowing they were his grandchildren, his own flesh and blood, how could her father refuse to take them into his home, especially after she made it clear that she no longer wished to be burdened with them, that they had no one else and nowhere left to go? Just as he'd no longer wished to be burdened with her once upon a time. He should be feeling plenty guilty about that by now, his soul desperately searching for some way to atone. And he couldn't ask for a better way than accepting responsibility for Michael and Felicia.

Her mind made up, she got them dressed in clean clothes and packed a few of their things in a small overnight case. The back of Michael's head was still terribly swollen and he continued to complain of a headache, so before they left she gave him twice the amount of aspirin prescribed on the label, tossing the plastic bottle in the case with their personal effects.

"Where are we doe-ing, Mommy?" he asked her as she pulled him down the hallway from his bedroom.

Unable to match her pace, he kept tripping over his own feet, but her firm grip on his upper arm kept him from falling.

"You and Felicia are going to go stay with your grandpa for a while. Not Grandpa Foree, 'cause he's dead, and not Grandpa Joe, but one you've never met whose name is Grandpa George. Can you say that, Grandpa George?"

Michael gave it a shot. "Gampa Dorge."

"Close enough," Camisa sighed. "When you see him, I want you to say, 'I love you, Grampa George.'"

"I yuv you, Gampa Dorge."

When she opened the front door to leave, Michael looked around behind them with a finger buried deep in his mouth. "Where Daddy go?"

"He went to look for Aaron," Camisa said tersely, saddling Felicia on her hip before yanking Michael's hand away from his face. She supposed it would be foolish to hope that all their bad habits would stay hidden until she was safely gone from Grandpa George's house, so she wasted no breath on any lectures.

The neighborhood in which George Gaston lived was fairly close to the downtown area. At one time it had been inhabited by the upper echelon, the doctors and lawyers and wealthy business owners. The houses were large and varied dramatically in design, conspicuously unlike the middleclass neighborhoods where most of the houses looked exactly alike except for the color of the clapboard.

But long ago the rich builders of these grand old houses had moved on to even greener pastures, the bigger, better, and more modern houses of the SunCrest addition. The present owners had nothing much to brag about.

The house bearing the address listed in the phone directory was at the end of the block, an impressive gray stone house with turrets that reminded her of a medieval castle. One thing was certain: her father wouldn't be able to plead poverty as an excuse for not taking Michael and Felicia.

A circle drive cut across the lush green lawn; Camisa pulled into it, suddenly ashamed of her junky car in comparison to the surrounding grandeur, faded as it was. Then she reminded herself that it, too, would be left behind; everything she'd ever wanted was waiting for her, including a nice sports car.

Staring at the red front door of her father's house, she felt her pulse begin to race. This will be a scene worthy of recording, she thought, assuming her father was at home. What the hell was she going to do if he wasn't? Try to foist the kids on to his present wife, who may not even know he had given up a daughter? She hadn't the faintest idea, but that wasn't going to keep her from knocking on that red door.

"We're here," she announced to Michael as she switched off the ignition. He stared apprehensively at the stone house through the dusty windshield while Camisa removed Felicia from her car seat. Pulling in a deep breath of courage, Camisa opened the driver's door and grabbed the handle of the overnight case loaded with their things. "All right Michael, let's go."

"I don't yike dis house," he announced with a protruding lower lip.

"This is a very nice house, Michael, a lot better than ours," Camisa growled at him. "Now come with me and don't make a fuss, or I'll crack your head some more!"

Sniffling, looking on the verge of a major crying fit, Michael reluctantly obeyed, scooting inch by inch across the seat to the open door. As soon as he was within range, Camisa snatched him out of the car by his shirt collar and dumped him on the concrete drive, resulting in a skinned knee. The dammed tears began to flow, accompanied by a loud undulating wail.

Camisa glared down at him. "You little shit!" she hissed, slamming the car door closed. "Quit being such a fucking crybaby, you hear me? Shut the fuck up right now, or I'll really give you something to cry about!"

Michael had heard this very same threat before, and knew that it wasn't idle. He silenced himself as much as he could very quickly, and under his mother's smoldering gaze, picked himself up. At that same moment the red door was opened by a middle-aged woman.

Hearing the door's hinges creak, Camisa turned around. The woman had bluish-gray hair and wore a plain black dress with matching pumps. A single strand of pearls encircled her wattled neck, and there was far too much blush on her cadaverous cheeks. Her eyes were a piercing cornflower blue, and they were taking in the sight on her circle drive with a mixture of curiosity and disdain.

"I believe you have the wrong house," she said to Camisa with the obviously put-on smile of a socialite. To further enhance her aristocratic demeanor, her voice carried a faint British accent.

The thoughts that went through Camisa's mind just then would have given the refined old candy-ass a coronary, and it was all Camisa could do to keep from saying them aloud so she could watch it happen. But that would hardly serve her purpose. So instead she pasted on a false smile of her own and said sweetly, "Oh, I don't think so."

The woman took another glance at Camisa's beat-up Chrysler, then at the two children, Felicia straddling Camisa's left hip and playing with her drool, Michael hiding behind her legs, still sniffling with a finger crammed halfway down his throat, the overnight case dangling from Camisa's left hand.

"This is the Gaston residence," the woman announced in a reproving tone as she stepped guardingly onto the front porch, leaving the red door standing open behind her.

Bending to grab hold of Michael's free hand, Camisa began walking toward the front porch where

FLESH AND BLOOD

the woman was now wringing her hands and glancing around nervously at the neighboring houses, as if afraid this little scene was being observed.

Get ready, you blue-blooded bitch, Camisa thought at the woman as their eyes locked again at a much closer distance. Here comes a ton of bricks. "George Gaston is my father."

The woman's cornflower-blue eyes widened in surprise or shock for an instant, then quickly narrowed into slits of anger. "I don't know what you're trying to pull here, miss, but if you don't get off this property in one minute, I'm going inside to call the police."

During the drive over here, Camisa had envisioned many possible scenerios, and this came very close to matching one of them. It was really no surprise that the new Mrs. George Gaston knew nothing of the daughter he'd put up for adoption twenty-three years ago. But a seedling of doubt suddenly sprang up, a base she hadn't covered. What if this was the wrong George Gaston? There was only one listed in the directory, but there could be another who had an unlisted number. And who was to say he even lived in Danville? He could live in Toledo, Ohio, or Bumfuck, Egypt, for all she knew.

Felicia was getting heavy. Transferring her to the other hip, Camisa sighed. "I'm not trying to pull anything, Mrs. Gaston. My name is Camisa Collins, and I found out last week that I was adopted out at the age of four. I also found out that my real father's name is George Gaston, and there's only one listing in the phone book, which gives your address. Maybe if I could just speak to Mr. Gaston for a few minutes? Is he here?"

"He's here, but you're wasting your time," the woman snapped. "My husband has never been married to anyone else, and he certainly never had any children except by me."

"So how old was he when you married him?" Camisa asked insistently, not yet ready to accept defeat. This had to be the right George Gaston, and he had to by-God take these kids off her hands, because otherwise she'd be forced to fatten the alligators at Reptile Gardens with their soft little bodies, and she'd really rather not.

Pointing a shaky arthritic finger at Camisa, the woman backed toward her door. "I don't believe that's any of your business, and I want you and that pile of junk you're driving off my property right now. If you're not gone in one minute, I'm going to call the police."

"Let her come in," a tired male voice spoke up from the other side of the red door. Camisa couldn't see the man who had spoken, but knew instinctively that the voice belonged to George Gaston, *her* George Gaston, her natural father. He'd been eavesdropping, and he was apparently willing to own up to his past, even if doing so cost him his second marriage.

His wife spun around, wearing a shocked expression. "George! Don't tell me she's told the truth!"

A few minutes later, when they were uncomfortably settled in a formal parlor stuffed with stiff pink and burgundy Victorian furniture, George Gaston confessed to his wife that he had indeed been married once before, and yes, Camisa was his daughter from that marriage, which had ended in his wife's suicide.

His present wife, Priscilla, was obviously devastated by this news. Her pale wrinkled skin paled even more, to make the blush on her cheeks stand out freakishly. Pressing a hand webbed with large blue veins and tipped with long red talons over her heart, she whispered harshly, "George, my God, I can't believe you would keep something like that from me. I suddenly feel as if I don't know you at all."

George's shoulders sagged, and right before Camisa's eyes he aged about twenty years. She remembered the vision she'd had that day in the nursery, of him tossing her playfully into the air. He basically had the same face, but what had been fat

FLESH AND BLOOD

then was now sagging flab. He'd lost a lot of weight, but not before his skin had lost its elasticity.

Looking wistfully at Michael, who was quietly sitting cross-legged at Camisa's feet, he said in a strangely hollow voice, "I take it you're my grandson. What's your name, boy?"

"His name is Michael," Camisa answered for him, "and this is your granddaughter Felicia." Held around the middle, the toddler was bounced gently on Camisa's knees for a brief horsey ride.

Sinking farther into her overstuffed burgundy chair, Priscilla moaned.

"Why did you come, Camisa?" George's large brown eyes lifted to meet his daughter's, though it clearly wasn't easy for him. "For answers, I suppose. But I promise you, you really don't want them. Let well enough alone. I can give you a little money"—at this Priscilla Gaston shot him a murderous look—"but please don't ask me to explain. And I'm sorry to have to ask you this, but I think it would be better for everyone concerned if you didn't come back."

Camisa's eyes narrowed in hatred. "I had no intention of coming back anyway, and I'm not here to ask for answers or money, although any of either of those you'd care to hand out wouldn't be rejected, *Dad*. What I want is for you to take Michael and Felicia. Some heavy-duty shinola's been hitting my fan, and I'm about one step away from a total nervous breakdown. And I've got no one else to turn to. My adopted family's kicked me out. So where else can I turn but to my own flesh and blood?"

Hearing this, Priscilla made a miraculously swift recovery from her shock. Springing forward in her chair, hands firmly gripping the armrests, she turned blazing eyes on Camisa. "Oh no, you don't. We're not taking in these two ragamuffins of yours. Over my dead body!"

Which could easily be arranged, Camisa thought with a petulant smile. Nudging Michael with her feet, she said in a syrupy voice, "Go over and give your grandpa George a kiss, Michael."

Priscilla's head swiveled to level her glare at her husband. "Surely you're not going to permit this! If you do, George, so help me God I will throw you out, and you won't get a red cent from me! Not one red cent!"

So this was all hers. Camisa's smile immediately drooped, then became a thin line of anger. Damn it, why did everything always have to go wrong, turn to a stinking pile of shit in her hands?

Obeying his mother's command, Michael timidly approached the strange man, who was looking back at him lovingly, but there was something mixed in with the sweetness, something very bitter that he'd never seen in the eyes of his other two grandfathers.

"You had another grandson," Camisa said coldly as George gathered Michael into his outstretched arms. She didn't know why she was telling him this, except maybe to inject something between him and his wife's ultimatum. If he was forced to give an answer, Camisa knew exactly which way the chips would fall. King George wasn't about to give up his castle, though he probably wouldn't mind shucking the ball-busting Queen.

Camisa cleared her throat and continued, "His name was Aaron. He drowned Saturday, five years old. His body was lost in the sea. But the police suspect me of foul play."

"These children are not moving in with us, George!" Priscilla spouted, smacking the armrests with her palms. "I will absolutely not have it, do you hear me?"

George hung his head and nodded sorrowfully. "I read about the incident in the newspaper. I'm very sorry, Camisa, very sorry, but there's nothing I can do except help you a little financially. I do have some money of my own," he said, pointedly directing this last statement at his firebreathing wife. Then an odd

FLESH AND BLOOD

expression crossed his face and he looked back down at Michael, who was standing between George's parted knees. Michael winced as the fingers of George's right hand again explored the back of his head.

"For God's sake, Camisa, the back of Michael's head is swollen out a good inch! I'm no physician, but I'd say that's got to be the result of a skull fracture! Were you aware of this?"

Camisa opened her mouth to say no, but decided to tell the truth instead. It would prove to them how unfit she was to be a mother, how much her poor little ragamuffins needed their responsible care. "Yes, he did it falling off a chair in the kitchen. I figured it was a skull fracture, too."

"Well, what did his doctor say?"

"I didn't see any point in taking him to a doctor. I mean, it's not like they can superglue his skull back together."

Her father looked stricken. "Don't you know skull fractures can be fatal? You should have put him in the hospital at once!"

"I think I've had about enough of this," Priscilla said, rising from her chair to stand rigid and straight-backed with both hands on her hips. "George, I'm going up to my room, and when I return, I expect to find these people gone. Then you and I are going to have a little talk."

"Yes, dear," George replied, giving the classic pussy-whipped response.

Priscilla stalked archly from the room, trailed by the scent of her exotic French perfume. Camisa toyed with Felicia's soft brown ringlets, imagining them dripping blood as her little head was crushed between tremendously powerful jaws and long jagged teeth. It would be Priscilla's fault, really.

For some time George sat silently on one end of a pink settee, leaning forward with his arms around Michael, his gaze cloudy and unfocused. His mind had taken him back in time, back to the years that still haunted him in nightmares. The memories flooded him with fear for Michael and Felicia.

"Being suspected by the police isn't all that's bothering me," Camisa said at last, when the silence became too oppressive. "Something really bizarre is happening to me psychologically. I think I've got a split personality."

Her father's eyes moved up and focused on her face, but he said nothing.

"Can't I leave the kids here for a little while? Just a week or two until I can get my shit together? This is a big house, I know you've got plenty of room. And the kids are really good. You'd hardly hear a peep out of them. Priscilla wouldn't even have to know."

George remained silent, but he was doing a lot of thinking. At the moment he was recalling the police composite he'd recently seen in the newspaper and the local television news, of a woman suspected of committing two homicides in the area.

A sick feeling stirring deep in his gut told him that he was looking at that woman right now, and had just heard her say she thought she had a split personality. Of that he had no doubt whatsoever, and he also knew that this other "personality" of hers was capable of unspeakable violence.

"I'll have to give that a little thought," he said carefully as he rose to his feet. "Excuse me, I need to use the rest room. Can I bring you anything to drink? Would the children like some cookies?"

Camisa shrugged. "Whatever."

When he had quietly disappeared down a dim marble hallway, Camisa put Felicia down on the thickly padded white pile carpet and reached for her purse, from which she removed a lighter and the pack of Virginia Slims she'd bought on the way. There were no ashtrays in evidence, and Camisa thought that Priscilla would probably have a cow if she came down

FLESH AND BLOOD

and smelled cigarette smoke, but she didn't care. There was a porcelain figurine of three bluebirds clinging to a gold birdbath handy for use as an ashtray, and if Felicia behaved normally, there would be more than cigarette smoke to smell.

George returned about five minutes later with a serving tray. On it were cups of milk and oatmeal-raisin cookies for Michael and Felicia, and a glass of iced tea for Camisa. He looked disapprovingly at her smoldering cigarette, but said nothing. Setting the tray down on a highly glossed coffee table, he returned to his place on the settee. Camisa noticed that his skin seemed very shiny, as if he'd stepped into a sauna while he was gone, and his hands were trembling. But she didn't think too much about it. If he was planning to pull a fast one on the Ice Queen, she supposed he had good reason to be nervous, not knowing that the fast one was being pulled on her. While in the kitchen, George had called the police.

"Camisa," he said gravely, "there's something I think you should know."

Until she had to get ready for her appointment with Dr. Jordan, Deidi spent most of Tuesday in bed. She'd called Tom the night before and told him she was near collapse, which was true, but he'd only agreed to give her the day off when she informed him that the stakeout had been a washout, and the killer's trail was now colder than the abominable snowman's prick.

As she showered and washed her hair, she kept wondering why Kurt hadn't returned to pester her some more about Suzanne. She'd slept off and on, but surely she would have wakened if the shithead had pounded on her door. It just didn't seem plausible that he would give up so easily, but maybe the sight of Hughman's impressive incisors had finally fostered some wisdom in Kurt's little chauvinistic brain. Deidi wanted to believe that, had to believe it because otherwise she had to face the possibility that her dream about stabbing him to death—to a bloody pulp—had in fact been reality.

Assuming for torture's sake that it was, it would be easy enough to confirm. All she'd have to do is call the Mermaid Inn. Checkout time was hours ago; the body would have been found by now. But after she was dressed with her makeup carefully applied and her hair blow-dried, she only threw the telephone a furtive glance before leaving. Hughman, who had very much liked having her around all day, whined softly when she closed the glass door between them.

As always, Dr. Jordan seemed happy to see her, and as he ushered her to the contoured couch, did his best to put her at ease. "Now Deidi, I want you to remember that you are completely safe here; nothing bad is going to happen to you. Whatever's lurking hidden in your past is undoubtedly very ugly to you, but this time you are going to look at it, you're going to take that bull right by the horns, and you're going to handle it just fine."

Acknowledging his optimistic words with a skeptical grunt, Deidi stretched out and closed her eyes, adjusting her body until she was comfortable. She then took several deep breaths and let them out slowly, knowing that was the first thing he would ask her to do.

After taking his own place and leaning over to start the reel-to-reel tape recorder, Jordan began the lilting rote that would soon put Deidi deep into a hypnotic state. It took a little over five minutes, and after a brief pause, Jordan began the regression, starting her at age seven but moving her quickly along down to six and then five, stopping at four.

"You are now four, Deidi, four years old. Look around you and tell me what you see. Don't be afraid; I want you to remain calm and relaxed. There is nothing to fear, nothing will harm you in any way. The truth will only set you free."

It was raining, the sky filled with dark, gloomy clouds. Dressed in a sleeveless pink cotton jumper, her fifth birthday only a couple of months away, Deidi was standing out on the screened back porch watching the raindrops dance on the glistening grass. Now and then a persistent robin swooped down to tug on a stubborn earthworm.

To the left of the wooden porch steps was a small patch of broken dirt. Frowning, Deidi forced herself look at it, at the little cross made of popsicle sticks that marked it as a grave. Mittens had been run over by a car and killed, her mother said. He was dead, and that meant he had to be buried in the ground.

Deidi didn't understand the concept of death at all. Staring at the patch of sodden dirt, she thought Mittens must be very unhappy being buried like that. He liked to jump around and play, and chase strings. He liked to lap warm milk and climb trees with his sharp claws, to stalk birds.

"I see where Mama buried Mittens," Deidi mumbled languidly to Dr. Jordan.

"Mittens was your pet?"

Deidi nodded. "Kitty cat. Black with white paws," she answered in a little girl's voice, and went on in the same voice to describe the rest of the scene as it unfolded.

Surreptitiously she opened the screen door and stepped down from the enclosed porch to the wet green grass, her expression full of pity. Poor Mittens. Buried so deep in the ground, how could he even breathe? But Mama had decreed that the grave would be left alone. Death was final, irreversible. Whatever that meant.

Standing away from the porch in the warm rain she was soon soaked to the skin, but she felt no concern for herself, only her dead cat. Then suddenly a voice

D. A. Fowler

spoke to her through the porch screen, startling her. Deidi looked up.

"Who is it, Deidi?" Jordan prodded, seeing the distress and confusion on her face.

"I don't understand. It's me," she whimpered. "I'm looking at me. I'm in two places at once, but that can't happen."

"Don't get excited," the psychologist soothed. "Calm down, just relax, and let's talk about this. Could it be your twin, Deidi? Is it possible you have a twin sister?"

"Go ahead and dig him up," her double on the porch sneered. "I know you want to. I dare you. I double dare you!"

A loud roll of thunder rumbled across the sky as Deidi looked back down at the grave. Though the rain was warm, she found herself shivering.

"I dare you," the girl with her face and hair repeated tauntingly, and a jolting revelation immediately flashed through Deidi's brain. The girl was her sister. Her identical twin. Something bad must have happened to her at some point, something final and irreversible. But that still didn't explain why she'd never been mentioned by her parents even once in all the years she was growing up.

Down on her knees she went, ignoring Dr. Jordan's gentle inquiries. She'd been double-dared to dig Mittens up, so that was exactly what she was going to do. Her sister giggled at her for getting so much mud on her jumpsuit, predicting that when their mother saw it, she would throw the biggest hissy-fit Deidi ever saw.

With her fingers bared into claws, Deidi began to rake at the rainsoaked earth, pulling up large clumps and tossing them aside, knocking down the popsicle-stick cross she'd made, all the while encouraged by her sister to keep going, keep digging, Mittens was down there somewhere.

Finally, about six inches down, Deidi uncovered a

patch of muddy black fur. She poked it with her dirty fingertips, but Mittens didn't move. Only the worms were moving in the hole she'd dug, several partially exposed brown earthworms and quite a few small white ones.

"Well, pull him out," her sister hissed.

At that moment another significant revelation surged to the brink of Deidi's conscious mind, but receded before she could grasp it. She wanted to scream, because she knew it had been important, something she really needed to know.

"Calm down, Deidi, calm down. Take a deep breath for me. Come on, deep, deep breath. That's it. Everything's just fine, you're doing great. Tell me what's happening now. What's going on, Deidi?"

She told him, "I'm pulling Mittens out of his grave."

His body was curled and stiff, and her eyes bulged in horror when she saw a tangle of worm-infested guts hanging from a split in his side. The smell hit her a second later, the worst smell she'd ever known, and it almost made her puke. But she certainly saw the light; dead things had to be buried in the ground because they stunk worse than skunks. She immediately hurled the stiff carcass back into the muddy hole.

Watching through the porch screen, her twin snickered, then abruptly turned her head toward the kitchen door and said, "Uh-oh." Giving Deidi one last glance, she ducked below the screen and hid. A few seconds later the kitchen door opened and a woman strode out on the porch.

Deidi felt her heart lurch into a gallop as knowledge hit her in the head with sledgehammer force. It was the same woman she'd seen at the front door with a baby in her arms when the mother of the boy they'd bitten went to tell on them. The woman she'd glimpsed in Grammy's casket. She was her real mother, their mother. Not Hannah Marshall, whom Deidi had called Mother all these years. This woman's name was Arlene, and when she saw what Deidi had done, her features instantly formed an expression of anger and disgust.

Flinging open the screen door, she stomped down the steps and, with her hands on her hips, approached the spot where Deidi was kneeling. Glaring down at Deidi's frightened, upturned face, she bellowed, "What in God's name is *wrong* with you? Didn't I tell you to leave that grave alone? Don't tell me you wanted to play with your dead cat! I can't believe you did this! What are you, some kind of ghoul?"

Thrashing her head back and forth on the contoured couch, Deidi began to sob. "Something's wrong with me, Mama said so, but I don't know what it is. I just know it's something *bad!*"

"It's all right," Dr. Jordan soothed. "Everyone's got a dark side, Deidi, it's nothing to be ashamed of. It's just part of being human. It doesn't mean you're evil or bad. Relax, now, take it easy. Breathe deeply, you're making a lot of progress."

It took a little while, but Deidi finally calmed down enough to proceed. Dr. Jordan instructed her to seek out those memories that troubled her most; she was strong enough to face them now.

Suddenly it was dark. At first she thought it was still the middle of the night, but the lighted digits on her Mickey Mouse clock told her it was just before dawn. A noise in some other part of the house had wakened her, but she couldn't remember what it had been.

She closed her eyes to go back to sleep when she heard it again; a muffled cry. She sat up, listening intently. The sound didn't come again, but she was pretty sure it had been made by her baby brother, Eric.

Curious now, she slipped out of bed and crept down the narrow hallway, which was softly illumined by an orange night-light. The door to the nursery was ajar, and she stuck her head in to see if he was waking up, hungry for his bottle. But the nursery was also aglow with orange light, and she could tell that Eric wasn't in his crib.

Thinking that her mother must have taken him to the kitchen, Deidi headed in that direction, acutely aware of the predawn silence. It occurred to her that some amount of noise should accompany the fixing of Eric's bottle, and its absence began to fill her with apprehension.

"No," she croaked aloud, a disturbed look covering her face like a storm cloud. "I don't want to go in there."

"In where, Deidi?" Jordan prodded.

"The kitchen. Don't make me go in there, no. I can't."

"Yes you can. It's only a memory now. Go on, Deidi, it's perfectly safe. Remember, I'm with you every step of the way. Nothing's going to harm you."

The kitchen was not only silent but dark. Standing on wavering knees in the adjoining dining room, she told herself firmly to hurry back to bed and pull the covers up over her head until this terrible day was over. But her feet, with a mind of their own, carried her slowly forward.

When she reached the archway, hugging herself, she was greeted by an unexpected wave of warmth. By then her eyes had grown accustomed to the dark and she could make out two shadowy figures on the floor. The larger of the two sat cross-legged, the smaller one squirming in the hollow between the larger one's legs. The smaller figure was Eric, and something had been stuffed into his mouth to keep him quiet.

The heat was coming from the oven.

Deidi felt her mind totter on the brink of disintegration. "Oh God," she moaned, reaching up to grab two fistfuls of her hair. "Oh God, oh God, no, *no!*"

"What is it, Deidi? Tell me."

Her twin rose gracefully to her feet, leaving Eric on the floor. "You know, everything was great till Eric came along. You hate him, too, don't you? 'Course you do. Well, I'm sick of him getting all the attention."

Deidi stared open-mouthed at their baby brother on the floor, her heart beating as fast as a captured bird's. "You can't—can't—"

"Why not? They won't know which one of us did it, so I won't get in any trouble."

Which one, which one of us did it. Deidi's mind began spinning like a catherine wheel, casting off hideous memories: Eric with his diaper pins undone so they would stick him when he crawled, Eric imprisoned behind the collapsed bars of his crib with shaving cream all over his face, Tabasco sauce in Eric's apple sauce. *Which one of you did this? I want to know THIS INSTANT!*

Which one? Deidi looked around and saw that she was surrounded by look-alikes. The kitchen was full of twin sisters, all of them looking at her with dark, hateful eyes.

The one who had encouraged her to dig up Mittens bent down and picked Eric up by his feet. The dishrag fell out of his mouth, and at once the silence was broken by his terrified cries. Deidi clamped her hands over her ears, unable to bear the sound, but still it came through, searing her brain, her soul. Her evil twin quickly stuffed the rag back in, and a few of the others helped her open the oven door. A blast of intense heat rolled out with a malodorous cloud of gray smoke, bringing malevolent smiles to all the identical faces.

"No, don't! Please don't!" Deidi fought to save the baby, but was held back by the throng of mirror images, which in truth was only Dr. Jordan trying to keep her from hurting herself.

An agonized scream burst from her lungs when Eric was thrown into the oven, landing on his back on the bottom grill. Instantly a horrible sizzling sound filled her ears, and the odor of charred flesh assaulted her nostrils. Again the rag came out of Eric's mouth,

FLESH AND BLOOD

followed by a bloodcurdling wail that made Deidi feel like she'd been punched in the stomach. She fell to her knees and vomited on the kitchen floor.

A moment later she heard the sound of the oven door being slammed shut. Inside the flameless inferno, Eric continued to scream like a tortured banshee for what seemed an eternity but couldn't have been more than five or ten seconds. The ensuing silence, dead silence, was short-lived. From the other end of the house, their mother's voice: "Eric? Oh my God. George! Eric's not in his crib!"

15

When Judson Hendricks left the police station for the Mermaid Village Apartments, he was surprised to find Deidi lounging against his car. She was smoking a cigarette and staring absently at the dark clouds gathering in the blue Florida sky.

"Where were you this morning?" he asked amiably, moving directly in front of her to get her attention. "You sure picked the wrong time to slack off. The Patton/Bagget homicide cases are all wrapped up."

"And you're completely full of shit." She smiled.

He sighed. "True. Well, I was just on my way to the Mermaid Village Apartments, but all I ate for lunch was a Snickers, so I'm starting to get pretty hungry. How about you?"

"I never turn down anything if it's free."

"Except Julio's burritos."

"And venereal disease."

Hendricks unlocked the passenger door to let her in. "Don't worry, I'm not taking you to Julio's." He decided to let her come to her own conclusion about the other matter.

They barely exchanged a word on the way to a German delicatessen called Frank's Furt, known as Frank's Fart to all the kids who knew the gassing

FLESH AND BLOOD

power of sauerkraut. On the outside it looked like an old Army fortress made of rough-hewn logs, with a huge wiener stretched over the entrance.

They'd barely exchanged two words on the way over; soon after leaving the police lot, she had turned on the music radio, cranking the volume to a level that almost made him wince. But he didn't ask her to turn it down; it seemed she'd forgiven the admittedly deplorable stunt he'd pulled yesterday evening, and he didn't want to push his luck.

Grateful for the relative quietness of the deli, he dove hungrily into his hot pastrami with Swiss cheese on an onion bun. She only nibbled at her ham on rye and fidgeted with the salt and pepper shakers, her mind obviously a million miles away.

Washing down his last bite with a long swallow of dark beer, Hendricks waved his hand in front of her face. "Hello, anybody in there?"

She jumped slightly, her eyes snapping into focus. "Oh, sorry. What were you saying?"

He recognized the golden opportunity for a wisecrack, but managed to restrain himself, realizing where the adolescent impulse was coming from. He was beginning to like her very much, too much, actually, and the only defense he had was flippancy. To hell with it, he thought. Be real.

"I wasn't saying anything, but now that you've returned to Earth, you wanna tell me what's going on up there? You look a little upset."

She pushed her plate aside and reached into her purse for a cigarette. "I am upset. This afternoon my shrink forced me under hypnosis to remember some terrible things about my past, that happened when I was a little girl."

"You want to talk about it?"

Lighting the tip of her cigarette, Deidi's eyes narrowed, one side of her mouth raised in a sneer. "That's what I pay him for. But if you want the information for your personal horror file, here it is.

First I dug up my dead cat, whose guts were hanging out and crawling with maggots. Then I watched my baby brother get thrown into a hot oven and roasted to death."

Hendricks felt his pastrami sandwich start to back up. He forced it down with a few more swallows of beer. "Jesus Christ!"

"He had nothing to do with it," she quipped, taking another drag of her cigarette, her expression hinting that she was getting some kind of deranged pleasure from watching his emotional reaction to her news.

"Who—Who did do it?" he stammered, his face looking suddenly pale.

She leaned forward with both elbows on the table until the edge was supporting her breasts. "They never found out," she whispered.

Hendricks was confused for a second. She had seen it happen, right? So she also should have gotten a look at the perpetrator. Then he theorized that it had been a stranger, someone she didn't know and couldn't identify. "You'd never seen the person before, is that it?"

Exhaling smoke from the side of her mouth, she abruptly sat up straight and changed the subject. "It's hot as hell in here, can we go?"

His mind still crowded with questions about the gruesome murder of her baby brother, Hendricks finished off his beer, then went back to the counter to order two sandwiches to go. Among the questions, wisps of an old memory teased him, never showing enough to inspire total recall, but he was almost certain that at some point down the road of life he had heard something about a baby being killed in a hot oven.

Back in the car he said, "If you're not feeling up to doing what I'm sure will only turn out to be more fruitless legwork, I can run you by my house, which is only about ten blocks from here, and when I'm

FLESH AND BLOOD

finished I'll come back and take you and the kids to a movie."

She gave him, in his opinion, a very odd look which was impossible for him to interpret. "Your kids are home?"

"Well, they'd damn well better be."

"All right," she said, turning her face toward her window, and she said nothing more until he pulled the car into his driveway. In the uncomfortable silence, Hendricks had asked for answers to all the questions that were plaguing him, but none of them passed beyond his lips. It was quite clear that she didn't want to discuss the tragedy any further.

When he pulled up the driveway, she commented offhandedly that he had a nice house, as if she'd never seen it before.

Hendricks couldn't help but smile, remembering how drunk she was that night. It wasn't surprising that she didn't remember it; besides, it had been full dark when they'd arrived.

"Well, it sure beats the shack I grew up in."

Inside they found Jeremy and Lacey at the kitchen table playing Monopoly. After giving Deidi a shy, fleeting smile, Lacey complained to her father, "Dad, Jeremy keeps stealing money out of the bank when I'm not looking!"

Hendricks chuckled. "You should know by now not to let him be the banker. Anyway, it's time to put the game away and wash your hands. Here's your supper." He set the white sack he was holding down on the edge of the table.

Jeremy looked at the artwork on the front of the sack and made a face. "Ew, Frank's Fart burgers!"

Lacey cupped her hands over her mouth and giggled.

Hendricks gave his son a warning look. "All right, that'll be enough of that. Now do what I said or suffer the consequences."

"We're going to suffer them anyway," Jeremy said snidely. "The attack of the silent deadlies! I hope you got us a couple of gas masks, too."

"I'll gas-mask you," Hendricks warned with a foreboding frown, taking a threatening step closer with his hands on his hips, and Jeremy promptly began helping his sister put away the game. Hendricks quickly turned away to conceal the smile that was fighting to override his sternness.

"He's not always this crude," he muttered under his breath to Deidi, who had wandered into the kitchen to study a mobile the kids had made out of soft-drink cans and other odds and ends. "Sometimes he's worse."

"Boys will be boys," she responded dryly.

Hendricks studied her while she plucked at the mobile, making its components dance and spin. There was nothing he could put his finger on, but he could swear something was different about her today. Maybe what he was sensing was just the result of her confrontation with those horrible childhood memories. What a terrible experience that must have been, and it would probably take her a good while to work through it.

When Jeremy and Lacey returned from washing their hands in the bathroom, Hendricks told them to sit down and listen up. "I'm sure you two remember Deidi Marshall from the park last Sunday."

"Yeah," Jeremy piped up. "She was the one with the killer dog."

Hendricks smiled wanly. "That's right. She's going to stay with you while I do a little snooping around the Mermaid Village Apartments, which shouldn't take much longer than an hour, two at the most. When I get back, we'll all go out to a movie. Well, whether you two get to go or not depends on how you behave while I'm gone. Understood?"

"Ten-four," Jeremy barked.

FLESH AND BLOOD

Lacey rolled her eyes. "We'll be good, Dad. We always are."

Hendricks dispensed their sandwiches, pickles, and chips with a light kiss on each fair forehead, reminding them of the Kool-Aid in the refrigerator if they wanted something to drink.

Deidi accompanied him to the front door. "You behave yourself, too," he said with a wink, planting a kiss on her lips, which remained conspicuously unresponsive.

"What will you do to me if I'm bad?" she asked in a low, childishly insolent voice when he pulled away. "Put me in handcuffs, then spank me with a belt on my bare bottom?"

Much to his embarrassment, Hendricks felt himself blushing. Was he supposed to take this as some kind of hint? He never would have guessed Deidi Marshall was the kinky type, but some of the most unlikely people could dàmn sure throw you a curveball. "Only if you insisted."

She laughed and said as she closed the door, "Don't work too hard."

Hendricks was two blocks from the Mermaid Village apartment complex when he got a call on his portable police radio to return to the station immediately. Swearing softly, he turned left at the next intersection and headed south.

What now, he wondered cynically as he attached the magnetic cherry dome to the roof and picked up his speed. Respectful of the swirling red light, drivers ahead of him began to pull over. He thought how utterly fucking typical this was. Anytime he made plans, the Universe conspired to screw them up.

When he arrived at the station like a hurricane, the sergeant on duty at the front desk directed him to the interrogation room. "Maybe you'd better stop by the bathroom first," he warned as Hendricks started for the corridor, "'cause you're sure enough gonna shit."

Too harried to linger long enough to ask what the hell was meant by that, Hendricks hurried on, his irritation giving way to a consuming curiosity about who—or what—was awaiting him in the interrogation room.

There were two uniformed officers standing guard outside the door. Upon seeing Hendricks, one of them took a formal military step into the hallway and opened it for him. Suffering a slight case of butterflies in the stomach, Hendricks entered the smoky room, not bothering to acknowledge the courtesy. The door was shut behind him.

There were two other men in the room, but Hendricks didn't see them. His eyes focused solely on the one person sitting at the table, and his first thought was that this had to be some kind of practical joke, and not a very funny one. Silence fell like a lead blanket.

"What the hell are you doing here?" he asked Deidi when he finally located his voice, mentally taking in the fact that she had changed clothes since he'd last seen her, which was maybe a whole twenty minutes ago.

One of the other men, Lieutenant Fairbanks, cleared his throat. "This woman says that her name is Camisa Collins, which her driver's license confirms."

Hendricks stepped a little closer to the table shaking his head slightly, his expression stamped with disbelief. "No, no way. I was with her less than half an hour ago, and her name is Deidi Marshall. I'd swear it under oath." Leaning over the table, he looked directly into eyes. "What's this all about, Deidi? What's going on, talk to me."

"My name is Camisa, you prick," the dark-haired woman hissed at him. "And I want out of here right now! You haven't got a shred of evidence against me! Not that I've done anything wrong," she added with downcast eyes, an unconscious gesture that told the three trained observers she was lying through her teeth.

It was then that Hendricks noticed her fingertips. They all bore thick, crusty scabs. Scenes at the restaurant flashed in his mind's eye; there had been no scabs on Deidi's fingers. And even if something had happened to them in the last twenty minutes, they'd had no time to heal, to scab over.

So this wasn't Deidi, couldn't be. His head stopped spinning a little. But she could damn well pass for her twin sister. The resemblance was utterly astounding. They were exactly alike, except for the clothes and the scabbed fingers. Exactly. Even smoked the same brand of cigarettes.

"We got a call from a guy by the name of George Gaston," Fairbanks said in a tired voice, crossing his arms as he leaned against the vending machine behind Hendricks. "Mrs. Collins came to his home this afternoon wanting him to take her two youngest children, one of which has a skull fracture. She's the mother of the boy who drowned last Saturday."

"Which you assholes have wrongly assumed to be my fault," Camisa muttered angrily, puffing on her cigarette like there was no tomorrow. "I know you've been checking around, asking personal questions about me. But I tried my best to save Aaron, and Michael fractured his own damn skull falling off a chair. Ask him, he'll tell you."

"But the reason he called us," Fairbanks went on, "is he thinks she might be the suspect wanted in the Patton/Bagget slayings. And she does fit the composite very well. She says she accidentally burned her fingers taking a hot baking dish out of the oven, but if you ask me, I'd say she was intentionally trying to get rid of her fingerprints. I wonder what her collection of steak knives looks like, and if one of them is missing. She told Gaston she thought she had a split personality."

Camisa glared up at him. "Fuck you."

Hendricks pulled out the chair across from her and sat down heavily, still totally dumbfounded by her appearance. Then suddenly an exciting thought pierced the numbness in his brain: the parrot, and the way he'd reacted to Deidi, *who was the spitting image of the woman before him.*

"Why were you wanting George Gaston to take your kids? Were you planning to leave town?"

"Maybe, maybe not," she quipped, blowing smoke in his face.

"Where were you last Wednesday night around two A.M.?" he asked, waving the smoke away and coughing slightly. The bitch was really asking for it, especially if she was in fact *the* bitch, which he was strongly beginning to believe. The system could put a very uncomfortable squeeze on the hapless people caught in its gears if it wanted to.

She crushed out her cigarette in a gold aluminum tray and stared daggers at him for several moments. Finally she bit out, "I was at home. In bed. Asleep."

"Can that be verified?"

She threw up her hands in disgust and exclaimed, "I don't have to take this shit. Where's the phone? I want to call a lawyer. I have the right to do that, don't I?"

Hendricks slumped down in his chair wearing a slight grin. "Yes, you do. But if you haven't done anything wrong, there's really no reason for you to have a lawyer present. All I want to know is if your whereabouts on the night in question can be verified. What about your husband? Wasn't he there with you?"

"Her husband's a truck driver, out on the road every Monday through Friday," Fairbanks answered for her. "So all she's got is her word." The way he said it, Camisa's word was every bit as good as Charles Manson's.

Again Hendricks thought about the parrot, and was about to mention it just to see her reaction when the door to the interrogation room opened. All four of the room's occupants turned to look as the uniformed officer who had admitted Hendricks entered and came to a crisp halt. Then from behind him a woman cautiously stepped into view, and at that moment Hendricks did come very close to shitting in his pants.

It was Deidi. At least, he thought it was. Again. But she still wasn't wearing the same clothes she'd had on earlier.

The men watched the two women's eyes connect and hold. The air was charged with tension so thick it was almost visible. Deidi's mouth had dropped open slightly; after what seemed another ice age, her jaws snapped together, breaking the spell. "You," she said accusingly.

"Well hello, sister," Camisa said with sarcastic emphasis on the last word. She smiled, but her eyes were full of hate.

Deidi started to shake all over. "You did it. I know it was you. I saw you do it that morning in the kitchen. You threw Eric into that hot oven."

"Like hell," Camisa shot back, jumping to her feet. "It wasn't me, I just watched like you did. Blythe's the one who did it! There's three of us, you stupid bitch; Daddy dearest filled me in while waiting for the cops to come and take me away. A was for Mommy Arlene, then B was for Blythe, C was for Camisa, and D was for Deidi, identical triplets born in rapid succession and in that order, two minutes apart, I think he said. And then of course E was for baby brother Eric."

Now it was Hendricks's turn to be slack-jawed. "There's *three* of you?"

"That's what I said," Camisa affirmed with a sneer. "And we were quite the nasty lot, according to Daddy. Somebody took out all our sugar and spice and added something that wasn't nice at all. But he admitted that he always thought Blythe was the worst. He never really doubted for a moment that putting Eric in the oven was her idea, but he put all three of us up for adoption anyway, because he didn't want to be reminded. By the way, our mother hung herself two days after Eric's death. She didn't want to be reminded, either."

Hendricks suddenly paled. "Oh my God. Blythe . . . she's with my kids!"

Camisa nodded toward Deidi. "How do you know *she's* not really Blythe?"

"I know," Hendricks said tersely as he sprang from his chair, almost knocking Deidi over in his haste to leave the room. He didn't waste any time apologizing; all he could think about at the moment was alerting the dispatcher to send all available patrol units to 1204 Viking Drive, with specific orders to lay some fucking rubber.

16

Their father hadn't been gone five minutes when his new girlfriend began to make Jeremy and Lacey very nervous. She sat down at the table with them to watch them eat, all the while wearing a strange little smile that suggested she was thinking something dirty.

Then she started asking them weird questions. "You two look a lot alike. Are you twins?"

Jeremy and Lacey gave each other disparaging looks. "No way," Jeremy said. "He's a year older than me," Lacey added, "unless you're counting mental age, then he's only about five."

"And she's still in diapers," Jeremy retorted.

The woman directed her next question at Jeremy. "Can you read Lacey's mind sometimes, tell what she's thinking?"

His eyes momentarily met hers. There was something a little frightening about her intense stare. Quickly returning his gaze to his sister's face, he answered with a shrug, "I dunno. Maybe sometimes, like once I knew she was writing a letter to our mom instead of doing her homework like she was supposed to. But she'd try to hide her paper every time I walked by, so that's probably how I figured it out."

"What about you, Lacey? Can you read Jeremy's mind?"

Lacey smirked. "Even if I could, I wouldn't want to."

The woman's strange smile slowly disappeared as she looked from one to the other. "Can either of you read *my* mind?"

Coming from the stranger's lips, and combined with the way she was looking at them, it was a chilling question. Both children shook their heads uneasily.

"Well, I can read yours," she said tauntingly. "I'll prove it. Just a minute ago, Jeremy, weren't you thinking about a pet bird you once had, wishing it hadn't flown away?"

His mouth dropped open in amazement. "How did you know that?"

Ignoring his question, the woman turned to Lacey. "And you, weren't you wondering if I'd been to bed with your father yet?"

Lacey blushed instantly, and opened her mouth to deny it, but knew that the guilt was already written across her face in big letters. She closed her mouth and said nothing, casting her eyes downward.

"How do you do that?" Jeremy repeated nervously, feeling more uncomfortable with this woman by the second.

"I'm psychic," she announced in the same way she might have said "I'm Catholic" or "I'm a vegetarian." "But not very," she went on, rising from her chair to casually pace around the table, trailing the fingers of her left hand along the edge. "Actually I was a little surprised that I could get inside your heads. I thought it was something special that I could only do with my sisters. And then I can't always, even if I really want to. It just sort of happens on its own, usually when I least expect it."

"Is it okay if we go play in the backyard?" Lacey asked timidly. She'd heard all she wanted to hear of

FLESH AND BLOOD

this weird woman's spooky talk and wanted to get as far away from her as possible.

As if a switch had just been thrown, their father's new girlfriend suddenly looked like a massive thunderstorm about to happen. "I'm talking to you!" she snapped, her eyes riveting on Lacey like dark, roiling clouds. "How can you be so rude?"

Jeremy and Lacey exchanged worried glances, and they could certainly read each other's mind now. They we're both thinking: Uh-oh. Extreme Bitch Alert.

"As I was saying," the woman went on, resuming her casual saunter around the table, which now seemed pretty menacing, "I thought I could only read my sisters' minds. I have two sisters, you know, and both of them look exactly like me, to a T. We're identical triplets."

Jeremy and Lacey, with no appetite left to finish their sandwiches, sat watching her circle them, offering no response.

"We've been separated a long time, twenty-three years to be exact. They forgot all about me, but I never forgot them. Well, once in a while I could tell they'd plugged into my mind, even though I was halfway across the country. They've done it a lot since I came back to Danville a few weeks ago, especially Camisa. She's my kindred spirit as well as my flesh and blood. Deidi fights her dark nature, or at least tries to. She doesn't always win." At this she issued a low, throaty chuckle, her eyes taking on a faraway look as she recalled a memory that was apparently amusing to her. After a second or two she snapped herself back to the present and continued, "I made myself a vow at the age of ten that I would come back someday and find them, and then the three of us would teach this stinking world the meaning of the word vengeance. They haven't had it as rough as me, but they've been through some shit over the years. Of course, nothing like being dragged to a new city and enrolled in a new school every few months, most of the time living out of suitcases in some fleabag hotel or cramped apartment overrun by cockroaches. And those were the good memories. Juvenile Hall really sucked. Anyway, I finally decided it was time to keep that vow, though I hated leaving Vegas and its endless supply of free-wheeling tourists. But my sisters didn't understand what was happening. Camisa thought she was living two separate lives, and Deidi thought she was losing her mind. Oh well. The party's over, so to speak. It was fun, though." She paused for a moment and laughed, the most wicked laugh Jeremy and Lacey had ever heard.

Jeremy was starting to wish his father hadn't been so adamantly against keeping a loaded gun in the house.

Abruptly the woman's laughter ceased, and Jeremy almost peed in his pants, thinking she'd read his mind about the gun. But she said nothing, just resumed walking around the table, and when she passed behind his chair, her fingers trailed across his shoulders, causing him to shudder.

"But there is a problem," she said, her voice lowered an octave. "I made a mistake, said a little too much in front of a certain parrot. Your father is a very smart man, you know. Very good detective. The other day I picked my sister Deidi's mind and discovered that he was alarmingly close to finding me." The children sat in shocked silence as she strolled over to the kitchen counter where she'd left her purse, their minds frantically putting the puzzle pieces together. About the time they reached the same conclusion, that this woman was the killer their father was looking for, she turned around holding a steak knife she had removed from her purse, leaving no room for doubt.

"I work at the Mermaid Inn, you see. Morning shift registration clerk; the owner handles the afternoon and graveyard shifts. Right now there's a man lying

FLESH AND BLOOD

dead in room seventeen. I killed him just for the hell of it, but it'll be a while before he's found. I made a voucher that said he'd paid a week in advance with a credit card, and hung a Do Not Disturb sign on his door."

Tears were streaming down Lacey's face. "Are you going to kill us, too?"

"No, of course not," Blythe Richmond said with a look of surprise, as if that was the most ridiculous question she'd ever heard.

Jeremy didn't believe that for an instant. He'd seen too many movies in which the killer openly confessed his or her crimes knowing it didn't matter because the listeners would soon be dead, incapable of repeating what they'd heard. "Then why are you telling us all this?"

"Well, I'm afraid I am going to have to kidnap you," she answered matter-of-factly. "If I have you two, see, your father won't dare to come after me. But I'll let you both go just as soon as he sends me the million dollars' ransom I'm going to demand. With that kind of money, I can pay a plastic surgeon to give me a whole new face, and then I can go anywhere in the world I want and live happily ever after."

Lacey drew in a sharp breath. "Our dad doesn't have that kind of money! He'd never be able to get a million dollars!"

"Maybe he'll win the lottery," Blythe said with a dour smile. "Now both of you, very slowly get out of your chairs and come in here with me. Do not try to run away, because I guarantee you that I am very fast myself and at least one of you would be caught. I don't think I have to tell you what would happen after that."

Her warning was totally unnecessary; both kids were so petrified they could barely move. Trembling visibly, their eyes wide blue saucers that reflected their terror, they simultaneously rose from their chairs and walked woodenly into the kitchen shoulder to shoulder. Blythe ordered Jeremy to find something with which she could tie their hands, and in one of the kitchen drawers he located a ball of thick twine, which he accidentally dropped on the floor when he tried to hand it to her. She scowled, telling him when he stooped to pick it up that he'd better think twice about pulling any stunts.

Next she made them stand facing the wall while she cut two three-foot lengths of twine with the steak knife. She tied Jeremy's hands together behind his back first, binding them at the wrists so tightly he could hardly stand it, but he was too afraid to complain. His instincts told him to be as cooperative as possible, just play it cool, don't piss the bitch off, and sooner or later their dad would rescue them. Like she said, he was a very good detective.

Lacey started sobbing while her hands were being tied behind her back, which seemed to delight her captor. "What's the matter, little girl? You want your daddy? You scared?" After she finished knotting the two ends of the twine, Blythe whipped the girl around and growled into her face, "You'd better be." She had no intention of kidnapping them; even if she wanted to, how the hell could she when she didn't even have a car? She'd only told them that to keep them manageable, otherwise they would have flown in sixteen different directions, panicked and hysterical, fighting her tooth and nail, and one or both might have escaped. They were going to die, all right. So was their father.

"Now both of you, march yourselves straight to the bathroom."

Jeremy turned and looked at her suspiciously. "What for?"

"Because I have to potty," she answered in a sarcastic falsetto, "and I can't trust either of you out of my sight. So march!"

Jeremy reluctantly took the lead, shuffling stoop-shouldered toward the main bathroom down the hallway off the dining area. His heart was beating so fast he was afraid it might explode. His mind filled with silent prayers that she was telling the truth about just needing to pee, or shit, whichever she had to do. She could both pee and crap right on his face for all he cared, so long as she didn't use that sharp knife on them.

When they were all standing inside the rather stale-smelling bathroom, its brown porcelain countertop marred with water spots and smudges of toothpaste, the bathtub's interior dulled by a wide ring of soap crud, Blythe closed and locked the door. Leaning against it, she smiled at the two blondheaded children staring back at her with such wide, frightened eyes. Why rush? she silently asked herself. There was plenty of time; the pig said he'd be gone at least an hour. And these two scared little rabbits would be so much fun to play with.

"Guess what?" she asked them, her smile turning to a sneer. "I lied. I don't have to use the potty at all."

"You are going to kill us, aren't you!" Lacey wailed, again breaking into sobs. Tears streamed down her cheeks like tiny rivers, and her teeth began to chatter. Her whole body was shaking so violently it looked as if she were having an upright seizure.

Jeremy's heart seemed to stop beating for a few moments. His brain was screaming denial of the situation, completely incapable of comprehending his impending demise. This simply could not be for real, could not be, no way. Only in the movies did things like this happen. Not to them. Oh God no, not to them. He became aware of an electrical buzzing in his head, and a huge black nothingness tried to send consciousness-killing tentacles through the top of his skull. Breathing like he'd just finished running a mile, he fought to hold on, and won.

Blythe leaned against the counter with an impatient look on her face. "Lacey, how many times do I have to tell you I'm not going to kill you? You and your brother are worth a million bucks to me alive; I'd be stupid to kill you."

"Then why did you bring us in here and lock the door?" Lacey returned, still sobbing.

"Because the bathroom's where you always go to play dirty games. Don't tell me you two have never sneaked in here and shown each other what you've got."

In spite of his overwhelming fear, Jeremy flushed with embarrassment. Lacey's face was already red from crying. "Gross!" Jeremy said with a grimace. He'd never even seen his sister in her underwear, nor did he have any such desire. And Lacey had never seen what he had, saying it wasn't worth the money he was asking.

Blythe smiled, absently rubbing the blade's knife under her chin. "I take that for a no. Well, you're both going to get an eyeful now. Who wants to be stripped first?"

Lacey's sobs became louder than ever, the sound echoing off the tiled walls, but Jeremy began to get a grip on his emotions, his heart quieting to regular palpitations. His brain, eager to believe in salvation, had dismissed the overwhelming threat of their being in a death trap. The woman was some kind of pervert, as well as a killer. Better to be humiliated and live than rebel and die.

"I'll be first," he mumbled, feeling more heat rush to his cheeks. He thought they must be glowing brighter than Rudolph the Reindeer's nose.

"All right, then get over here," Blythe demanded.

Lacey's wails grew even louder as Jeremy slowly moved forward, his gaze glued to the floor. When he was only another step away, Blythe grabbed him roughly and turned him around to face his sister, then began unbuttoning the top of his blue jeans. "Don't you close your eyes, now," she warned Lacey with a look that sent chills up the girl's spine. "I mean it. If you close your eyes or look away, Jeremy will have to pay for it. I'll cut him with the knife. And shut up your fucking crying, it's starting to get on my nerves."

Like magic, Lacey silenced herself instantly, but tears continued to pour from the corners of her eyes, and she couldn't help the sniffling. No one would have guessed, but at that moment she was very close to breaking into hysterical laughter. Her salty tears were so blurring her vision that she wouldn't have been able to tell a doll from a truck if it was put right in front of her face. If only she could beam that message to Jeremy. It would be their private little joke, a little anecdote they could tell their friends when this horrible ordeal was over and the woman was safely behind bars.

Suddenly, in the midst of pulling off Jeremy's jeans along with his underwear, Blythe's head snapped up in Lacey's direction. "Bend over and wipe your eyes on that towel hanging behind you, and turn off the waterworks."

Lacey jumped as if she'd been slapped. Her thoughts had been beamed all right, straight to the wrong person! Her urge to laugh died quickly. This situation was scary enough without having to worry that every thought was being monitored. Sometimes thoughts were very hard to control. What would happen if one slipped about her being a psycho bitch from Hell?

Blythe snapped her fingers. "Get over here, Lacey. Right now. Come on, we haven't got all year."

The seconds ticked by, and Lacey's feet remained firmly in place. Finally Blythe, aware of the passing time, lost her patience. "All right, get into the tub, Jeremy," she said angrily.

Quivering, Jeremy obeyed, and Blythe leaned over to pull up the metal lever under the spigot that closed the drain. Wearing a sinister smile, she patted him on the cheek with the serrated knife blade. "You dirty, dirty boy. Don't you feel dirty? You are, you're filthy, just like all boys who grow up to be filthy men like my adoptive father. The bastard's wife knew what was going on, the fat pig, but she never did anything about it. He started in on me the second night I was there, and I screamed for her to help me, but she just turned the television up louder. After nine years of that fucking shit I took off on my own, but not before using some hydrofluoric acid to make sure his dirty prick never had any more fun. Anyway, you're just as filthy, so I'm going to give you a bath."

She reached out and turned on the hot water full blast.

Only the hot water.

Jeremy bolted upright, looking fearfully over his shoulder at the gushing flow from which wisps of steam was beginning to drift. "It's too hot!" he screamed at the top of his lungs. "It's too hot, it's too hot!"

As he scooted to the far end of the tub and struggled to get on his knees, Lacey screamed for Blythe to turn on the cold water before Jeremy got burned. Blythe looked at her stonily for a few seconds, then quick as lightning backhanded her and sent her careening to the floor, her head hitting the edge of the toilet bowl on the way down. It didn't knock her out, but it caused a great deal of pain. The small room was a deafening din of screams and rising steam as the tub slowly began to fill with scalding water.

Several miles away at the police station, an incredulous Judson Hendricks had just looked at Camisa Collins and exclaimed, "There's *three* of you?"

Jeremy, screaming his lungs out, was flopping about in the tub like a fish out of water, unable to escape the encroaching water without the use of his hands. Finally, with his feet turning tomato red, he bellyflopped over the side, but Blythe caught him and forced him back inside the tub. Still curled on the floor, Lacey strained forward and sunk her teeth into Blythe's ankle, her will to fight no longer restrained by the knife's threat. The psycho bitch from hell was trying to kill her brother.

Blythe roared much like a lion when Lacey savagely bit into her, applying all the pressure her jaws could muster, which was sufficient to break the skin and give her Achilles tendon something to think about for at least a month. "You little bitch!" she raged, turning to yank out a handful of Lacey's hair. But Lacey was so wired on adrenaline she hardly felt it, only a slight tingling numbness on that side of her scalp, and continued to sink her teeth deeper.

Jeremy was thrashing insanely as the water burned him like fire. He'd almost lost his voice from all his screaming. Now hoarse, barking coughs erupting from his lungs in rapid succession. His mouth was stretched wide and distorted in an agonized grimace, his eyelids pulled back so far that the whites were visible all around his blue irises, what could be seen of them through the haze of steam. The water was getting deep enough so that his spastic movements were flinging stinging drops of water on Blythe and Lacey.

Blythe took notice of the stings, but at the moment she was far more concerned with making the human snapping turtle at her ankle let go. Gripping the knife, she stabbed the point through the back of Lacey's right hand.

The maneuver worked; Lacey had a much higher than usual tolerance for pain, but this was one she couldn't ignore. She opened her mouth to howl in pain, and Blythe quickly pulled her ankle free.

Incensed by the sight of her own blood, she jerked the knife out of Lacey's hand and stabbed her again through the lower arm. Lacey filled the room with a shattering scream, but abruptly cut it off midway to listen.

The only remaining sound was that of the water splashing into the tub.

Something black and cold suddenly enveloped Lacey, a thought so terrible and totally unacceptable it made her heart threaten to stop beating. "Oh my God," she whimpered.

"Got awful quiet in here all the sudden, didn't it?" Blythe hissed, reaching for the towel on the rack to wrap around her ankle, thinking she should clean and disinfect the wound as soon as possible. Surely there was some hydrogen peroxide or alcohol around here someplace. And she was going to need some antibiotics, too. Someone had once told her that human bites were a lot worse than dog bites because the human mouth carried more germs. An amazing fact considering a dog's usual habits.

And oh, was she going to make the little bitch very, very sorry she did this. She'd make her watch her father die, then her own death would be slow and exquisite torture.

Lacey was sobbing openly again, knowing in her heart that her brother was dead. Random images ran fleetingly through her mind, Jeremy in all his moods, things they'd done together, minor spats they'd had, times when they were the best of friends. This was too terrible to be true. God, she prayed, please wake me up from this nightmare.

Blythe turned off the water, then grabbed Lacey by the hair. The room had become suffocating, like a hot sauna, and Blythe couldn't stand to stay in it a moment longer. Peering inside the tub through the mist, she saw Jeremy's boiled red body floating facedown with small air bubbles breaking the surface around his head. He must have gone into shock or something and blacked out, she thought.

Dirty boy all clean now.

"Come on," Blythe growled at Lacey, pulling her by the hair toward the door, Blythe limping in pain on her injured ankle. She closed her hand around the knob and had just started to turn it when she suddenly stiffened and said, "Oh, shit! Oh, *fuck!*"

Lacey didn't ask what she was cursing about. Her brain was all but paralyzed by the fact of Jeremy's death. As Blythe yanked open the door, letting in a rush of cool air, Lacey received an explanation anyway.

"They're coming, fucking pigs out the ass! I just had a flash on Deidi, and she's following them!"

Lost in the depths of severe trauma, Lacey felt no elation at the news. It was too late. Jeremy was already dead, and she might as well be. She felt dead.

Blythe, muttering more obscenities under her breath, frantically dragged Lacey out into the hallway. "I've got no choice, I'm going to have to use you as a hostage," she said, giving the fistful of Lacey's hair a cruel twist. "Damn it to hell! Does your pig father keep a gun around the house?"

Lacey didn't answer.

Blythe held the knife up to the girl's throat. "Answer me, goddammit!"

"No," Lacey sobbed, now starting to shiver all over. After being in the overheated, steamy bathroom, the conditioned air of the house was chilling to her bare skin.

"Well, fuck a duck!" Blythe spat, roughly guiding Lacey through the dining room. In the living room she hurried to the front windows to take a cautious peek outside. Much to her dismay, when she pulled aside the curtain, she saw a patrol car with its lights flashing careen around the corner up ahead, proceeding like a charging bull in her direction after coming out of its skid.

Unable to fully express her anger at that moment with expletives, Blythe flung the curtain back and screamed. A tiny smile appeared on Lacey's lips, although she was unaware of it. Her mind was presently preoccupied with the throbbing pains in her right hand and forearm and the blood that must be dripping all over the carpet.

Having released her fury via a full primal scream, Blythe felt quite a bit calmer. In a matter of seconds she managed to get out from under the control of her emotions and take the driver's seat behind the quiet engine of cunning.

I am going to get out of this, she thought, taking a deep breath. *All I have to do is keep my cool, be very careful and make no stupid mistakes.*

"There's a lot more on their way," Blythe said calmly to Lacey as she lowered herself catlike to the long earth-toned couch in front of the windows, pulling the girl down with her. "So let the fuckers come. We'll just sit right here and wait for the emcee of this pig convention to show up, which should be any minute now. All I can say is, your dad better be a reasonable man, Lacey. Your life depends on it."

As Blythe predicted, the car driven by Judson Hendricks roared up less than a minute later to join the five police cruisers parked helter-skelter in the street. Three had their doors opened and acting as shields for the officers crouched behind them with their service revolvers drawn and aimed at the front door. Four of the officers had been dispatched to the backyard to cover the rear exits. Neighbors stood gawking from their porches or windows.

"Someone's been looking out that front window," one of the officers informed Hendricks as he approached carrying a megaphone. "But other than that, nothing's happened."

En route to the scene, Hendricks had informed the patrol officers by radio to do nothing but seal off the area and keep an eye on the house until he arrived, fearing that any overt action might bring harm to his kids, if they hadn't been harmed already. But he couldn't allow himself to think like that or he'd fall apart on the spot. He'd never been more frightened in his entire life. Why the fucking hell hadn't he listened to his instincts, the voice that told him before he left that something was wrong?

His hands were shaking badly as he took a few cautious steps into the front yard, where he then switched on the megaphone and lifted it to his mouth. *"Blythe!"* Through the amplifying instrument, his voice had a raspy, mechanical quality. *"Can you hear me? Open the window, I want to talk to you!"*

After a brief delay of perhaps fifteen seconds, the curtains fluttered and the window was raised about three inches. Through the crack, a woman's voice responded, "I'm not going to talk to you like this, asshole! Toss your gun away and come inside! And take your clothes off so I'll know you're not hiding anything!"

Jesus Christ, Hendricks thought. All the neighbors were looking at him. But how could he refuse? His kids' lives were on the line. *"All right,"* he blared back. *"Just give me a minute!"*

None of the officers snickered. There was nothing the least bit funny about this situation, but hopefully when they looked back on it later they could laugh and tease him about his shapely legs, Hendricks thought.

Hendricks was not a very religious man, but he began praying like a fanatic as he removed his clothes. One of his prayers was that he would be allowed to keep his shorts on at least, but all the rest were for Jeremy and Lacey. They had to be all right, or he would never be able to forgive himself. All the lectures he'd given them on safety, all the precautions he'd taken to make sure they would always be safe. Then what does he do? Brings a psychotic killer right into their home, leaves them alone with her. If that wasn't the epitome of irony, he didn't know what was.

When he was stripped to his shorts, socks, and shoes, Blythe yelled at him through the window that he could come in now, but he'd by-God better not try anything funny, and the rest of the pigs had better keep their distance.

Hendricks picked his feet up one at a time and moved them toward the front door to his house. He felt like a marionette on strings, strangely numb. He imagined himself as a man being marched to the gallows, a man who had not yet resigned himself to death but who knew that fighting it would be useless.

The door was unlocked. Swallowing a fist-sized lump in his throat, he turned the knob and pushed the door inward. Stepping over the threshold, he looked to his right and saw Blythe perched on the edge of the couch with her knees apart. His little girl was sitting on the floor between them with her hands behind her back, Blythe's feet planted between Lacey's thighs ostensibly to prevent escape, as if the knife being held at her throat wasn't enough. Tears welled up in his eyes. Dear God, what had his daughter been put through? And where the hell was Jeremy?

Before he could ask, Lacey told him. "She killed Jeremy, Daddy! Killed him in the bathtub with boiling hot water!"

"I'll do the talking," Blythe hissed, smacking Lacey on one of her bare shoulders.

Hendricks went chalk-white, eyes rounding in horror. "No," he whispered, feeling the pain in his chest worsen considerably, making him fear he might be having a heart attack. He was certainly entitled to one. "No," he repeated louder, shaking his head adamantly, refusing to accept this package of ultimate misery. It couldn't be true. He fucking wouldn't *let* it be true!

Without asking "Mother may I", he bolted for the hallway that lead to the bedrooms and the full bathroom. A moment later a loud anguished wail was heard, followed by the splashing of water as Jeremy's body was presumably removed from the tub. That water still had to be mighty hot, Blythe thought. The pig had to have burned himself, and the idea made her smile. She told Lacey what a stupid pig her father was, thinking her brother could be revived after this much time. The little bastard was a goner for sure. And Lacey responded by saying, "I hope they shoot your head off," which earned her another smack, this one very hard on her right cheek.

FLESH AND BLOOD

Hendricks remained gone for several minutes, and Blythe began to get antsy; she wanted out of there. Being surrounded by pigs all wanting her hide was not one of her favorite pastimes. Undoubtedly he was back there giving the dead body CPR, still hopeful of reviving it. Then the wailing sound of a siren could be heard in the distance, rapidly getting closer. Blythe surmised there was a telephone in one of the bedrooms and the pig had called for an ambulance. Well, no way in hell was she going to allow a bunch of paramedics in here.

"Hendricks!" she bellowed. "Get your ass in here!"

He appeared half a minute later with his son's limp, red body in his arms. Hendricks looked like a man who had been to hell and back a dozen times. He was a broken man with the haunted eyes of a concentration camp survivor. "You've got to let me take him out to the ambulance," he croaked. "I got his heart beating again just a minute ago, but then it stopped. The paramedics have equipment, a portable defibrilator and respirator . . . he's still got a chance. Please!"

Blythe smiled. "By all means do what you have to do. But hurry back, I'm fast running out of patience." She figured that granting him this gargantuan favor would make him more receptive to her demands.

Throwing Lacey a tortured glance, Hendricks rushed out the open door with his son. The ambulance had just turned onto their street. Blythe watched through the window as two of the uniformed officers rushed up to meet Hendricks and take the boy from his arms.

"Now maybe we can get down to business," Blythe muttered, noting that a television news crew had arrived since she'd last looked out the window. So had Deidi. Blythe couldn't tell what her sister was thinking, but her expression indicated that she was very distraught. Blythe did, however, psychically connect with Camisa at that moment. She was pacing in circles in a jail cell, furious about being charged with felony child abuse. Blythe thought that was terribly funny, considering all Camisa had done to her other boy, Aaron. Blythe had seen it all through Camisa's mind. So they got her for the wrong kid, but she was definitely guilty of the crime. It was just like Camisa, though, to be so self-righteous, to whitewash her dirty deeds with inane justifications. Blythe never made excuses for her wickedness. She knew that her soul was black as the ace of spades, and she sated its appetite for cruelty and perversion with relish.

The paramedics had laid the boy on a stretcher that was now being quickly loaded into the back of the ambulance. The doors were closed and secured, the lights and siren reactivated. The rear tires sprayed loose bits of gravel on nearby spectators as it sped away on its crucial mission.

Hendricks watched until it was out of sight, his shoulders slumped under the crushing weight of guilt. He no longer gave a shit about his neighbors seeing him in his underwear. Undoubtedly the news camera was turned on him right now, getting juicy footage for the ten o'clock broadcast, but he didn't care about that, either.

Suddenly a soft voice spoke up behind him. "What happened, Judson? Is he going to be all right?"

He turned and looked at Deidi, a strange sensation stealing over him. Here was the woman he thought he was falling in love with, and she bore the exact image of the woman he'd like to murder with his bare hands. "She drowned him in the bathtub, in scalding hot water. If he lives, it'll be a miracle," he said in a dull voice, his eyes moving past her face to the house beyond. "I'd better get back inside before she does something worse to Lacey."

Deidi touched his arm lightly. "Maybe I can help. After all, she is my sister."

"And you're still a reporter. You'd use anything to

get a good story, wouldn't you?" His gaze was full of scorn, and he walked away without giving her a chance to defend herself.

Back inside the living room of his house, he found Blythe and Lacey in the same position as before. "Let me guess," he sighed heavily, leveling Blythe with a stony gaze. "You want a million dollars and a jet full of gas. Lacey will accompany you as a hostage, and after you've safely landed on some remote Pacific island, you'll send her home with a lollipop."

A slight grin curved one side of her mouth. "Now that's what I call an offer impossible to refuse. Can you really arrange all that?"

Hendricks felt the rage building in him now, overshadowing the guilt and sadness. What he wanted to arrange was the slow twisting off of Blythe's head. But only after all her other limbs had been amputated in the same manner. "Sure. I can turn straw into gold, too, and sprout fairy wings from my back to fly you there myself." He paused, bringing his hands up to his hips in a conscious attempt to appear as formidable as a man in his skivvies could. His voice took on an edge of steel. "Here's the real deal. You let my daughter go in the next ten seconds, and maybe you'll make it out of here alive. There's a couple of sharpshooters out there that could put a bullet dead center in your forehead from two hundred yards, and they're not nearly that far away."

The petulant grin on Blythe's face was instantly erased. "You want to play hardball, fucker? I'll cut your daughter's throat open right here and now. You willing to pay that high a price for my head?"

Lacey's eyes widened as she looked pleadingly up at her father.

Hendricks silently seethed. Blythe wasn't buying his bluff, and he didn't think she was bluffing him now. Nothing really mattered but getting his little girl back safe and unharmed. "You know I'm not. All right, I can get you a car and five thousand dollars, but Lacey doesn't go with you. I'd trust the Devil himself before I'd trust you."

Much to his chagrin, Blythe started laughing heartily, as if he'd just told the funniest joke she'd ever heard. It took almost a full minute for her to get it under control. "What kind of fucking idiot do you think I am? Without Lacey, my name is Game and it's open season." Then her face suddenly brightened, the proverbial light bulb going on over her head, heralding a brilliant idea. "Call for Deidi. Tell her to get in here."

Hendricks wasn't sure what Blythe was up to, but it was sure to be something he wouldn't like. But like it or not, she was presently calling the shots. He reluctantly stepped into the open doorway and called out Deidi's name, motioning with his hand for her to come.

While they were waiting, Blythe explained her plan to Hendricks. "When Deidi gets in here, you're going to get out and shut the door behind you. In exactly five minutes all three of us will come out. But you won't know which is me and which is Deidi, because in those five minutes we may or may not trade clothes. Your sharpshooters won't be able to shoot, because they might be plugging the wrong one. We'll all three leave in that car you promised with five thousand dollars in cash, and you won't have to worry about Lacey because Deidi will be with her to protect her. At the appropriate time, I'll let both of them go. Now that's a deal *you* can't refuse."

Hendricks was forced to admit to himself that the bitch was pretty damn smart. It was a clever plan, maybe clever enough to ensure her escape. But it also gave him some assurance about Lacey's safety. Maybe Deidi had news ink for blood, but unlike her sister Blythe, she was a decent human being. She wouldn't allow anything bad to happen to Lacey.

Just then Deidi timidly stepped over the threshold.

FLESH AND BLOOD

She avoided looking at Hendricks, instead directing her attention toward Lacey and Blythe. The concern written on Deidi's face evolved into deep distress when she saw Lacey's condition. "Oh my God," she whispered.

"It's going to take me at least fifteen minutes to get my hands on that money," Hendricks said bitterly to Blythe.

"Then you'd better get your ass moving," she responded in kind.

Still keeping her eyes averted from his face, Deidi asked him, "Do you have any bandages for her hand and arm?"

"Bandages? What for?"

Lacey's arms were behind her back, and her dried blood blended well with the brown carpeting; Hendricks hadn't even guessed that she was wounded, and didn't understand how Deidi could know.

"I saw . . . I had a vision of Blythe stabbing Lacey in the hand and arm," Deidi answered softly, casting her evil sister a reproachful glance.

Hendricks felt an emotional explosion coming on, an explosion of such magnitude that his body began trembling like a rocket on the launch pad halfway through the countdown. It was all he could do to keep from flying across the room to smash Blythe's face into a shapeless mass of bloody clay.

Blythe made a childish face at Deidi. "Tattletale. Shall I tell him about the vision *I* had last Sunday? Of what happened in your bedroom, and what you did afterward?"

Deidi gasped, eyes widening in fear.

But Hendricks, not caring in the least right then about what had happened in Deidi's bedroom, raged, *"You stabbed my daughter?!"* He took a few threatening steps toward the couch with his fists clenched, but stopped short when the knife blade was pressed up against Lacey's throat.

"I'll be okay, Daddy," Lacey squeaked, blinking

back fresh tears. "It doesn't hurt that much anymore."

"The sooner you get back with that money, the sooner she'll be released so you can get her to a doctor," Blythe reminded him.

Still trembling with bottled rage, Hendricks pointed a finger at her. "I don't care how long it takes or what it takes, I'll get you for what you've done to my kids." And with that he stormed out, slamming the door behind him.

Several moments of silence followed, finally broken by Blythe's casual comment that Hendricks sure had a temper.

Deidi stared at her incredulously. "What the hell do you expect? You drowned his son in scalding water and stabbed his daughter. He's supposed to snap his fingers and say 'Oh darn'?"

"You know what they say about people who live in glass houses, so just shut up and go get two long-sleeved shirts out of his closet. I've got to be able to hide this knife so they won't be able to tell us apart when we leave."

Deidi's eyes narrowed. "Supposing you do know everything, then you also know I was only guilty of protecting my dog. What about you? What the hell is your excuse for all the things you've done?"

"I don't need any excuses," Blythe spat. "Just go get the damn shirts before I decide to carve my initials in this kid's face."

Seeing the fresh wave of fear leap into Lacey's eyes, Deidi bit back the counterthreat that came to mind and hurried to the master bedroom.

17

Fifteen minutes later Lacey's knife wounds were cleaned and bandaged, as was Blythe's bitten ankle. To hide her incriminating wound, Blythe had Deidi also get them each a pair of Hendricks's socks to wear. Blythe had decided that she and Deidi would not exchange clothes, but would just put on the detective's long-sleeved shirts, making it impossible for the police to tell which of them was concealing the knife.

"Now when we get out there," she said in a low, don't-dare-fuck-with-me voice, "you two will remain absolutely silent. Not a word out of your mouths, and no body language either, no signals or blinks or head nods or any bullshit like that. If you do, I'll open Lacey's throat from ear to ear. Got that?"

Deidi and Lacey nodded solemnly.

"Deidi," Blythe continued, "we'll each take one of Lacey's arms. You'll be on her left, and you'll place your free hand, which will be covered by the left sleeve cuff, over her left collarbone. I'll do the same on the right. Don't even think about trying any heroics, like yanking her away from me. Believe me, I've got a very strong grip. So that's how we'll proceed to the car.

We'll all get in on the driver's side and sit together in the front seat. Deidi, you'll be driving. As long as you two behave as I've instructed, it should go very smoothly. And when I feel the time and place is right, I'll dump you two off and be on my merry way."

Deidi sighed. "You're crazy if you think you're going to get away with this. Why don't you give yourself up? There's no way in hell they're just going to let you off scot-free. The car will undoubtedly have a tracing device hidden somewhere in it. Anywhere you go, no matter how fast or confusing your trail, they'll find you. And they'll kill you, Blythe. Don't kid yourself. You've hurt, maybe even killed, one of their own."

"I'll bet your car doesn't have any fucking tracing device," Blythe said, turning her head a moment to peek out the window. There were now so many spectators gathered behind the police barricade that if she didn't know better, she'd think there was going to be a concert. The fifteen minutes were up, she knew, so where the hell was Hendricks and that money? Turning back to Deidi she added, "So we'll take your Corvette. It'll be a little crowded, but what the hell. Thanks for letting me know about the tracing device; I never would have guessed. Believe it or not, I've never been in this type of situation before."

"It is a wonder," Deidi said dryly.

Blythe smirked. "I knew you were going to say that."

"I have to go to the bathroom," Lacey piped up in a small voice.

Deidi rose from the wicker fan chair in which she was sitting. "I'll take her."

"Yeah, right out through a window." Blythe laughed. "God, you of all people should know I'm not stupid enough to fall for that. You wouldn't, would you? Well, we're a lot more alike than you'd care to admit, sister. The only real difference is, you *think* evil while I *do* evil. And you'd better believe that there's a very, very thin line between the two. You are what you *think,* not what you eat. And all that you do is guided by who you are."

"What is this, Philosophy 101?" Deidi snapped, incensed at the audacity of those words, trying to put both of them in the same rancid barrel. Their faces and bodies might be identical, but there the similarity ended. Blythe was a snake, worse than a snake. She was a heartless sociopath who deserved to die horribly, her body riddled and torn with bullets. Deidi personally had no claim to sainthood, but knew she certainly had never done anything to qualify for a firing squad.

"I have to go!" Lacey implored, bouncing her knees impatiently.

"Then go," Blythe grumbled, taking another peek out the window. "Right there where you sit, if you can't hold it. Your father is already three minutes late and I don't feel like fooling with you. I can't take any chances on something going wrong."

"The door can be locked," Deidi said, her tone firm and deliberate, as if she were speaking to a very young child. "For God's sake, let her go to the toilet, Blythe."

"I don't do anything for God's sake," Blythe hissed. "So just shut the fuck up. You're not the one running this show, and don't you forget it."

Frowning deeply, Deidi sat back down in the wicker fan chair and buried her face in her hands. Lacey began to whimper softly.

"Here he comes," Blythe said a few seconds later, peering again through the slight part she had made in the curtain. Hendricks was sitting shotgun in a white sedan, obviously an unmarked police car. He had put his clothes back on. A uniformed officer was at the wheel.

The crowd in the street parted to let them through. Moving slowly, the driver guided the sedan halfway up Hendricks driveway, parked it and switched off the engine. Then both men got out, Hendricks carrying a fat bank envelope. He cut across the yard, hurrying toward the front porch when Blythe shouted through the window for him to stop. Hendricks froze.

Seeing that she had his full attention, she went on in a loud voice, "I want everybody back, and that includes you! Put that bank envelope on Deidi's dashboard, we're taking her car!"

From the crestfallen look on the detective's face, Blythe could tell that her sister had been right on the money about the tracing device. She owed her one, although, as Blythe reflected, she had never been very faithful in repaying favors. "Don't just stand there like a fucking moron! Do what I said, and get everybody back, and I do mean *way* back! I don't want anybody rushing us!"

Now Plan B had been shot all to hell, his expression said, and despite her nervousness, Blythe couldn't help but smile. All the bases were covered now, surely. A lot of rough road lay up ahead, but with her looks and worldly wisdom, she'd survive. The fittest always did.

It took another five minutes to get all the people moved back far enough to meet Blythe's satisfaction. During that time, unable to hold her bladder any longer, Lacey had been forced to urinate in her shorts. The act filled her with hot shame and she began to cry.

It was finally showtime, and Blythe was in no mood for tears. "Shut up, Lacey, it's only piss. Besides, it's my lap you're going to be sitting on. I'm not exactly thrilled about it myself."

The aspect of making Blythe the slightest bit uncomfortable was enough to cheer Lacey out of her crying jag. It even put a little smile on her face, which Deidi was relieved to see.

"Okay, here we go." Blythe stood up, then helped Lacey off the damp carpet to her feet. Deidi stood also, her mind working frantically to formulate some plan of action through which Blythe's control might be overthrown. But no potential plan was free of risk,

FLESH AND BLOOD

and with Lacey's life at stake, any risk at all was too great.

They stepped out on the front porch together, Deidi on Lacey's left, Blythe on her right. From across the street Hendricks studied them closely through a pair of binoculars, and to save his soul he couldn't tell which was Blythe and which was Deidi. He wondered why they were both wearing one of his shirts and a pair of his socks, but the reason for the shirts dawned on him when he saw how the cuffs were pulled up over their free hands. Obviously Blythe would identify herself by holding the knife openly. Unknowingly staring straight at her now, he saw no indication in her expression of the pain she had to be suffering by walking normally on her injured ankle.

As they slowly moved down the steps as one, he concentrated on his daughter's facial expressions, hoping she would give him a subtle indication of which woman had the knife up her sleeve. But Lacey didn't even look up; she kept her head down, her eyes glued to the ground, the way she always did when she felt embarrassment or shame. His heart reached out to her achingly. He wanted so bad to hold her in a soothing embrace, plant kisses all over her face, say all the words she needed to hear to make everything all right with her world again. If such words existed. No matter what happened now, their lives would never be the same.

Hendricks had been lying about the two sharpshooters. There was actually only one. But Officer Bill Skiles, the stocky young man standing at Hendricks's right, could sure as hell aim a gun. According to several reliable witnesses, Skiles had shot five consecutive beer bottles off a fence post from a distance of 215 yards.

Skiles now leaned toward Hendricks and asked in a gruff whisper, "Can you tell them apart? If I just knew the right one, she'd be down before you could say good-bye."

"That would be nice," Hendricks sighed, "but I can't tell. Dammit! The bitch just might pull this off."

The trio had crossed the yard and stood now at the curb. Deidi's Corvette was parked on the other side of the street. One of the TV news hounds, a tall redheaded woman in her late thirties, held a large microphone over a policeman's shoulder and shouted, "How much money did you get?"

She received no answer. Lacey was the only one to even give her a glance. The rest of the crowd remained hushed, as if they were all holding their breaths. Many of them probably were. This was the drama's climax, the big payoff they'd been waiting for. God forbid they miss anything.

Then something happened, something totally unexpected. The identical women and the long-faced little girl between them had just stepped into the street when a flapping commotion was heard from the direction of the mimosa tree on the other side of Hendricks's driveway.

Startled by the noise, Blythe turned in time to watch the large green bird, which had been perched silent and unseen on a high branch, take wing with a loud, prolonged squawk. She noted with dread that it looked exactly like the one in that smelly boat cabin, but surely it wasn't. Then she remembered Jeremy's unspoken wish for the bird who had flown away to come back. Rather than leave the parrot on the boat to starve, Hendricks must have brought it home with him, given it to his kids for a pet. Looked like Jeremy's wish had been fulfilled. But so what? Her injured ankle was fucking killing her; all she cared about at the moment was getting off her feet.

Still squawking, the parrot, now the center of attention, made a wide circle above their heads. Although Blythe refused to believe that the bird was going to cause a problem, she didn't at all like the way it was circling overhead instead of flying away, like she thought it should. She wasn't entirely convinced it was the old man's bird, but generously supposing that it was, it was still just a stupid-ass bird with a brain the size of a pea, and it didn't have enough intelligence to understand what had happened in that cabin. What did fucking animals, especially birds, know about death? Man was the only species that comprehended its mortality.

In spite of all this mental armory, Blythe still felt the urge to hurry, get in the car and roll up the windows fast, but she couldn't without appearing conspicuous. Discreetly nudging Lacey forward, she took her eyes off the flying parrot and decided to ignore it, but that was pretty hard to do when it squawked from above: "Hell of a storm brewin' up, Cyrus!"

It was the same damn bird, all right. No question about it now.

And when she looked up again from the middle of the street, something else became crystal clear. He most certainly *was* going to cause a problem. He was diving straight at her!

In spite of her intense effort to remain calm, cool, and collected, Blythe totally freaked. She shrieked and her arms rose automatically to shield her face, which automatically raised her shirtsleeves to reveal the steak knife clutched in her right hand. And the moment she let go of Lacey, Deidi grabbed the girl and bolted for the other side of the street, where they were greeted by a very grateful Judson Hendricks and several other officers. The crowd cheered thunderously.

Lacey broke into tears. Wrapping his arms around her fiercely, Hendricks began weeping silently, along with all who were witnessing the scene, including macho marksman Bill Skiles. He wept, but managed to say, "Shall I shoot the suspect now, sir?"

Blinking the tears from his eyes, Hendricks turned his attention to the event taking place in the middle of the street. Cyrus the Parrot versus Blythe the Demon.

Place your bets, ladies and gentlemen. Odds are three to one in favor of the parrot.

Cyrus had rocketed straight for Blythe's face, but at the last possible moment he banked to her left. His outstretched claws made a passing grab at her upraised left hand, succeeding in making three long bloody gashes on the back of it, starting an inch or so above her wrist. She screamed and thrashed the knife blade in the air, horror leaping into her eyes at the sight of her new wounds.

Now this is justice, Hendricks thought. "No, not yet," he told Skiles. "I'm enjoying this too much." He knew that newspeople were present, and he'd probably get raked over the coals for allowing this to continue. He might even face a suspension. Big deal, he smiled to himself, even as his heart lay crushed under the burden of Jeremy's condition. Big fucking deal.

As Cyrus circled for another dive, it was obvious that Blythe had made an executive decision to make a limping run for Deidi's car, which came complete with strong windows (which had to be rolled up) ignition key, and five thousand dollars.

There was only one problem. There were at least a hundred people standing in the street, blocking both ways. But of course to Blythe the Demon, that wasn't really much of a problem. The thick wall of bodies would just slow her down a little, is all. She'd mow down an order of nuns if they didn't move.

Hendricks opened his mouth to shout an order for her to immediately throw down her weapon and place her hands over her head, that if she didn't comply she would be shot, but she was already opening the driver's door.

Before she had it open wide enough to permit, entry, however, Cyrus dove down for Round Two. This time his formidable claws hooked into her scalp and hair. Wings still beating, he dragged her, screaming and stumbling, several feet away from the car, his

FLESH AND BLOOD

sharp beak pecking at her hands and fingers as she fought to defend herself. Then she tripped, compliments of her bad ankle, landing hard on the pavement with Cyrus's claws tangled in her hair. The throng pressed in closer, neighbors quibbling over the most advantageous standpoints, despite the police restraints.

Squawking frenetically, his wings beating the air in wild panic, it was clear that Cyrus was now trying to escape, but he was caught. Still, he was scoring more points for Rufus, doing Blythe some considerable damage in his bid for freedom. Her forehead had been nearly sliced to ribbons, and great chunks of her hair had been pulled out.

But unfortunately she was scoring some points of her own. One of his wings was broken, so he wouldn't be able to fly now, and she'd managed to stab him deeply underneath that same wing.

A woman's voice cried out from the sidelines, "Please, somebody stop this! Stop her before she kills that poor bird!"

Activated by her plea, one of the officers quickly stepped forward, but before he could take any further action, Blythe again jabbed the blood-smeared blade into the parrot's body, this time stilling all motion. The woman burst into sobs while the rest of the crowd hissed and booed.

"Facedown with your hands behind your back," the officer who'd stepped forward growled at Blythe, drawing his pistol.

Forcing herself to accept defeat, she did as she was told. But she had not lost all hope. There was always the chance they would put her in the same cell with Camisa. . . .

Epilogue

On a Sunday a little over year later, Lacey took Hughman out to the backyard to play Frisbee, although Hughman's idea of the game was to catch the flying disk and play keep-away. Watching them head for the back door, Hughman's stubby tail wagging a mile a minute, Deidi felt a warm glow spread over her, bringing an affectionate smile to her lips. Her previous aversion to motherhood had completely dissipated.

Hendricks and Deidi had been married for two months now, but she still hadn't confessed what Blythe had threatened to reveal on that terrible day about Suzanne, how Hughman had killed her and she had covered up his crime. Suzanne was still listed as a missing person, and her parents had spent a small fortune on private detectives trying to find her, refusing to believe that she had drowned. At times Deidi was plagued by guilt about this, and kept telling herself that someday she would tell her husband everything. But not until after Hughman had passed on to Dog Heaven, which hopefully wouldn't be for many years yet.

When charged with the murder of Harlan—blood matching his type had been found in trace amounts on the oblong chain-saw blade in the garage—Camisa finally admitted she also "accidentally" killed her young son Aaron. She adamantly claimed she'd killed Harlan in self-defense. Found guilty on two counts of second-degree murder, she was sentenced to life in prison. Custody of Michael and Felicia had been awarded to Harlan's parents.

Flora Bushbaum's body had been discovered when another neighbor began noticing the smell of her decaying flesh. Her murder was rightfully attributed to Blythe Richmond, along with the murders of Larry Patton, Rufus Bagget, and Kurt Flannigan. For these crimes Blythe was sitting on death row waiting out her appeals.

"What are you thinking about?" Judson asked her, scooting a little closer on the couch. "You've got one of those Cheshire cat smiles on your face again," he added, focusing his full attention on his beautiful wife.

"I'll never tell," she teased.

From a few feet away a gravelly voice echoed, "I'll never tell."

"You'd better not, Cyrus," Deidi warned. Sometimes she wanted to wring that bird's neck for repeating private things she'd said aloud to herself or Hughman. Even so, she had grown pretty attached to him, now that he no longer went berserk at the sight of her. It would have been a tragedy if Blythe had succeeded in killing him, too, but as it turned out, he'd only fainted from fright when she stabbed through his broken wing.

"We have ways . . ." Hendricks said in a low, sexy voice as his fingers began creeping up Deidi's blouse.

"You could try them all back in the bedroom," she responded, snuggling up to him and moaning with pleasure when her palm pressed against his bulging hardness. "But Jeremy should be getting back from his mowing job any minute now, and you still haven't put a lock on that door."

FLESH AND BLOOD

Cyrus ducked his head and repeated a phrase he'd picked up from Lacey a few evenings ago when she was doing her math homework: "I hate this stupid crap!" which made Judson and Deidi laugh so hard they both fell on the floor and died simultaneously of massive heart attacks.

Just kidding.

THE DEBUT OF A BRILLIANT NEW SERIES!

V.C. ANDREWS®

Ruby

The bestselling novels of V.C. Andrews have captivated millions of readers worldwide. Now, hot on the heels of her magnificent Cutler family saga, comes a thrilling new series. RUBY, the first book, takes us to the heart of the bayou, where Ruby Landry lives a happy, simple life. But innocence can't last forever....

Available from Pocket Books
mid-January 1994

And look for
PEARL IN THE MIST,
the next novel in the thrilling new
V.C. Andrews series.

From the Bestselling Author of Terror and Suspense
ROBERT R. McCAMMON

- ☐ BAAL   73774-0/$5.99
- ☐ BETHANY'S SIN   73775-9/$5.99
- ☐ BLUE WORLD   69518-5/$5.99
- ☐ BOY'S LIFE   74305-8/$5.99
- ☐ GONE SOUTH   74307-4/$5.99
- ☐ MINE   73944-1/$5.95
- ☐ MYSTERY WALK   76991-X/$5.99
- ☐ THE NIGHT BOAT   73281-1/$5.50
- ☐ STINGER   73776-7/$5.99
- ☐ SWAN SONG   74103-9/$6.99
- ☐ THEY THIRST   73563-2/$5.99
- ☐ USHER'S PASSING   76992-8/$5.99
- ☐ THE WOLF'S HOUR   73142-4/$5.99

ALL AVAILABLE FROM POCKET BOOKS

Simon & Schuster Mail Order
200 Old Tappan Rd., Old Tappan, N.J. 07675

Please send me the books I have checked above. I am enclosing $_____ (please add $0.75 to cover the postage and handling for each order. Please add appropriate sales tax). Send check or money order–no cash or C.O.D.'s please. Allow up to six weeks for delivery. For purchase over $10.00 you may use VISA: card number, expiration date and customer signature must be included.

Name _____
Address _____
City _____ State/Zip _____
VISA Card # _____ Exp.Date _____
Signature _____ 663-02